LONGHORNS

LONGHORNS

Victor J. Banis

CARROLL & GRAF PUBLISHERS
NEW YORK

LONGHORNS

Carroll & Graf Publishers
An Imprint of Avalon Publishing Group, Inc.
245 West 17th Street, 11th Floor
New York, NY 10011

AVALON
publishing group incorporated

ISBN-13: 978-0-78671-952-5
ISBN-10: 0-7867-1952-4

9 8 7 6 5 4 3 2 1

Interior book design by Maria Fernandez

Printed in the United States of America
Distributed by Publishers Group West

For my longtime editor, and old friend,
Earl Kemp—who really is Chapter 1.

Looking for Victor Banis

The publication of Victor Banis's *Longhorns* is a major event for gay publishing. Not simply because it is a terrific novel and a great read—any reader who knows Banis's work will expect that—but because it marks the re-emergence of one of America's most talented, most interesting, most entertaining, and certainly most productive fiction writers back into the mainstream of gay letters.

But who is Victor Banis? And why has hardly anyone heard of him?

Victor J. Banis is probably the best-kept secret of gay literature. He is foundational to what we now know as gay male letters, yet mostly unknown. My own history with Victor—who can be fairly described as a genius of gay male pulps of the 1970s—is emblematic of this irony. I've written expansively about gay male culture for nearly forty years, and yet my first encounter with Victor was a few years ago.

I first spoke to Victor J. Banis about four and a half years ago. I had been looking for him for months but to no avail. For over two years I had been working on a collection of gay pulp fiction for St. Martin's Press that was eventually titled *Pulp Friction: Uncovering the Golden Age of Gay Male Pulps,* and the lawyers demanded—somewhat unreasonably, I thought—that I secure copyright permission for all of the works I was going to reprint. This was a complete nightmare as most of these authors were dead, or wrote under pseudonyms, or were actually nonexistent, their "names" simply inventions of pulp publishers slapped onto manuscripts turned out by hacks. I mean how do you track down someone named "Jack Love"—the author of the 1967 novel *Gay Whore?*

For weeks I Googled, I did research, I contacted people—such as legendary gay writer Larry Townsend—who I knew had some connection with the pulp industry in the 1960s. In my research I had made some interesting discoveries. I wanted to use a chapter from Victor Jay's *The Gay Haunt,* a 1970 sexy, gay ghost story published by Traveler's Companion. I had discovered, through some used-book Web sites, that "Victor Jay" was also "Don Holliday" as well as Victor Banis, as well as Lynn Benedict, and Jan Alexander, and Jay Vickery, and J. X. Williams. I had a cache of gay male sex pulps by Jay, Williams, and Holliday and they all did have a similar style. In fact, Don Holliday's series—there were nine of them—*That Man from C.A.M.P.* was a minor cult item among pulp enthusiasts. It was so popular at the time that Phenix Publishers (who had done several books in the series) also published *The C.A.M.P. Cookbook* that was co-authored by Holliday and "Lady Agatha."

But how could I find this person, who had more names than Martha Stewart has ways of brightening up your prison cell? There were no hints on Google, and I had run out of leads from the book covers. Suddenly, in a brilliant Sherlock Holmes moment, it dawned on me—the white pages of the phone book. I went online and typed in "Banis, Victor"—that seemed the least invented of the names, and "Victor Jay" looked like a spin-off of "Victor J. Banis"—and sure enough, there was a Victor J. Banis living in San Francisco. On a chance I called the number, and the phone was answered by a soft-spoken man. I introduced myself and said I wasn't sure if he was the Victor Banis I was looking for. Our conversation went something like this:

"Well, if you're Michael Bronski who writes for the gay press I probably am."

"Are you also Victor Jay?"

"Yes."

"And J. X. Williams?"

"I am."

"And Don Holliday?"

"Oh, yes."

"And Lynn Benedict and Jan Alexander?"

"My god, you know everything."

"And Lady Agatha?"

"Oh, no. That's someone else."

I was totally relieved. Finally, someone could give me permission to reprint a chapter from *The Gay Haunt,* but even better—I had discovered Victor Banis/Don Holliday, etc., etc. (who like Edgar Allen Poe's "The Purloined Letter" was hiding in plain view), in the San Francisco telephone directory. Victor and I corresponded and finally met in 1999 when we did a reading from *Pulp Friction* in San Francisco—along with Ann Bannon, Michelle Tea, Michael Nava, and other writers—and he has since become a friend as well as an invaluable source of details about the history and the workings of the 1950s and 1960s pulp industry.

Victor's literary output is prodigious—he estimates that he has written more than 150 novels under his own and numerous other names. Victor emerged as a writer during the late 1960s when writing gay and straight pulp novels for the then burgeoning pulp markets that had opened up when the U.S. government began to relax national censorship laws. Victor covers his career as a pulp writer in his memoir *Spine Intact, Some Creases*—published in Europe and due out in the U.S. shortly from Wildside Press—but his modesty presents him from being clear about the obvious truth: his writings, and the writings of many other pulp writers in the 1960s and 1970s really formed the basis for popular gay male literature. Sure, writers in the late 1940s and 1950s such as Gore Vidal, James Barr, John Rechy, Fritz Peters, Charles Jackson, Lonnie Coleman, and Gerald Tesch laid the foundation for a contemporary gay male literary tradition, but it was the pulp writers—with their wide grasp of genre, use of humor, and astute targeting of social mores, not to mention love of the sexual detail—that were hugely responsible for a popular tradition of gay male fiction.

This can be best seen in *The Man From C.A.M.P.* series that Victor produced over a two year period in the late 1960s. The inspiration for the series is obviously the popular-at-the-time *The Man From U.N.C.L.E.* television series, which first aired in 1964. This was, in turn, a spin on the even more popular James Bond series, which was at the height of the first wave of its popularity. Victor's first *C.A.M.P.* book was the 1966 *The Man*

From C.A.M.P. and his ninth, and last—published two years later was *Blow the Man Down.* In those nine books—each written in about five days—Victor managed to pin down with élan and a superb, often outrageously tacky, sense of humor a gay male sensibility that is distinctly mid-1960s. By this I don't mean the sort of Andy Warhol, Carnaby Street, paisley shirt mod look that we now associate with Austin Powers, but rather a distinctly political sensibility that bridged the old homophile movements and camp (often closeted) sensibility and the new bolder and more overtly angry liberation movement that was to be born in 1969. In spite of, or maybe because of, their outrageous silliness *The Man From C.A.M.P.* books were—and are—deeply and scathingly political.

Before we get to that, let me quickly describe these remarkable books. That man from C.A.M.P. is Jackie Holmes: a secret agent who works for C.A.M.P.—a secret worldwide organization, connected to no government, whose mission is "the protection and advancement of homosexuals." C.A.M.P.'s main enemy is B.U.T.C.H.—Brothers United to Crush Homosexuals—although they also fight other assorted villains. (Readers at the time would have instantly understood that B.U.T.C.H. was a parody of SMERSH, the brutal Soviet secret spy organization in the Bond books, or THRUSH, the international crime syndicate at war with U.N.C.L.E.) In each of the nine novels Jackie—who looks like a "weakly, thin homosexual, effeminate and anything but athletic" but is actually amazingly fit and can "run with the speed of a gazelle and out-fight opponents twice his own weight"—manages to outwit the evildoers from B.U.T.C.H., help stamp out queer bashing, avoid international disasters. He also manages to have sex with most of the men he meets, often in the line of work. Jackie is mostly a bottom and can drive his sexual partners to the heights of pleasure.

While most of the C.A.M.P. books are on the silly side and filled with cultural in-jokes—*Gothic Gaye* features a gay rock star named Dingo Stark—and obvious (but often funny) sexual innuendo, they read amazingly well today. Banis has a sharp sense of style and an even sharper sense of humor. While no one is going to mistake them for high literature, they are consistently fun and charming. But the real—political—importance of the *C.A.M.P.* books is that they were for the time truly revolutionary. While Banis cloaked the books in the language and the inflection of a gay male camp sensibility, the undercurrents here were much more serious. The *C.A.M.P.* series not only took the idea of gay oppression seriously (indeed, Banis codified it into an organization) but was able to imagine a successful way of fighting homophobia. By—literally—queering the idea of James Bond, Victor Banis invented the first fictional gay hero whose sole job was to protect—and promote—homosexuals and homosexuality. This was, in the mid-1960s, a radical idea.

But even more than that, Victor Banis's invention of Jackie Holmes as a effeminate (if strong and agile) gay man was a shocking twist on the accepted notions of gender roles at the time. One might have imaged a gay hero who was big and masculine—that might make some sense—but a queen? Impossible, and culturally unacceptable, except in the pages of *The Man From C.A.M.P.* And to push the envelope even further—Jackie Holmes was a bottom. With the publication of the first book in the series Victor Banis overthrew a century of gay stereotypes and invented something shockingly new and culturally powerful.

Now, four decades later, Banis is slyly taking on a new genre: the western. To think of *Longhorns* as a "gay western" is to miss the point. It is that—and many readers will also see it as a response to *Brokeback Mountain* as well—but it is also a queer meditation on a traditional, idealized American icon: the cowboy. It would be tempting to say that Victor Banis is queering the American cowboy the way that he queered James Bond. But the reality is that the American cowboy is already pretty queer. In a culture that demands flagrant heterosexuality from its heroes the cowboy eschewed female companionship and chose instead to live his life with his fellow buckaroos. There is already an extensive body of critical writings about the queer cowboy and frontiersman in American literature—from Leslie Fiedler's classic 1948 essay "Come Back to the Raft Ag'in, Huck Honey!" to Chris Packard's excellent 2006 *Queer Cowboys: And Other Erotic Male Friendships in Nineteenth Century American Literature*—so there is no need to write about that here. *Longhorns* is a terrific novel, but like *That Man From C.A.M.P.* series, it is also a marvelous work of social criticism as well. As with other pulp novelists—Richard Amory's *Song of the Loon* series or Dick Dale's *Gay on the Range*—Victor is attracted to the western not so much as a traditional genre, as for what it can tell us about contemporary today. His characters here— Buck, Red, Les—are as much prototypes as Owen Wister's eponymous hero in the classic 1902 *The Virginian,* but they are also insightful, and playful, commentaries on gay life today. But don't take my word for it—just read *Longhorns*. After all of these years, and all of his many novels, Victor Banis is back—this time under only his own name—and that is reason enough to be happy.

—Michael Bronski

March 2007

Michael Bronski is the author of *Pulp Friction: Uncovering the Golden Age of Gay Male Pulps* (St. Martin's Press, 2003) and other books. He is a Visiting Professor of Women's and Gender Studies at Dartmouth College.

Chapter I

They were herding cattle, out on the range, when he first showed up, late of an afternoon.

"Looks like we got company," Red said.

Les looked in the direction Red was staring, toward the far horizon, where a distant speck gradually formed itself into a cowboy on a brown and white pinto.

Visiting strangers weren't common on a roundup. It had never happened to him personally, but Les had heard tell of a time or two when that had meant trouble of one kind or another for the herders—rustlers, they said, or *bandidos*, though a lone rider wasn't likely to be much of a threat with a dozen or more cowboys gathered around.

Still, he broke off working with the boys and strolled out to meet the stranger as he rode into the camp in a cloud of dust. Les wore his six-shooters on his hips, and he did not draw them, but he hooked his thumbs in his wide leather belt, where he could get to them quick if he needed to, and if there was a faster draw in Texas, he had never met him. The cowboy jumped off his pinto, hitched his pants up, and swaggered over to where Les was standing.

"I heard you was herding some longhorns, thought you might could use an extra wrangler," he said in the way of greeting, extending his hand. "My name is Buck."

"Mine's Les." Les shook his hand and looked him over. The boy wore an old shirt, worn but clean, and those new pants, dugris, that had come up from the Bahamas—but the fellows called them dungarees, and said they were way more comfortable than the old-fashioned woolies—and he had a fancy-looking pair of snakeskin boots on his feet, white, with curlicues of black and green.

He wasn't more than eighteen years old, maybe nineteen, his skin already leather-colored from the Texas sun, and he stood only five foot nine inches, ten at the most, fine-boned and small-built, but wiry. His hair, a tangled mass of wayward curls as black as obsidian, reached almost to his shoulders, and his eyes, in the fading light, were nearly as dark. An old-fashioned Winchester long rifle was slung over his shoulder, and he wore a Colt on one hip, and a Bowie in a leather sheath on the other. Despite his size and his youth, he had a cocksure air about him, like a man who has just wrestled the puma and is waiting for you to send in the grizzly.

Les himself was six foot three, broad of shoulder and chest and narrow of hip, his long legs bowed outward, like a pair of parentheses that contained his cowboy history within them. A life out of doors had etched fine lines around his mouth and eyes, and bleached his fair hair almost to a whiteness, but the thatch of it on his chest was reddish yellow still where his shirt hung open. He looked exactly like what he was, a long-time cowpuncher who was man enough for just about anything that might come up, and damn well knew it.

"You Indian?" he asked the newcomer.

"Half," Buck said. He seemed unembarrassed by the fact, though not everybody around these parts took kindly to half-breeds. "Daddy was a trader, leastways so I always heard, but I never knew him. Mama was a Nasoni. A Nasoni princess, she used to claim, but she didn't live no royal kind of life, seemed to me."

"Nasoni? Don't believe I know that tribe," Les said.

"Northeast Texas, was where we come from. Gone now. Mostly died out the last century, or swallowed up by the Caddo, except for a few of us stragglers here and there." Buck said. "Texas is a Nasoni word though. It means friend. Guess that's why I'm so doggone friendly." He grinned again and looked Les up and down. Something about the way he looked at him made Les oddly uncomfortable, and he shifted his weight from one foot to the other and glanced down.

"Them's fancy boots," he said, his eyes settling on them.

"Thanks. I traded a fellow down in Galveston for them," Buck said.

"Must have given him something pretty special," Les said. "For a pair of boots like that."

"Mighty special, to tell the truth."

Something about the way he said that made Les think maybe he did not want to follow that subject any further.

"You new around here?" he asked instead. "I don't recall seeing you about San Antone when I been in town."

"Come from Oklahoma, but I been down Galveston way for a spell. Just come up from there. I was looking for some work, and fellows I met on the trail mentioned your name, said you was herding and that I should ride out to find you. Mighty glad they did, now that I set eyes on you."

Which Les thought was an odd thing to say, but he glanced past the kid just then for a moment to where some of the boys were working on the makeshift corral, and his attention was distracted. "Best make that fence a little higher, Red," he called across to his Segundo. "From the look of them clouds yonder, appears like we might get some weather tonight."

When he looked back at the newcomer, Les found Buck's eyes down, an intent expression on his face. Les looked too, and realized Buck was staring at him, staring right at the bulge of his crotch.

"What you got on your mind, boy?" Les said sharply.

"I was just thinking," Buck said, seeming not to mind at all that he had been caught with his eyes where they were, "'bout some of the things them sailors taught me down in Galveston. Things I had never even heard of back in Oklahoma. I tell you, them sailor boys is truly something. I got me a fair education, is sure."

"Well, they ain't no sailor boys here," Les said, doubly annoyed because they had been herding cattle out here on the prairie for several weeks now, and his prick, on the alert for any prospects, had took instant note of the attention it had gotten.

Still, one of his cowhands, Rex, had taken a fall a couple days before and broken an arm and had to ride back to the ranch—you weren't much good one-armed on a roundup, and a man who couldn't work was a man who was in the way—and Matt had come down with a bad case of the trots and couldn't stop shitting, and that had kept him in camp for two days now. They had been a bit shorthanded to begin with when they had set out; so the plain fact was, he could use an extra hand, and out here, there wasn't much to choose from.

"I reckon you can stick around for a day or two, see how it goes," he said. He glanced down at those fancy snakeskin boots, not a speck of dirt on them, and added, spitefully, "I'm guessing you can ride okay. We got no room here for sissies."

"Well, now, seeing it's you, and now that I have set eyes on you, I would surely love the opportunity to show just how well I can ride," Buck said with a flash of teeth in his sun-leathered face. "I got the time, if you got the inclination, and that big old patch of mesquite over there looks private enough to me."

"I expect I'll see you on your horse soon enough," Les said, hoping without much hope that he had misunderstood the suggestion.

"Oh, a horse, well, I guess so," Buck said. He turned and started toward his pinto, his shiny spurs jingling, but he looked over his shoulder to add, "I can ride them, too, case that's what you meant."

Watching him go, the jaunty swing of his narrow hips and his round little butt in those close-fitting dungarees, Les wondered if he had just made himself a big mistake. He had a bunch of grizzled cowhands here, working the roundup. It wouldn't do to have no trouble amongst the boys.

'Specially not that kind of trouble.

• • •

The Texas longhorn was the descendant of the cattle the original Spanish explorers had brought with them in the sixteenth century, but since then the cow had gone wild. Narrow-hipped, swaybacked and bony, the longhorns had adapted to the Texas wilderness with a vengeance. They could fight off the wolves and the wildcats of the plains, even a bear. They ignored the hardships of blizzard or drought, and could travel incredible distances without water and without seeming to tire. They lived now mostly in the "black chaparral," a no-man's-land of mesquite, of prickly pear cactus, and the sharp-thorned *paloverde*, home to the rattlesnake and the fierce-tempered *javelina*.

No man pretended it was easy to catch the longhorn in his natural backyard. On the other hand, any man who could, owned them. They were there for the taking, and they were the ideal animal for the long, arduous cattle drives to the railroad heads in Kansas and Nebraska, where they were shipped to Chicago and New York and the other cities back east.

Les and his boys had herded nearly a thousand head by this time, and would shortly bring them to the ranch to fatten them up some and prepare them for the drive up the Chisholm Trail. Though it was only the tail end of spring, the weather had turned unseasonably warm, as hot as Hades, an ominous harbinger of one of those violent summer storms that could blow up out of nowhere and sweep like a wildfire across the open plain. The cowhands worked with sweat streaming down their faces and kept an anxious eye on the sky, white-gray with an ominous bank of yellow smeared clouds massing on the far horizon. So far, they'd had no trouble, and they were all looking forward to heading home;

but a spell of bad weather could change everything in a minute.

Thinking about the new man as he strolled toward the chuck wagon a little later, Les figured that they wouldn't be out here more than a few days longer, a week at the most. Even if he was a mite queer, the Nasoni couldn't likely cause too much mischief in the time they had left.

And the extra help would be welcome.

Les was sleeping lightly that night in the weighted heat, when Red shouted his name from somewhere nearby. Just as Les opened his eyes, a sheet of lightning lit up the prairie sky.

He scrambled up, instantly awake. He was still fully dressed except for his boots. Cowboys slept in their clothes on a roundup. You had to be ready at all times to move fast. It didn't take him but a minute to shake the scorpions out of his boots and wrestle his feet into them.

"Better wake everyone, right fast," he told Red while he grabbed up his saddle. A bad thunderstorm could stampede the cattle. The temporary corral the cowboys had erected held the cattle penned well enough with things peaceful, but it wasn't likely to withstand the onslaught of a thousand or more charging longhorns. It was the worst kind of luck on a roundup, the thing every wrangler feared and prayed wouldn't happen: a prairie thunderstorm.

Distant thunder rumbled ominously. In the next flash, he could see that every man was up already and hastily saddling his horse. There was no need for him or Red to issue anybody orders. Everyone on a roundup knew the danger and what had to be done. If the cattle stampeded, the only necessity was to stop them. How, you couldn't be sure until you had tried and done it, or failed.

The cattle were on their feet, too, testing the air and milling about nervously and lowing their trepidation. The cowboys riding guard began to sing, not very well, but their off pitch crooning sometimes helped to calm the cattle. A dozen baritones sang in as many different keys, "Did you ever hear of sweet Betsy from Pike . . ."

"Looks bad," Les said, swinging onto his palomino. Already mounted, Red said nothing, but his face was grim.

In another flash of light, Les saw a rider wearing one of those new rubberized "slickers" that were supposed to be impervious to the rain, though Les personally thought they were ugly as sin. The light was gone too quickly for him to see who was wearing it, though.

In the next moment, he forgot cowboy and slicker altogether. The cowhands were singing louder and louder still: "Says Betsy, you'll go by yourself if you do, singin' toora-li loora li loora-li ay . . ."

The air was denser, heavier, and the movement of the cattle more restless, their calls more worried.

An ear-splitting clap of thunder rent the air, and seconds later, a blinding blue flash, so intense you could almost smell it, set the night afire. In the blackness that followed, Les was sightless for a moment, but he didn't have to see to know what was making the earth tremble beneath them. The cattle were stampeding!

Hardly any of the cowboys were even aware that the storm had finally unleashed torrents of rain that poured down on them in wind-blown sheets. It was the thunder and lightning that had spooked the cattle to where they broke right through the fence of that corral. The riders cursed aloud as they rode in pursuit of that thundering, bellowing herd, charging now across the rangeland, heedless of where they were going, driven only by their primeval fear.

Les rode for all he was worth, the palomino nearly leaping out from under him. You had to outrun the cattle, get to the front of the herd. That was the only way to turn a stampede. Once, twice, lightning flashed, and he could see not only the herd but Red close alongside him, and just off to their right, that rain-slickered cowboy, riding hell-bent for leather.

The ground shook beneath the pounding hooves. Despite the rain, he could feel the heat of a thousand rangy bodies and the cowhide smell filled his wet nostrils. The palomino snorted wildly, his heart fair to bursting with the effort of his speed. Les could see nothing ahead or below. One misstep, a prairie dog hole, a fallen branch, and horse and rider would both end up with broken necks, but there was no time to think about that. The banging of horns together was like the clicking of castanets in one of those fandangos the Mexicans were fond of dancing, but this was a deadly dance they were at now, and the darkness and the thunder-drums and the alto cries of the cattle only made it more eerie.

The sky turned blue white again, and glancing aside for an instant, Les saw that they were alongside the leaders of the herd, him and Red, and somehow the rain-slickered rider had gotten ahead of them, pounding stride for stride in a life or death race with the front-running bull. To turn the cattle from their headlong flight, the cowhands had to literally push them aside, and that meant convincing the leader. If that cowboy fell now, if his horse stumbled even for a second, those charging hooves would pound horse and rider, and rain slicker too, into the dust of the Texas rangeland.

The palomino was steady. Les thanked the day he had bought him and almost laughed to think he had cursed how much the horse had cost. A pain shot up his leg as it was crushed between two massive bodies for a moment. He clung tight to the reins. There was nothing he could do now but ride for all he was worth and trust in the horse—and God, too, of course, but at the moment the palomino was closer to the heart of things.

It was the cowboy in the slicker, though, who counted for the most now, riding at the hell-post with the look of a wild animal himself, shouting "Hi-yah. Hi-yah," at the top of his lungs like some kind of storm-crazed demon and leaning all but horizontal out of his saddle to wave his Stetson in the very face of the lead bull—and, miraculously, he began to have his way with the bull, forcing his will on him. The longhorn bellowed in protest, but he was turning now from the headlong flight of his path. The cattle directly behind him began to yield to Les and Red's determined coaxing and to veer as well, and once the leaders had started, the others followed, the cowboys urging them on. A slowly forming circle of longhorns wound in and in upon itself, until cattle were bumping into cattle, and none of them knew which way to run or could find an open path for it.

The stampede was stopped. The rain had lessened, the thunder grew more distant, and it had been several minutes since they had seen more than a far-off flash of light. Les and the palomino were both gasping for air. He leaned down and patted the horse's sweaty neck, and whispered in his ear what a fine fellow he was. The horse snorted disdainfully and tossed his head, as if reminding him that he could certainly be expected to know his job, thank you all the same.

There was no telling till morning how many head they had lost. Until then, the boys would have to take turns riding a containing circle about the gradually calming cattle. With daylight the herd would be penned again, the corral repaired, and the damage assessed.

For all the effort and all the risk, though, Les felt oddly exhilarated as he rode back to camp, his heart still beating fast. Cookie's campfire already glimmered in the darkness where he hurried to brew his thick bitter coffee by the gallon in his big enameled pot, to keep the men awake. The coffee and a pinch of salt and an egg were wrapped up together in a piece of cloth, and when the water was boiling mightily, the egg was crushed and the entire bundle dropped into the pot, and the pot set aside to steep. It was like creek mud, the boys liked to say, but they drank it gratefully, and you weren't likely to fall asleep after a cup or two.

The cowboys were milling about noisily, laughing off their fear and slapping one another on the back, and saying, "God damn," and "Son of a bitch." Les swung off his horse next to the campfire. Red was already there, and when he saw Les he strode quickly across to him, calling as he came, "Man, did you see that fucking kid ride? I never seen nobody could ride a horse like that my whole damn life!"

"The one in the slicker? I saw him," Les said, "But who the hell . . . ?"

He didn't need to finish his question, though, because the new man rode up just then and jumped down from his horse in one graceful leap. He shed the slicker, and threw it across his saddle, and his little pinto snorted and tossed his head.

"Hoo-ee," Buck shouted, walking over to them, and grinning from ear to ear like he hadn't a few minutes before been no more than a heartbeat or two away from ending his days. "That was some excitement, wasn't it? Sure got the blood all stirred up, I will say." He reached behind him and rubbed his hands heartily up and down over his butt. "I swear, it makes me want a good ridin' myself, to take the edge off, if someone was of a mind." He cast an unmistakable glance at the bulge of Les's crotch. To Les's embarrassment, the boys standing nearby saw it as well, and whooped with laughter, too keyed up from the stampede, and too impressed with what the boy had done, to take any offense.

Red clapped a big hand on Buck's shoulder. "Say," he said, a wide grin on his homely face, "Why don't you and me go put them horses away, and we can take care of them saddles while we are at it?"

"I'm your man," Buck said. "I reckon my saddle could sure use a little taking care of right now, the way it is tingling." He returned Red's grin, and started away with him, but he looked back to wink at Les, which produced another round of guffaws.

One or two of the cowboys looked after the departing pair wistfully. It was kind of hard not to take notice of Buck's round little butt, the way he strutted and the way them dungarees of his fit it like a second skin, and they had all of them been out here on the prairie for several weeks now, and there weren't many that did not think a butt looked prettier to them now than it might have when they had set out.

Les had been herding most of his life and he was no fool. He knew that sometimes on the trail, one or the other of the men would slip away to somebody else's bedroll for a spell. Everyone just pretended they didn't notice anything or hear the noises that followed. You never could tell: it might be you feeling the need real bad the next night. Truth was, once or twice Les had almost wished someone might creep over to his bedroll, but they never had, him being the boss and all. Almost wished, but not quite. That just plain wasn't his style.

He never paid much attention to that shit when it happened, though, and he had never attached any importance to it, either. He figured that was just a matter of hot nuts, and what was available, which was pretty limited out on the range. This new guy, though, was something different. Les was beginning to think the boy was a real sternwheeler.

He suddenly realized that his eyes too had strayed to Buck's curvy little bottom. He had a fleeting notion that he wouldn't have much minded taking the edge off his own pent-up energy.

He turned away in disgust and thrust that thought determinedly from his mind. *Shit,* he told himself, *next thing you know I'll be taking him serious, all them damn fool remarks of his.*

The little fucker sure could ride, though.

The rain had stopped altogether by the time Buck and Red finished settling the horses in the pen, and a big silver moon had found her way through the ragged clouds that lingered overhead.

"Looks plenty dark over yonder," Buck said, indicating a large stand of mesquite off some ways from the camp. "If you was serious about having yourself a ride."

"I'll just hang these saddles on the fence," Red said, breathing a little faster and not from the work, "Whyn't you go on over there and make yourself to home. I'll be along real quick."

"I'll be awaiting," Buck said, and sauntered off in the darkness. Red looked after him for a minute, and hurried to get the saddles stowed.

Red had been riding the range, herding cattle, since he wasn't much more than a boy, and a man got over being too particular about things over the years. He reckoned he liked a woman as well as the next man, but there weren't any women on a roundup, and not much else to choose from, although the boys joked sometimes about how a cowboy got to be called a cow-poke, and he figured some of them weren't altogether joking. He hadn't any taste for that kind of thing, but he had learned long ago that there was plenty of pleasure to be found in other ways and he wasn't the least bit squeamish about savoring it when the opportunity offered—and Buck had sure enough offered.

By the time Red joined him, Buck had already shed his britches and he was on his knees on the ground, his head cradled in his arms like he was sleeping, but his little butt was raised in the air in plain invitation, stark naked and just waiting for Red to help himself. In the moonlight it looked silver and sleek, and Red needed no encouragement. He tugged himself free of his trousers and dropped to his knees behind the half-breed, and spit in his hand and felt for the opening. The moon scurried behind the clouds and the night went darker.

"That's powerful tight," Red said.

"It stretches," Buck said, and wriggled a little.

It did, too, though it stayed plenty tight. Red worked his way in cautiously, wanting to make it as easy as possible for his partner.

"You ride pussyfootin' like that, cowboy, it ain't no wonder them longhorns paid you no mind a while ago," Buck said over his shoulder.

"I reckon once't I get settled in the saddle, I can show you a thing or two about riding," Red said gruffly. He forgot about being cautious and began to ride his partner in earnest, holding Buck's taut little hips firmly in his big, work-calloused hands and plowing in and out at a fast clip that quickly got faster and then faster still, till his own butt was nothing but a blur of movement in the darkness.

Red had kind of wondered for a minute, back in camp, if maybe Buck hadn't just been horsing around, but it was clear now that he hadn't been. He was making it mighty plain that it was pleasuring him as well, moaning and sighing and twitching around, which only made it that much better for Red. And he liked being rode hard, too, apparently, since Red was really going to town on him by this time, letting him have it for all he was worth, and mightily enjoying every minute of it himself.

It had been a couple of weeks or more since anyone had slipped into his bedroll at night, and him being Les's right hand, his Segundo, it didn't seem exactly proper for him to go looking for anything amongst the other boys unless they came to him for it; and with that, and the way Buck was working his butt, it didn't take more than a minute or two before Red groaned and swore aloud.

"Holy shit!" he moaned between clenched teeth. He stiffened and rammed it home hard and let fly, it seemed to last forever before it finally dwindled and stopped. He knelt over Buck's bent form without moving for a long time, getting his breath back, and savoring the afterglow of what he decided was surely the best fuck he'd ever had in his life.

"Partner, you must have been saving that up a bit," Buck said after a bit, wriggling happily.

"Been a while," Red said, regretful when he began to grow soft and all too quickly slipped free. "Mighty obliged to you. Hope I weren't too rough, but that little butt of yours would get a dead man to sprout, you ask me."

Buck laughed. "Don't see no point getting in the saddle if you ain't going to ride good," he said, and then, more thoughtfully, "It did go awful kind of quick, though, didn't it? 'Course, that's the way it is when it's been a while for a fellow, you get a chance, there's no way you are going to hold it back."

"Sure ain't. Sorry, I was so fast, though, like you say," Red said with a little chuckle, shaking his head. He paused, and added, "'Course, one shot don't mean the shooter's empty, if you follow me. If you was to stick around a bit, I expect there is plenty more where that load come from, once't I get my breath back."

"I wasn't fixin' to go anywhere for a while," Buck said. "Not now, you got me all woke up, that frisky riding of yours." He rolled on his back and looked up. The moon had watched them one-eyed through a hole in the clouds, but now she sailed into view again, round and beaming. "You got any smokes on you?"

Red sat up, found his tobacco pouch and his papers, and quickly rolled a cigarette. He kept his lucifers in a shirt pocket, wrapped in oilcloth to keep them dry, and he took one out and struck it on the heel of his boot. The match flared brightly. He lighted the cigarette from it, took a puff, and handed it to Buck.

They smoked in a companionable silence for a few minutes, comfortable without talking, passing the cigarette back and forth, the night air smelling of tobacco and man-sex and damp mesquite. Nearby, one of the horses chuffed noisily and another scolded him for it.

"Anybody ever ride that range boss?" Buck asked after a bit.

"Les? You might as well forget all about that, buckaroo," Red said, surprised by the suggestion. "Ain't nobody ever got up enough courage to creep over to his bedroll of a night. Old Les is as ornery as one of them longhorn bulls, and about as tough, too."

"Yep, I can see that," Buck said. Just at the moment, though, he couldn't get old Les out of his mind. Something had happened to him, the minute he set eyes on that good-looking cowboy. It was like some spark had jumped between them and set him on fire. He had never felt anything like it before.

He had a sudden picture in his imagination, of Les's long legs, bent with a lifetime of riding horses—pleasure bent, them sailors down in Galveston used to call it—and thick with muscles, and he could picture them bare, and the hair glinting on them, and he imagined how those powerful legs would feel wrapped tight around him. The thought made his dick tingle and stretch.

"Say," he said, "You about got your breath back yet?"

Red flipped the cigarette away, its red tip arcing into the darkness. "That saddle still warm?" he asked, kind of shy. Looked like this was his lucky night.

Buck turned on his side, his back to him. "You want to know, I reckon it is still slicked up real good from last time, oughtn't to have too much trouble getting back to where you was," he said.

"Well, then," Red said, scooting happily up behind him and feeling for the opening again, "Let's us ride a spell, buckaroo."

Chapter 2

Les was on his way to the chuck wagon the next morning, having slept a bit later than was his custom, when he heard a single gunshot. The sun was barely over the horizon. Even the stones on the ground cast long shadows in the dirt, and his own shadow might have belonged to some giant. It happened sometimes that by this point in a roundup, the boys had begun to get testy, and high jinks would occasionally erupt among them, but it was surely too early in the day for anything like that. Still, he veered from his path and went to investigate, just to be safe. Cowboys could be a feisty bunch.

He found a cluster of the boys standing around Buck, who held his long rifle at his side. Little Joe was some distance away, scuffling in the prairie grass like he was looking for something, the others watching him. As Les joined the group of waiting cowboys, Little Joe shouted, "I found it," and bent down and lifted a good-sized jackrabbit up by its ears, holding it aloft for all of them to see. There was an approving chorus of shouts from the boys.

"Looks like we have us some rabbit for dinner," someone said, and someone else cried, "Hooray for the Indian."

"Buck shot it, Les," Red said. "Must have been forty yards away if it was an inch. Got him with one shot, too."

Les gave Buck an approving nod. "That's pretty good shooting, boy," he said.

"Guess I can shoot," Buck said modestly, but he beamed when he said it.

"How is your draw?" Jack asked him with a sly grin. He had been feeling a mite miffed since the night before. It wasn't his usual habit, but he had been known to slip over to Red's bedroll from time to time at night. Every once in a while he kind of enjoyed being rode, especially the way Red did it, fast and furious, like one of those jackrabbits Buck had just shot. It got a fellow's blood really stirred up, and it always seemed to him like he sat better in his saddle the next day for it.

Like some of the others, though, he had taken notice of the new man's shapely little bottom, and he had seen the satisfied smile on Red's face when the two of them came back to the camp the night before, and he had sort of made up his mind that he would get himself a sample of that himself, to see what made Red smile so—only, Red and the new boy had been thick as thieves since then, looked like you couldn't separate them with a crowbar; and the only time that kid wasn't hanging on whatever Red had to say, he was making eyes at Les. It didn't seem like he had any mind for anybody or anything else.

Which kind of set wrong with Jack, and put him up to a bit of mischief.

"Now, Jack," Red started to say, but Buck cut him off.

"I reckon I am as fast as the next one," he said. "Faster, maybe, than lots of them, if I don't want to brag."

"Why don't you draw against old Les, there?" Jack suggested.

"Don't be talking foolishness," Les said, and would have gone back to the chuck wagon where he had been headed, if Buck hadn't spoken up real quick.

"Suits me," Buck said, and added, too quick maybe, "if Les ain't afraid to draw against me, that is to say."

"Les ain't afraid of nothing," Les said, testy like. "The sooner you get that idea firm in your mind, boy, the better off you'll be."

"Umm hmm," Buck murmured, sounding doubtful. "'Course, I can see why the range boss wouldn't want one of his cowhands showing him up. Especially if it was just a little half-breed."

Les was not a man to shy away from a dare, and he swung around sharply now on his heels, feet planted wide, his knees bent outward, and raised his hands just above the handles of his six-shooters. His stance was upright, stiff-looking, in fact, and to anyone who didn't know him, it might look like he was a greenhorn gunslinger. The cowhands knew better, though.

"You talk mighty big, boy," he said. "Anytime you are ready, you go ahead and draw."

Buck crouched low in the typical gunslingers stance, paused for a moment with his right hand suspended above the single holster on his hip. He and Les regarded one another across the patch of dirt between them, the boys around them looking back and forth, happy for a little fun to break their routine.

Buck made a quick grab for his Colt. It wasn't halfway out of the holster before Les had drawn both of his and fired a single shot into the ground between them, the dust spitting upward.

Buck blinked and gaped in astonishment. He had never seen anybody that quick. Les's hands had been nothing but a blur, it was like one second, his guns were in their holsters, and the next, they were in his hands, like it was magic. Buck shook his head admiringly, wide-eyed and a bit envious, too, and gave a little chuckle. He shoved his gun back into its holster.

"Damn," he said, "You always shoot that quick?"

"I was taking my time," Les said, which might have sounded to some like bragging, but which the others knew was probably the truth. "Figured I would give you a chance to show what you could do."

"I guess I know when I have been topped," Buck said.

Les holstered his shooters. "Take a lesson from it, boy, be careful who you challenge in the future," he said. "The next fellow might not shoot at the ground."

"I see your point," Buck said. Then, one of those goofy grins of his split his face. "Say, speaking of topping someone, and you saying just now you ain't afraid of nothing, I got an idea." He dropped his eyes to Les's crotch. A couple of the boys laughed aloud. "Seeing now as how quick you can shoot, why, it wouldn't take no time at all if you and me was to . . ."

"Being afraid and not having a mind for something are two different things," Les interrupted him. He turned his back and strode quickly away. Buck stared after him, his thoughts written plain on his face for anyone to read. A few of the boys exchanged smiles and winks. Nobody had ever known Les to get interested in anything like that; but they had never known anybody who had lit out after it the way the new boy was.

It began to seem like things might get interesting before they were over.

Later, Red found Buck off by himself in the mesquite, practicing his fast draw.

"Ain't no use," Red said, "You ain't never going to be faster than Les. I don't reckon anybody is. Nobody that I have ever seen, leastways."

"Even if I don't, it can't hurt me none to get faster," Buck said.

"Well, now, that depends on how you look at it," Red said. "If you was willing to take some advice from an old cowpuncher."

"You ain't so old," Buck said, smiling at him. "Not too old, as I can say for certain. And I expect your advice is worth listening to, you being the kind of man you are, and us being friends, seems like."

"Seems like to me, too," Red said, grinning shyly. He had never had anybody attach themself to him the way Buck had, and it was hard not to bask in the glow of Buck's obvious admiration. The fact was, he liked the boy, aside from that other business, which had been plenty enjoyable—but the kid had a friendly way about him, he seemed to brighten things up, just being there. "Least, I hope so. But, what I was about to say, is, fastest draw and best shot ain't the same thing, boy, and it is my way of thinking that the second of the two is the more important."

"I ain't sure I follow you, exactly," Buck said.

"Well, see, most of the quick draw artists, the ones you hear about, why, they more often than not end up dying young. The El Paso Kid, say, I expect you heard about him. Everybody said he was the fastest gunslinger in the west, but hell, he wasn't any older than you when he died in a gun fight."

"Well, why did he then, if he was so quick on the draw?"

"That is just the point I am making. You draw that fast, ain't no time to really take aim, the quick draw man just kind of shoots in the general direction. Sometimes he gets lucky, and sometimes he don't. But, I seen me a bunch of gun fights in my days, and most of them, it was the fellow who took a bit more time, and aimed his gun instead of just firing blind, who walked away when it was over. You take Les and me, say, if we was to have us a fight, which we ain't, of course, but if we did, why, Les would get the first shot off, for sure. I ain't anywhere near as fast as he is, probably not even as fast as you are, but I can shoot as straight as the next man. So, I reckon if him and me were to draw, and we was any distance apart, I'd have a fair chance that he would miss with his first shot, and before he got another one, I would have time to take real aim, and I would probably have him plugged."

"I never thought about it like that," Buck said.

"Best thing for you is, you set your mind to shooting as straight as you can, which you are already powerful good at. The better shot a cowboy is, the better his chances are, and don't you let it worry yourself none about that quick draw stuff. It makes a good showing, is all it is. Anyway, you wouldn't never get any better at it than Les, like I said, if you was thinking about some kind of rematch. Lots have tried, but he is still the fastest."

"Well, say, then," Buck said, his brow wrinkling thoughtfully, "how come he is still alive and them others ain't?"

"Les ain't a man to get himself into a gunfight, unless he was downright forced into it. Only time I ever saw him get that close, he said to the other fellow, why don't I just show you something, before this gets too far along, and I tossed a clod of dirt up in the air—not too far away from him, mind you—and when that other fellow saw how fast Les was, why, he lost all interest in it and walked away. But Les can do that because he is Les, and that same fellow might have wanted to call your bluff. I don't fancy seeing you with no bullet holes in you." He surprised himself by adding, "Reckon I like the holes you got a lot better," and grinned kind of sly like. Cowboys did what they did, but doing and saying were two different things, and they did not as a rule talk about what went on from time to time. There was something different, though, about the way it had been between him and the little Indian, even if Red didn't exactly know how to explain it to himself.

It was different, though. He was sure of that.

Buck laughed, not in the least embarrassed by the remark, as some others might have been. He put an arm about Red's shoulders, and said, "Say, I am sure grateful that I got me a friend I can learn things from."

"Seems like I might learn a thing or two from you, too, before we is done," Red said, and they laughed together, relaxed and each of them discovering that he savored the other's company.

The fact that Buck was the hero of the stampede was not enough for him to earn his keep, though, as Les saw things. They still had cattle to round up, to make up for what they had lost in the storm. It was one thing to be able to ride like the devil, but Les figured Buck would have to do more than that if he meant to stay.

A lot more than that, seeing as Les was not real particular about having him around, being the sort he was.

Riding and roping of course were the most important things when it came to herding longhorns, but the territory dictated costume as well. It was important that a cowboy knew how to prepare himself for chasing the cattle through that dangerous chaparral, where mesquite and *paloverde* could rip the skin right off a carelessly dressed rider.

Even hot as the weather still was, Buck had donned the same kind of close-fitted jacket made of denim that the other cowhands wore, and heavy leather chaps covered his trousers. Fancy as they were, those snakeskin boots of his appeared sturdy enough at least, and he had further protected them with the heavy *tapaderos* that covered his stirrups. At least he looked like a real wrangler, Les thought when he studied him in the morning, and not somebody just playing at it.

"You know how to rope these bastards?" Les asked him before they set out. "It ain't like roping horses."

"I know a few tricks," Buck said with his usual ornery grin. "I expect I could teach you a few new ones if you had a mind."

Sitting saddle alongside Les, Red gave a little snort of laughter, but he quickly smothered it and made his face all innocent when Les glowered at him.

"It's them longhorns want learning," Les said dryly.

Unabashed, Buck said, "Well, I can do this," and quickly demonstrated the essential lasso throw of the cow herder: the basic *mangana*. Les nodded, unimpressed. Any cowboy worth his chaps could do that in his sleep.

"And this," Buck said, and showed them the *lazo remolindeado*, the whirlwind bow, which was a damned sight more difficult, and which he threw so fast you could hardly see the rope as it sailed through the air.

"And this one," he added, not yet finished, and did the throw that was the trickiest and the most critical of all for roping longhorns, the *media cabeza*, or half head, the loop thrown behind one ear and horn and in front of the other and the under jaw—the throw that a cowboy needed for a really mean cow. A longhorn could weigh eight hundred to a thousand pounds. A badly cast rope could spell disaster for horse and rider.

The other cowboys watched Buck's demonstration and nodded their approval. They could see that he was as good with a rope as he was with a horse—about as good, in fact, as Red was, and except for Les himself, they all knew Red was the best roper there was. Buck's little pinto, too, seemed to know exactly what was expected of him, without the need of any direction from his rider.

"That boy is damn good," Red said approvingly.

"Appears he is, at some things," Les said. "'Course," he added, without looking in Red's direction, "you'd know better about one or two of them, I reckon, than I would."

Red blushed, but he had worked with Les most of his life, and he wasn't much inclined to be shy with him. He said, "Seems to me like he's plenty willing to teach you what he knows, if you was interested."

"Long as he knows about roping longhorns, is all I care," Les said, and to the others, "Let's ride, boys, we got some cows to catch. We lost a couple dozen head last night, got to make up for them if we ever want to see that ranch again."

Red stared after Les briefly as he rode away. For a minute there, it had almost sounded from the tone of his voice like Les was peeved about something. He thought about how he and Buck had gone off together the night before. They had been the objects of considerable teasing—some of which he was sure was nothing but plain old-fashioned jealousy—from some of the boys when they came back to camp. It had been mostly of the good-natured sort, though. Wranglers slept close to one another under the stars. They were close together all the time, day and night, and they shared just about everything but their hats and their guns. The result was, there weren't many secrets in a cow-boys' camp.

Les had not joined in any of the teasing that had gone on. He had, in fact, ignored altogether their little trip behind the mesquite, but he certainly must know exactly what the two of them had been up to back there.

Les was an old cowpuncher, though. He had been on many a drive and many a roundup, and he knew the kinds of things that went on sometimes, and that had never bothered him any before.

Red decided that he must have imagined that moment of sour beans. He couldn't believe that Les cared the least about him riding Buck a couple of times—in memory, the second go round had turned out to be even better than the first; that little fellow had sure got something in his mind in between times that had got him worked up real special.

Anyways, it always seemed to Red like a cowboy worked better after he'd gotten some of the orneriness drained out of him good, kind of got him relaxed and of a mind for business.

All the boys knew that, even if they never exactly talked about it. Les was no fool, though. He knew that as well as the next one, regardless that he didn't get himself taken care of.

Maybe that was the problem, Red thought. They had been out here a while. It wasn't like there was any shortage of boys who would have been happy to see to things for the boss man, either. Buck was not the first, nor the only one, Red felt sure, who had thought about that, even if he was way more open about it than the others.

Red had better sense, though, than to say any of this out loud, not to Les, and not even with them being such old friends. Unlike some, he still had all his teeth, and he reckoned he would like to hang on to them a bit longer.

He kneed his horse and rode to catch up with Les.

Their first time out, Les let Buck ride along with him as a "spotter," so he could get himself a better idea of what the kid could do. Catching longhorns wasn't a job for anyone who didn't know what he was doing, fancy roping or no, and he didn't want no fool half-breed getting himself hurt, and then they would have him to take care of.

They rode a ways in silence. Les wasn't a talkative sort, but he was aware of the kid looking over at him often, and it made him feel a little uncomfortable, considering what he suspected might be on the boy's mind. After a bit, thinking it would be safer, he stirred himself to make some conversation.

"Where'd you learn to ride the way you do?" he asked.

Buck shrugged. "Indian blood, I guess," he said, and then added, "If I was to tell you the truth, it's this here pony more than it is me. He is the smartest horse I ever did see." He patted the pony's long neck affectionately.

"He's a good horse, I can see that," Les said. One thing every cowboy respected was a man who knew his horses. For most cowboys, his horse was his best friend. "I reckon you know how to ride him well enough, though."

Buck accepted the compliment with a nod and an embarrassed smile, but he was pleased by it. He did not figure Les was a man given to flattery. "That's a handsome palomino you got there, too," he said.

"Yep. He is a pretty good one, old Silver." Les glanced over and saw the boy looking at him funny like. "What are you thinking?" he asked, suspicious.

"I was just thinking, as long as we are comparing what we got, how about if . . . ?"

"Don't even finish saying it, boy," Les said, frowning. He ought to have known, he thought, aggravated again.

"Wouldn't bother me none, if that is what is worrying you," Buck said, "I mean, about your palomino being bigger than my pony, which I can plain see for myself."

"Well, maybe he is, and maybe he ain't," Les said. "I don't let nobody mess around with my stock, is the thing."

A red-tailed hawk had been circling above them, and now they watched him swoop down from the sky. There was a quick movement in the brush and a moment later he soared upward again, a field mouse caught in his talons, and disappeared against the blaze of the sun.

Buck felt an odd sense of kinship with that mouse. It seemed to him like something had swooped down out of nowhere, and had taken hold of him, something strange and different, and mighty powerful, and it seemed like there was nothing he could do now but let it carry him where it would. He had known lots of other cowboys, and some of them had been plenty nice to look at, he reckoned, but he had never felt about anybody before the way he did about Les, had felt about him almost from that first moment he rode into the camp the day before and saw him standing there, his thumbs hooked on his belt, his eyes, blue like that turquoise they sold down in Mexico, looking him up and down. He wanted the range boss, plain and simple, but in some way that was unlike how he had ever wanted anybody else before him.

He didn't figure, though, that Les was ready yet to hear anything like that from him. Just now, it was plain that he was set against it. Buck was not a man who was easily discouraged, however, when he had made up his mind to go after something, and he had sure fire made up his mind that somehow or other, he was going to have his way with that good-looking cowboy riding alongside him, despite what Red had said to discourage it. He figured it was going to take some doing, was all, but hell, that had never bothered him before. Sometimes, it just made the prize all the sweeter when it was won.

The way to do that, in his mind, was that the more you learned about a fellow, the easier that might make things down the road, and he set himself to learning what he could. If he was that field mouse, as he saw it, he was like the hawk, too, gliding across the sky and waiting for the mouse to show him where to pounce.

Sooner or later, Les would show him. He was sure of it.

"How old are you?" he asked aloud. He could see right up front that Les was not a man who talked much, and even less when it came to talking about himself, but there was a trick that Buck had learned long ago, which was that if you wanted to hear, the best way was to tell. Most folks, if you told them something unusual about yourself, would try to top it, and in that way, you could get them to say all kinds of things about themselves that they otherwise wouldn't tell. As for his own life, Buck did not think that it was anything very special, since he was nothing but a cowboy and a drifter—but it was different, he reckoned, different enough, anyway, that it generally did the trick, and got another man to open up about himself.

"Forty-one, come the fall," Les said. "How about you?" Which was the question Buck had hoped him to ask, taking the bait he had been offered.

"I don't exactly know, to tell the truth."

"Well, you got a birthday, ain't you?" Les asked. He had never heard of anybody who didn't. A fellow had to get born, didn't he?

"I guess so. Must have, I'd say, but I don't know when it is. Don't think my Ma ever told me."

Which surprised Les. He hadn't ever heard of that, either. "Your Ma alive?" he asked.

"No, she passed away when I was just a kid, trying to give me a baby brother. I never did know my Daddy, so I just sort of lit out. We had been drifting all along anyway, the two of us, so it wasn't much different, me drifting on my own."

"Sounds like you was pretty young, to be on your own like that."

"Ten, maybe, something like that. Might have been twelve. But, they's folks don't mind looking after a little guy for a spell, if he has growed up early in some ways. If you catch my drift. I reckon I probably got randy younger than some boys do, so I didn't mind too much, mostly."

Les thought about that for a moment, Buck being on his own, so young. He supposed that explained a thing or two. Still, his own life had not been no featherbed, either. He didn't want to leave the impression that it had.

"I got an early start my own self, I reckon," he said.

"How is that?"

"Well, now, that ranch, the Double H we been branding the cattle with, I wasn't but about twelve years old myself when I first come there," Les said, glad to pursue a safe subject, which he hoped meant Buck had been successfully discouraged from any further interest along those other lines. He shifted his balls around in the saddle to make them more comfortable and, remembering who he was with, took a quick look in Buck's direction. Buck seemed not to have noticed, though. His eyes were straight ahead. Les relaxed a bit and gave his balls another little tug.

"We come from Ohio to begin with, see. My Pa was an army man, and old man Cameron, too, they was both at the war, and they neither one of them come back. Anyway, the Double H, that was the Camerons, Henry and Harriet, and when he was killed, Miz Cameron was left with the ranch, and when Ma and me came out to look for work, Miz Cameron hired her on to look after the house, and they put me to doing whatever I could do outside."

"Seems to me like you was pretty young at that, to be working on a ranch," Buck prompted. He was discovering that he even liked the sound of Les's voice, now that he had got him talking—low, husky, like. It kind of made Buck tingle in all the right places. Damn, if that man didn't plain set him afire.

"I was, but I was big for my age, and strong, and I worked hard," Les said. "I knew if we didn't make good at the Double H, things were going to be bad for us, my Ma and me, so I did everything I was told, and twice again as much, too. Wasn't long, two, three years, maybe, before I was just about running things."

Les thought about that, about how that had come about, him being foreman, and hardly more than a kid himself at the time. "See," he said, almost like he was thinking aloud, "The foreman she had then wasn't good for a lot, liked his whisky over much, and he was stealing her blind to boot. So after a spell, Miz Cameron said she was unhappy with him, and she asked me if I couldn't do the job, and when I said I expected I could, she fired him, and made me foreman, even though I was barely dry behind the ears. I had to prove myself a time or two, you understand." He looked sideways at Buck, who seemed to be listening intently. Maybe he wasn't so big a fool after all. "There was some didn't fancy taking orders from a young fellow like me."

"I'll bet that's when you got to be so quick on the draw, wasn't it?" Buck said.

Les glanced at him again, surprised he had seized on that so fast, and nodded. "True enough," he said. "I got challenged once or twice. They got over it, though, when they saw how it was. I was pretty strong, too, good with my fists, if I do say so.

After a bit, seemed like everybody just settled their minds to things.

"Then, a couple of years later, when my Ma died, Miz Cameron decided she would be more comfortable in town. I expect she missed having a woman's company. I just been kind of handling everything since. Once a month or so, she comes out to see how things are going. Or, lately, seeing as she is getting up in years, I ride into town to see her."

It was a long speech for him, and when he had made it, and he caught a glimpse of the kid kind of smiling to himself now, like he had a secret, Les had an odd feeling, like he had maybe said too much, had told the kid things he hadn't ought to know, although he couldn't say exactly what that might be.

He hadn't told him anything, had he, except how he had come to be foreman?

Before you could catch the Texas longhorns, you had to find them, and that could be trickier than a body might think, out here on the open range where the cows were more at home than you were. The varicolored cattle were downright clever at concealing themselves in the brush and sometimes it took a keen eye to discover them. The two of them hadn't ridden more than a mile or so from camp when Buck waved his hat and nodded silently in the direction of a thick stand of brush a few yards off to Les's right.

Les had bought his palomino for its cattle experience. The horse paused just then in his stride and pricked his ears in the same direction Buck had indicated. At first Les saw nothing over that way but a seemingly solid wall of brush. Then, as if the wind had blowed a fog clear, he spied the twisted horns of a cow, neatly camouflaged by the mesquite. A lightning bolt of excitement burned down his spine. For all the years that he had been doing it, he had never got over the thrill of catching these devils. He spurred his horse and rode at the longhorn.

With a speed and agility that belied its size and clumsy appearance, the cow was up and tearing off through the brush. It looked to Les at times as if she was running straight at impenetrable patches of mesquite, but he was determined to go wherever the cow went. Still, it took all his considerable skill to stay in the saddle. Branches cracked and snapped around him, tearing at his chaps and the *tapaderos*. One thorny protrusion nearly took his eye out and left a trail of blood on one cheek. He bent down, flattening himself to the horse's straining neck, dodging as best he could and taking the blows he couldn't dodge. Ahead of him, the longhorn twisted and darted, vanished and reappeared—but Les saw with a surge of exultation that he was gaining on the cow.

The longhorn broke into a patch of open ground. This was the opportunity Les had been watching out for, the time to rope his quarry. If he let the cow reach the next thicket, it would be hard to find room to get a rope over her and he could be chasing her halfway across Texas before he got another opportunity.

His heart in his throat, he twirled his rope overhead and cast a loop spinning through the air. It floated like a feather, seeming interminably slow, and then, with an accuracy that made him grin with satisfaction, it settled neatly about the long, curving horns.

His horse, trained to the job, knew it was his turn to show his skill, and he tensed to take the strain when the cow reached the end of the rope. Now was the critical time for horse and rider. Sometimes the longhorn, caught on the rope, would turn and charge. Sometimes a cowboy roped himself a real *ladino*, a maverick that would fight to the death.

The rope tightened and held, and horse and longhorn were in a tug of war. The cow bellowed and bucked, but the horse held steady. Then, abruptly, the fight was over, and the longhorn began to obey the pull of the rope.

In the excitement of the chase, Les had all but forgotten Buck, but he rode up now, grinning ear-to-ear, and saluted with his Stetson. "Whoopee," he shouted, "Damn, I knowed the first time I laid eyes on you that you was born to the saddle. Sure would like to have been that palomino for a spell there, the way you was riding him."

"Reckon when you grow four legs maybe I'll put you to use," Les said, all huffy again. Just when he had begun to be comfortable in the kid's company, too. Damn fool had a way of rubbing him the wrong way, seemed like. It just took the fun out of things, and it got Les's back up, him saying things like that, when he ought to have seen straight off that he was wasting his breath.

"Ain't got four, but I got me a good sized third one," Buck said. "I'll bet you would be surprised to find out what I can do with that, if I was to show you."

"Maybe not," Les said. "Whyn't you take that cow back to the camp, boy, maybe you can get her interested in something along the way, and after that you can try roping one yourself. I don't guess I need me a spotter."

He turned his back and rode off to look for another longhorn.

Chapter 3

The different jobs were divided up among the workers on a roundup. Most of the boys, of course, rode out to rope cattle, and it took special skills to do that right. Some of the cowhands stayed behind, and waited for the longhorns to be driven back to the pen that had been quickly repaired after the stampede, and these boys had their own skills that were different from the ropers.

Little Joe was the head of the *marcadores*. It was his crew's job to see that the cattle were each one of them branded with the Double H brand, three uprights sharing a single cross bar, simple enough but hard for a rustler to transform into anything else.

The branding irons had been heating over a fire since morning, and when Buck brought the cow in and drove her into the pen, his part of it was done, and he rode back out to look for another. Joe took a red-hot iron from the fire and called over to Ben, "Bring her on over."

"Here's my new girlfriend, then," Ben said, and led the cow to where Joe waited, guiding her by her tail, held over her back to restrain her, and twisting it to make her go forward; but you had to hold the tail right, at the base, to keep from breaking it, and if a man was careless and stood behind her instead of off to the side like Ben was careful to do, he was likely to get kicked bad for his efforts. An angry longhorn had been known to cripple a man with a good kick.

Sometimes, with an ornery cow, they had to use the ear twitch, a loop of rope tied about the horns, and then a half hitch fastened about the ear, so that they could divert a cow's attention from what was being done elsewhere, and the *marcadores* had to master the rope casting harness as well, which made it possible for even a single man to tie up a cow without the danger of strangling her. This cow, though, was docile enough, now that she had been run down and roped.

"Hold her steady, there," Joe said, and he clapped the red-hot iron quickly and firmly against a haunch. There was a quick sizzle of burning flesh and a wisp of smoke. It seemed like the *marcadores* hardly ever got the smell of burning hair out of their nostrils. Of course the cow bawled loudly in brief protest. Regardless of how you had diverted a cow's attention, she was like to notice when that happened.

"Hang on to her now," Joe said, and when the cow would have bolted, Ben kept a firm grip on her tail, and called, "Whoa there, settle down, girl." Once you let go of a cow it could be the devil's own job to get hold of her again. A longhorn's memory was good, and afterward, given the chance, she would shy away from the men who had roped and branded her, and the job was only half done now, till the *ataleros* did their part of it.

It was the *ataleros'* job to smear lime paste on the fresh brands, so that they scarred properly. A brand had to last the lifetime of the longhorn. You didn't want one healing over and fading in time. They worked fast, while Ben kept his grip steady, and when it was finished, he let go of the cow's tail and she galloped a few feet away, lowing angrily, and slowed to look back resentfully at them.

Once all the longhorns had been properly branded, a *capador* rode among them and separated out the males and castrated them and put the testicles aside for Cookie's fry pan. The cowmen considered the cooked testicles a real treat and would vie with one another to see who got them.

Finally, a piece was nicked out of each longhorn's ear and put aside in a pile, so that when they wanted a count of the newly acquired herd, they could count pieces instead of cows.

A day's work lasted from just after sunup to nearly sundown, when the fading light made it too difficult to spot the cattle and too dangerous to chase them through the chaparral. Everyone worked hard, and by the time they rode into camp at the end of the day, they were ready for the ample meal that Cookie had waiting for them, and a night's rest, before it all started over again the next morning.

Most evenings, though, the boys gathered about the campfire for a bit before they settled into their bedrolls. Buck was there with them that night, sitting between Red and Jake, and looking like he had always been there. The weather was clear, with no hint of any more storms on the way, but they heard wolves cry in the distance, and they threw some more mesquite on the fire to keep it blazing high, and Les sent a couple of extra riders to watch over the herd, in case the lobos got close enough to try their luck.

One of the boys, Pete, began to talk about the home he had left behind in Dixie, and his dear old Ma who was still there, and how, come fall, when the work was finished up, he intended to go see her for the first time in years.

As tough as they are, cowboys are a sentimental bunch, and the others listened to him gravely, and nodded their heads, and some of them gazed into the fire and thought of the homes they had left behind. They talked often among themselves of their distant homes, and of going back for visits, but few of them ever did. It was a dream they liked to share with one another, but it had no more substance than the pungent smoke that drifted up from the fire, stinging their eyes when the wind blew at them. They were cowboys, and whatever roots they had once had, they had left them behind long ago. The Double H—and the open range—were as close as any of them had to a home now.

The fire popped and sparked, sending little embers into the air, and occasionally onto shirtsleeves or their trousers. From time to time someone got up and walked a few feet off to take a splashing leak. One of the boys, Matt, took a beat-up harmonica out of his shirt pocket and began to play an old war tune, slow and mournful, "Oh, stranger tread lightly, 'tis holy ground here . . ." The others grew still and listened, paying no mind to the bad notes, and gazing pensively into the fire.

Buck looked up and saw Les striding toward them, and like they were drawn by a magnet, Buck's eyes went straight to that bulge in the front of Les's trousers, and he smiled unconsciously at the sight of it.

Les had been thinking to join them, but as he neared, he saw Buck look up at him, and saw exactly where Buck's eyes went, which made him plenty sore. *Goddamit*, he thought angrily, *a man couldn't exactly hide his dick, it was just down there, wasn't it?* He'd had the same damn bulge in his pants most of his life, since he had grown out of being a boy, and course he had never tried to hide it none, wasn't something a man needed to be ashamed of, not and he had himself a hefty one, which he reckoned he did all right. But nobody else had ever paid any special attention to it before either, that he had ever seen—except for the girls at Miz Yolanda's in town, and, hell, they was paid to pay attention to a man's pecker.

The way he saw it, another cowboy wasn't even supposed to notice it, except maybe just out of curiosity, as to how his own measured up, which he supposed some fellows did. Buck wasn't the only one that had ever looked at him there. He had caught a glance or two from time to time, mostly envious like. It was just that Buck looked at it different from the rest.

Hell, for his own self, he had never taken no notice of what anybody else had down there, except for old Jack's, and you couldn't help but see that thing hanging down his leg the way it did, but, shit, all the boys made jokes about Jack's tallywhacker, Jack most of all. That was just funning. It wasn't like they were planning on getting any of it for themselves, except if one of them slipped over to Jack's bedroll of a night. He supposed one or the other of them might have from time to time, that was the way cowboys were, but if they did, they didn't talk about it afterward. Leastways, not with Les, who they all knew hadn't any mind for that sort of funny business.

All of them, anyway, but the new fellow, and now, shit fire, here he was, this damn fool Indian, looking like he was going to jump up and take himself a bite out of Les's dick every time he saw it.

It plain rubbed him the wrong way, and he changed his mind about sitting down at the campfire with the boys and strode on past instead, and went to check the horses, his expression all angry like.

Red saw the entire exchange, even the little hesitation in his step when Les changed his mind and went by without stopping, and he felt a pang of sympathy for the boy sitting next to him, and for the first time ever, he felt kind of irked at his old friend. It wouldn't have killed him, would it, to sit for a spell, just to be neighborly?

He almost put a hand on Buck's knee, to console him, and then thought better of it. Butt fucking off by yourselves was one thing, and nobody around the campfire would hold that against them, but you were supposed to leave that business behind the bushes when you were done.

"Say," he called across the fire to Matt, feeling oddly testy, "didn't they have no happy tunes at that damned war?"

Matt stopped in mid note, surprised, and thought for a moment, and then burst into a spirited jig. Cookie had finished his cleaning up by this time and was walking across just then to join them, and he cried, "Now, that's more like it," and commenced to shuffle his feet and dance about in the dust.

"Well, there," Buck said, giving a little whoop and jumping to his feet, "cut me in," and he began to dance with Cookie.

The others roared with laughter to see the two cowboys dosey-doing in the flicker of the firelight, Cookie bowing gallantly and Buck making a silly little half of a curtsy, and the boys shouted their encouragement. Two or three of them started to clap their hands more or less in time, and Pete to sing, making up the words where he didn't know them, his tune different here and there from the one Matt was playing on his harmonica.

" . . . With a three legged stool and a table to match . . . "

Standing off by himself at the *remuda*, Les smiled unconsciously at the clapping and hollering, and wished now kind of wistfully that he had joined the boys after all. Faint in the far distance, a coyote added his voice to the song. A tumbleweed rolled by at Les's feet, caught on the corral post for a moment, and then vanished into the night, and a couple of the horses chuckled softly to themselves, to see it go.

Les was a loner. Cowboys were, despite the camaraderie of the campfire. When you got down to it, a man sat alone in his saddle.

An odd kind of disquiet drifted down over him, though, like the prairie dust that settled endlessly on the brim of your Stetson and the tops of your boots, a feeling that maybe he had missed something, or it had missed him. It felt like there was something blowing past him with the manure smell in the Texas breeze, like he should put out his hand and take a hold of it before it was gone. Only, he didn't know what it was.

He shrugged it off, and started for his bedroll. A lot of foolishness, that's all it was. Anyway, morning came early.

" . . . And a hole in the floor, for the rooster to scratch."

What surprised Les over the next few days even more than the outrageous remarks Buck was always making, and the way he looked him over all the time, which he was downright shameless about, was that none of the grizzled cowboys in the camp seemed to take any offense at it.

Of course, Buck had proven himself the night of the stampede. These were tough hombres, and a man who could ride the way he had ridden and who had balls enough to take on a stampeding longhorn bull, could talk and act any damn way he wanted, was the general attitude. Buck had quickly showed, too, that he was no one trick pony and was about as good as any of them when it came to roping cattle—mostly, the boys agreed among themselves, because of that pinto of his, who seemed to read a longhorn's mind as well as he did Buck's.

The point was, he had earned their respect and he had it, and they didn't give a rattlesnake's ass about the rest of it. If anything, they seemed to take an amused interest in his blatant flirtation with their range boss.

Whatever else Les thought about him, by the time that he had been there a couple of days, Les himself had to admit that the Nasoni was earning his pay, and he was glad that he had taken him on—except for that damn foolishness of his, which he never seemed to tire of.

They had shortly made up for the cattle that had escaped in

the stampede, and had more than a thousand ear pieces in the pile. It was time to head back to the ranch. Les had early on made up his mind that, once the roundup was over, he would tell Buck it was time for him to ride on.

The way it was now, though, Buck was like some kind of hero to the cowhands. The boys had quickly come to appreciate his high spirits and his inexhaustible good humor, and since he was far away the youngest of them, it was almost as if he had become something of a pet to them, and that tomfoolery of his seemed not to bother them in the least—though as Les observed, it wasn't them it was directed at.

The upshot of all this was, Les saw that he couldn't fire him now without having an uprising on his hands. So, when it came time to head back to the Double H, there was nothing for it but that Buck had to come with them.

Anyway, Les consoled himself as they rode for home, what with all them horny cowhands out in that bunkhouse, Buck would probably find somebody who would be happy to give him those rides he was always jawing about, and everyone would be happy, and the damn fool would be well out of Les's hair.

Buck rode up to the ranch that first afternoon wondering what to expect. He had lived much of his life on horseback, and had taken part in plenty of roundups, but mostly afterward he just drifted on. He had hardly ever spent any time settled down on a ranch, and he would probably not have traveled back to the Double H either, if it hadn't been for Les. It was like he plain could not get the range boss out of his head. Couldn't get him out of a couple of other places, either, although he had drained one of them it seemed like a hundred times, thinking about him. So there was no drifting on for the present, and it was off to that ranch, and see what come of things.

A trio of scrawny-looking dogs came out to greet them as they rode up the lane, barking and howling at first, and then, seeing who it was, wagging their tales happily and dashing in and out through the horses' legs, making the horses whinny their disapproval and sidestep to avoid them.

The ranch house itself was a long, low structure that sprawled across the land as if it had been built a room or two at a time, without much plan on anyone's part. The front of the house was adobe and old, with a wooden porch that extended its full length and offered respite from the Texas sun. Strings of dried chilies, shiny and red, hung from the porch rafters. There were pepper trees scattered about the yard, their leaves making a carpet under them, and pecan trees, and a small stand of cottonwoods near a well.

Beyond the main house were various sheds and outbuildings, some of them obvious and some that he would have to explore later, and an enormous barn, and two or maybe three corrals for the horses. Past them was another enormous corral to which they drove the bawling, peevish longhorns, where they would be held for the next couple of weeks and fed to fatten them up for their long journey north.

It was all mighty impressive to a drifter like Buck, and when the cattle were penned, he rode into the yard with the others and looked about as he dismounted and waited to be told what he should do next. There were chickens in a pen, clucking with all the excitement, and a big red rooster strutted loose across the yard as Buck got off his horse. He fixed a steely eye on Buck and, seeming to find him wanting, turned his tail feathers to him and stalked away, nattering to himself.

Someone got up from a rocker on the porch of the main house and, hobbling down the steps with the aid of a stick, headed slowly but determinedly in Buck's direction.

It turned out to be an old, an ancient, Mexican woman. Buck figured she must be the oldest person he had ever seen. Her hair had probably once been raven black, but it was white now, what there was of it, and tied behind her with a piece of string. Her toothless mouth had fallen in on itself, and her skin was like parchment, dried and mottled, and with an odd translucent quality, so that you almost expected you could see her innards through it, the way you did with a baby bird.

She came, squinting, directly to where Buck stood, and peered closely at him for a moment, and leaned so close to his face, straining on her toes, that he half thought she meant to kiss him, and he had to resist the urge to lean away from her and her sour breath.

"Half-breed," she said, and turned her head and spit a stream of brown tobacco juice out of the side of her mouth, just missing one of Buck's snakeskin boots. She turned her back on him and made her laborious way back toward the porch.

Buck scratched his head. "Was that a welcome, or not?" he asked Red, who had come to stand alongside him.

Red just laughed. "Don't pay her no mind," he said. "That's just old Mama. Half the time nobody knows what she means by anything."

"Whose Mama is she?" Buck asked, the two of them leading their horses toward the stables with the other men.

Red shrugged. "Nobody's, I guess, nobody that I ever knowed. The story goes, she followed Cookie out here years ago. He tried to drive her off, beat her something fierce, way I heard, till old Miz Cameron told him he couldn't do that no more, and then he locked her outside, wouldn't let her come in the house, told her over and over to leave him alone, but she wouldn't do nothing but sit outside the door day and night, crying and saying she was his woman and she wouldn't go nowhere. So, finally, he settled his mind to the fact that she was here to stay, and here she still is."

"She is like Cookie's woman, then, I guess is what you are saying."

"I reckon you could say that, although I doubt that Cookie uses her that way anymore, seems like. They don't even share a bed any longer, if they ever did. Cookie's got him a little room off the kitchen where he beds down of a night, and she sleeps in that shed over yonder. 'Less he sneaks out there from time to time, but I kind of doubt that. He don't even go to the whore-houses with the boys anymore, says it would just be a waste of money for him."

"So, what does she do?" Buck asked, curious.

"Not much of anything, these days, being as she's so old, woman's got to be ninety years if she's a day, maybe a hundred, for all anyone knows. She used to help with the chow, and do chores around the house, but she doesn't get around too well anymore. She feeds the chickens, I guess. Mostly she just sits around in the sun and bakes her bones. 'Course, Les lets her think she is still doing her share, and she does what she can, cleans some from time to time, does some washing."

A man came out of the barn, walking with a crutch, and took the reins of Red's horse. Buck glanced down and saw that the man's left leg was missing below the knee. The deft way he managed on the crutch told better than words that it must have been gone for a while. Since the war, maybe, Buck thought. Lots of men had come back from that missing parts of themselves, seemed like.

"This is Big Joe," Red introduced him, "So we can keep him separate from Little Joe."

Buck had to stifle a laugh at that, figuring it would not be polite, since Little Joe, who had been on the roundup with them, stood six foot tall or more, and Big Joe, who looked not much younger than old Mama, was a good two or three inches shorter.

"This here is Buck," Red added. "He's going to be working with us for a spell."

"Howdy," Big Joe said, and extended a hand, balancing on his crutch with the ease born of practice, and gave Buck a friendly smile before he took their horses and led them into the barn.

"Seems funny, don't it," Buck said. If he had learned anything in the time since he had joined the roundup, it was that Les worked hard and expected his boys to do the same, which made it seem odd that he would keep an old woman around who did little or nothing, and a man with one leg.

"Funny what way?" Red asked.

Buck shrugged. "I was thinking on Big Joe, there, don't look like a man with one leg missing could exactly earn his keep on a cattle ranch. You'd think Les would let him go, wouldn't you?"

"Where would he go?" Red said. "It ain't like someone else would hire him. It's the same as old Mama. This is the only home they got. Same with Rex, too, when he took a fall and broke his arm on the roundup, that was afore you got there. He is still young and active, of course, but with that arm in a sling, hell, it'll be a week or more before he is good for much, but that don't stop Les from paying him either, every month. And he would you, too, if you was laid up somehow."

"That is right generous of him, seems to me," Buck said. "Never heard of anybody doing that sort of thing before."

"That's just the way Les is. See, some years back, we had an infection of hoof and mouth, wiped out the entire herd. There ain't nothing you can do about hoof and mouth, as you most likely know, but destroy the herd, to keep it from spreading. It was a sorrowful sight, I tell you. We dug these big trenches out on the prairie, and then we drove the cattle into them, and shot them, every last one of them, and then we buried them.

"We lost near two thousand head. That was the worst year there ever was for the Double H. Lost most of the boys, and them that stayed, like myself, we worked for no pay, and not much to eat, to tell the truth. Took the better part of two years before we were back on our feet."

"That Miz Cameron, though, she kept Les on, seems like," Buck said.

"Well, it wasn't Les's fault, she knew that. Wasn't anybody's fault, just one of them things that happens. Besides, Les worked without pay himself. He didn't have to, she tried to go right on paying him, but he knew it had left her plenty short, too, and she had to borrow from the bank just to keep things together, and anyway, he said, if his men was working without pay, he would do the same thing. Some of the boys, course, decided just to ride on. That was their own choice, though, not Les's, but he figured he couldn't argue about their going, since he couldn't pay them nothing."

"I reckon I would have stayed," Buck said, "same as you."

"Well, a fellow has got to make up his own mind about something like that, and there was no hard feelings on either side, with them that left. It's just the same thing, though, that I was saying, with Big Joe, and Mama. Les, he ain't a one for turning a cowboy out on the range once he gets to where he can't work, 'cause he is too old, or something that is no fault of his own, and Miz Cameron, she says that if that's how he sees it, it is fine with her.

"You take some ranches, see, you go one time and there is one gang of cowboys, and you go six months later, ain't a familiar face among them. You know the same as I do, cowboys can be a restless bunch. They come and they go as they please, like the tumbleweeds, just rolling along where the wind takes them. But now, you take the Double H, everybody pretty much sticks around. Except for you, well, I guess you are the first new hand he has hired in a coon's age, since we got over that hoof and mouth. I think the boys has all been here a year or longer, some of them five and six years. Shit, I expect Jake's been around the place ten years if it's a day. That's a long time for a cowboy to stay put. Les is just the kind of man a cowboy respects, and he treats them good, and he says in the long run, it saves him money, not having to break in new hands all the time, and it seems like the boys work harder for him than they do for anybody else."

"Is that why you stick around with him?" Buck asked.

Red chuckled and kind of shrugged. "Shit, old Les and me, we been riding together most of our lives," he said. "We are sidekicks. I wouldn't want to ride with anybody else. You'll see. You stick around a couple of months, you'll be thinking it's where you will want to stay too."

"He sounds like a pretty good man," Buck said, "The way you tell about him."

"Les is the best there is," Red said. "I never bowed to anybody in my life, but if I was to go on my knees before any man, it would be old Les."

Buck smiled to himself. He had a notion he would surely like to get on his knees in front of old Les, too; but he felt pretty certain him and Red did not mean it in the same way.

Chapter 4

Buck had always been an early riser, and his first morning at the Double H was no different. He woke while the windows of the bunkhouse were just turning a pearly gray with the approach of dawn, and lay for a few minutes listening to the boys snore. The air smelled of sweat and old cigarette smoke and stale farts and clothes worn long between washings, but he found the odd blend of scents comfortable and welcoming, a cowboy kind of aroma that he missed when he was alone on the trail.

He remembered all at once the dream he had been savoring, in which Les had been holding him in his arms. The memory, and the image that came into his mind of Les, made his morning erection stiffen still more. Unlike the rest of the hands, who slept in their long johns, he generally slept in the raw except when he was out on the trail, where you needed to be ready for anything that might come along. He yawned and stretched, and ground his dick against the coarse wool of his blanket. He briefly contemplated relieving himself, and thought better of it. That would wait, he decided. There was a whole new world outside the bunkhouse, waiting for him to explore.

He slipped from the bed and into his trousers, checked his boots for any critters, and tugged them on, and stole from the bunkhouse, careful not to wake anyone else. The sun was just tiptoeing over the horizon. The loner in him loved the early morning hours, especially having them to himself, when he could savor the solitude and the silence.

Only, it was not really so silent. The hounds came bounding up, sniffling and wagging, and he knelt to pet them and slap their rumps playfully. The birds in the pepper trees argued noisily among themselves over questions of territory and social matters, and in the distant henhouse, the old rooster bawled the day's orders to his harem. The windmill over the water tank creaked and whirred lazily in the morning breeze. Homely sounds. It had been a while since he had heard their like.

He made a visit to the outhouse, and went to the pump and splashed water over himself, and dried himself with his shirt before he put it on and tied his bandana at his throat. He yawned again and stretched his arms over his head, feeling young and full of sap, and thought maybe after all he ought to have seen to some pecker business before he left his bed, but he did not feel much inclined to go back to it. The sun had begun to gild the edges of a solitary cloud on the horizon and to smear the sky with bold streaks of yellow and pink, like a peach, to where you just wanted to stretch up and take a bite out of it.

He realized suddenly that he was not alone. The old Mexican woman, Mama, came out of the barn carrying a big feed sack, off-balance and leaning sideways with the weight of it, and headed in the direction of the chicken run, seeming not to notice him.

He caught up with her, and took the sack from her. She gave him a suspicious look, but she relinquished it without any quarrel. He carried it for her to the chicken run, and waited while she let the hens out of the house, the rooster leading the way and making it clear to one and all that he was the one who mattered the most in this enclosure.

She tossed feed on the ground in handfuls, the birds squabbling among themselves, pecking at one another and the feed, and sometimes climbing right on top of someone who was in their way.

When Mama had finished feeding them, Buck took the sack again and carried it for her back to the barn, and at her wordless directions, filled a couple of buckets with water from the horse trough and carried that to the chicken run and filled the old wash tub they drank from, stepping carefully around the still bickering hens.

A pail of slops by the kitchen door went to a pen off to one side of the barn where a trio of mud-caked hogs greeted them noisily and quickly went to work choosing the delicacies from their morning victuals.

That seemed to finish her chores. She stood in front of Buck and leaned in close to study his face, frowning, as she had done the day before, and her breath sour in an old-person way. "You're the half-breed, ain't you?" she said.

He grinned, hoping to put her at ease, and said, "Reckon I am, ma'am," and corrected himself, "señora."

He jumped when she unexpectedly put a hand down and took hold of his dick through the fabric of his pants, and seemed to measure it with her fingers.

"Injuns is always good at using them things," she said.

For a moment he was worried that she might expect a demonstration, but she seemed satisfied with just checking its size, and let go of it, to his relief.

She turned her back on him and hobbled away without another word. Watching her go, he tried to imagine what she might have looked like when she was younger, but like most young men, he lacked the knack to see youth where it had once been, and his imagination refused to color the white hair black, or fill out the scrawny hips and the withered legs. She was just an old woman.

When she had disappeared inside her shed, he laughed to himself, and gave his dick a consoling pat, case it had taken any offense. A finger of smoke had begun to point upward from the kitchen chimney. He figured—rightly, as it turned out—that Cookie must be already at work. Cowboys tend to wake up hungry, and a smart cook is up before them and ready when they do.

The kitchen door stood open. Buck opened the screen and let himself in, and found Cookie on his knees before his stove, stoking the fire. He looked up and nodded a greeting. "Guess you get up with the chickens, same as me," he said.

"I like to see the sun come up," Buck said.

Cookie got up and dusted the knees of his pants. "Coffee'll be ready shortly," he said.

Buck looked around the room. The kitchen was enormous. He guessed that it occupied the whole east wing of the house. There was an inglenook next to an open hearth with a spit on it, that looked big enough to roast half a steer, and two stoves, both of them of cast iron: a smaller one that was well used, and the newer, bigger one that Cookie had been stoking. That one had a top as large as the kitchen door and all sorts of modern conveniences like warming ovens and water baths. On the table beside it and hanging from ceiling rafters and on the walls was a vast assortment of pots and skillets and other cooking paraphernalia, much of it well used. There was a rusty-looking sink with a hand pump, and a glass-doored cupboard filled with unmatched crockery and cups and dishes, and next to it, a pie saver with pierced metal doors and its feet set in dishes of water to discourage the ants. A wooden table sat in the center of the room and dominated it, round and big enough that any number of hungry cowboys could crowd up to it, and covered with a red and white checked oilcloth with patches where elbows and hands and coffee mugs had worn through the pattern.

"Nice kitchen," Buck said. He had taken to cooking when he was just a boy, to care for his mother, and had found it a relaxing pastime over the years. Seeing a kitchen so up to date like this one, and so well equipped, made him think that he wanted to talk to Cookie later about putting his hand in while he was here.

"It is," Cookie agreed. "'Course, when the weather gets really hot, I'll mostly cook out yonder in the summer kitchen, keeps the house cooler." He paused to glance at his coffee pot, but the water was not yet aboil. "Come on and have a look around, if you like."

He led the way out of the kitchen and along a covered walkway, to the door into a dining room at the front of the house. The room appeared altogether too elegant for dusty cowboy boots, Buck thought, and he did not go inside, but only looked from the open doorway.

He had never seen anything so splendid. He figured it was like something out of a palace, though he had never actually seen one of those. A table that must have been fifteen feet long if it was an inch sat in the middle of the room, gleaming with a velvety patina from years of devoted waxing, and arranged along each side of the table were chairs covered in cowhide and trimmed at the arms and backs with horn, and overheard a hanging light made from a wagon wheel. At the far wall was a sideboard from which some silver pieces gleamed dully, and over that, a gilt-framed mirror in whose smoky surface he could just see their faint images.

"Don't nobody hardly ever use this," Cookie said. "Never was used much. Even when she was here, Miz Cameron mostly ate in the kitchen like the fellows, unless there was company. Same with the front room. But I keep them swept and dusted and all, clean as a whistle, just the way she always liked them. Can't ride anymore, hardly, 'cept to drive the chuck wagon, so I figure least I can do is keep things up in the house, so's they are ready for her if she should anytime decide to pop in. Old Mama, she helps sometimes. Not a lot of work to it, though, since nobody hardly ever goes past the kitchen. This here is the front room."

He indicated the parlor that took up the rest of the front part of the house. Heavy drapes were closed over the windows here, so mostly Buck saw shadows among shadows. He gave his eyes a moment to adjust, and when he did, he jumped back. From the far wall, a puma eyed him menacingly.

"What . . . ?" he started to say.

Cookie chuckled and moved past him to partially open a pair of green velvet draperies. In the dim light, Buck saw a whole wall of trophy heads staring down at him—not just the puma, but a bighorn sheep as well, and a buffalo, and a javelina and an antelope.

"Old man Cameron, he was quite the hunter," Cookie said. "Him and his buddy, Ray, they used to go off camping and hunting every chance they got. That was before the two of them went off to the war, course, and didn't come back."

The stuffed heads dominated the room, which was otherwise furnished as splendidly as the dining room next door. There was a pair of horsehair sofas, in frames of elaborately carved rosewood, and more of the hide and horn chairs, and brightly patterned rugs on the wood floors.

Cookie tugged the drapes together again. "Got to keep them closed. Everything fades in the sun," he said, and came back to where Buck stood in the doorway.

The house was built in a square shape, with a central courtyard in the middle, floored with red clay tiles, with a profusion of dusty green plants standing here and there in large clay containers. Flame-colored hibiscus filled one corner of the square and perfumed the air, and bougainvillea the color of violets climbed up the kitchen wall.

Cookie had shown him the dining room and the parlor from the covered walkway that ran around three sides of the interior, missing only the wing that held the kitchen, and which when the summer sun was at its fiercest, would provide welcome shade to anyone passing from one part of the house to another. A stone fountain stood in the center of the courtyard, trickling brackish-colored water and hung with gray-green moss. A dragonfly hovered near it, its wings iridescent in the morning light.

"Look like Mexican houses I have seen," Buck said, thinking that it was all very beautiful indeed.

"It was, to begin with. This part of Texas *was* Mexico at one time," Cookie said. "This was the hacienda of a Don Sebastiano, an important man, as I hear it, when San Antone was a Mexican pueblo. When the Camerons took it over, that was after Texas was independent of Mexico, they up and kept the old hacienda and just added on to it, to make it larger as they needed it. There's bedrooms along the west side, there," he pointed. "Miz Cameron's is the first one, the biggest of them. I keep that for her in case she wants to stay over when she comes out, which she don't much anymore, and there's a couple of extra rooms, for when they used to have company. At one time, there was lots of it, but that was long ago. And across the backside of the house there, that room was Les's Ma's when she was around, and the one next to it is his. Ain't any bigger than a breadbox, Les's room. Miz Cameron, she used to tell him all the time that he ought to take one of the bigger bedrooms, now that he is lord of the manor, as she says it, but he says his old one does him just fine. The one next to it there, that used to be for the old man's friend, Ray, when he would come to stay, which was pretty regular in them days. We just store things in it now, and at the other end, there, that little room just off the kitchen, that is where I sleep."

It was the grandest place Buck had ever seen, although his experience along those lines was limited. They stood for a moment, savoring the stillness of the courtyard with only the gentle plash of the fountain to break it. A bee came in from somewhere and cavorted a bit in the hibiscus, and flew off drunkenly to spread the word.

"Speaking of Les," Cookie said, breaking the silence, "That boy will be rising pretty shortly, he's not a one to lie abed either, and he will want his breakfast ready when he does. Reckon I had better get things moving along."

He left Buck where he was and headed back to the kitchen. Buck walked over to look at the fountain, and trail his fingers idly in the water. He drifted closer to the room Cookie had pointed out as Les's. Les would be stirring by now probably, and Buck pictured him in his imagination, stretching in his fading sleep, his prick morning-swollen. Buck lifted his head, scenting at the air, and almost thought he could smell it, that warm puppy smell they had on waking, musky and overlaid with the salt of sweat.

For a moment, he half thought about just going in there, catching him before he was full awake, seeing if he could get himself a little something going before Les had time to think about it and object. A stiff dick didn't take much convincing, in his experience.

He decided differently, though. What he wanted up his ass was not the toe of Les's cowboy boot. It was his experience, too, that a fellow might be dead set against it, and say no, no, no all the time, and mean it sincerely; but then maybe a time would come, it might be no more than a minute, when the latch that had been locked up tight all along was left open, whether by accident or because someone wanted what they did not know that they wanted, and if a fellow kept a lookout, and saw when that moment had come, why, he could push the door open and walk right on in, and he might be made plenty welcome. Then, things went as easy and as natural as if they had been planned for all along.

If you got in a hurry, though, and tried to push the door too soon, or you came to it late, why, it would stay shut tight on you, and then you were nothing but an intruder, and your visit unwelcome.

He would wait till Les left that door unlocked for him. He could usually tell, and he had slipped through many a door that had remained locked to others before him. He laughed to himself, happy just to be here, to know that Les was lying abed, maybe naked, no more than a few feet away from him. He almost felt as if he could look right through the walls and see him.

Savoring that picture in his mind, he went in search of Cookie.

The two of them were seated at the table, drinking Cookie's muddy coffee, when Les came shirtless into the kitchen a short while later, hair tousled and eyes still puffy with sleep, the golden hair on his chest glinting in the morning light. His pants were unbelted and there was the merest glimpse of more gold too where his fly hung half open. He looked kind of surprised to see Buck at the table with Cookie, but he only nodded briefly and mumbled "Morning," to them as he passed, and went outside, the screen door banging shut behind him.

He was back after a few minutes, his hair damp, and his fly, to Buck's disappointment, fully closed now. He went back to his room, and reemerged a minute later with a shirt on, tucking it into his trousers as he walked, and sat down heavily at the table.

"Sure is a fine morning," Buck said in a cheery voice, "Looks like it is going to be a hot one . . . "

"Boy, I ain't even had me a cup of coffee yet," Les said curtly, at the same time as Cookie set a big, chipped mug in front of him.

"Sounds like somebody must have got up on the wrong side of the bed," Buck said, undeterred.

"Ain't but one side I can get out of my bed on," Les said. "And I ain't a one for a lot of jawing before I have had my breakfast, if you get my drift."

"Oh, sure, I understand," Buck said. He set his lips tightly closed and made a locking motion with his fingers.

"Glad you do."

Cookie was back in a minute with an enormous plate that he set steaming in front of Les. There was a big slab of ham on it, in a mahogany pool of red eye gravy, and a half dozen fried eggs swimming in grease, a mountain of pinto beans studded with strong-scented onions, and two thick slices of bread, brown from the oven and shiny with bacon drippings.

Les took one of the hunks of bread, and poked it into the yolks of the eggs, and dipped it into the gravy, and began to chew on it enthusiastically. Buck watched him with undisguised pleasure. He liked to see a man who enjoyed his food. It generally meant his other appetites were pretty good, too. He looked at Les's mouth while he chewed, and found himself wondering what those firm lips would feel like against his own. An image came into his mind: he was lying naked on his back, and Les was atop him, his weight heavy and warm. Les's knees pushed his legs wide apart, and one of those big hands reached down between them . . .

He suddenly realized that Les was looking quizzically across the table at him while he ate.

"Somethin'?" Les asked around a mouthful of food. Buck started to answer, and remembered that he wasn't to talk. He clamped his lips shut and shook his head instead.

Les took a big forkful of beans and began to chew on them, but he continued to stare steadily at Buck for a long moment.

Buck got the message finally. He pushed his chair back from the table with a noisy scrape of wood on wood. "Reckon I will mosey outside," he said, hoping Les would tell him to stay, but he did not. Les did, though, look after him from under his brows as Buck went out. The screen door banged again.

"Reckon we had better fix that screen door," Les said to Cookie as he brought the coffee pot over to refill his cup, "if we're going to have crowds of folks coming in and out all the time regular before a man has even had his breakfast."

It didn't bother Buck at all though that Les had been grumpy like that. He himself always woke up happy and raring to go, but he had known lots of men that woke up like grizzly bears. That was just how some men were. He thought it mattered a lot more how they went to sleep, and he liked to send them off to dream land well contented when he got the chance. Hopefully, sooner or later he would get the chance with Les, and then he could wake up as mean as he liked, it wouldn't make no difference to him if he did. Once you got what you wanted off a man, well, hell, he couldn't take it back, could he? He had never heard of a load going back into where it had come out of.

The sun was up now, already hot and bleaching all the color out of the sky. There was still no one else to be seen, but he could hear voices from the bunkhouse, engaged in friendly banter, so the other hands would be emerging soon. He looked around and scratched at his balls absentmindedly, and went to explore more fully than he had before.

He skirted the shed where old Mama had disappeared earlier, not wanting to encourage any further interest on her part in the size or performance of his dick, and found the summer kitchen Cookie had mentioned, just off the main one. It was smaller than the one inside, of course, but it was almost as fully equipped, except with only one stove and a smaller hearth, and it had windows on every side to encourage any breeze that happened by.

There was a woodshed not far from that, to save carrying firewood any long distance to either of the kitchens, and a springhouse, dark and cool and damp, the reflections off the water dancing on its stone ceiling. A couple of hams, wrapped in cheesecloth, hung from the ceiling, smelling of pig and mold and the mesquite over which they had been smoked.

Not far from the springhouse he found a kitchen garden, in need of some weeding, but filled with vigorous-looking plants that would soon become potatoes and tomatoes and chilies, and what appeared to be different kinds of beans, and one or two things he wasn't sure of. He thought maybe between chores he would have a go at some of them weeds.

He had been in the barn the night before, and knew that it was lined on both sides with stalls for the horses, and there was a small buggy parked in there as well, and a larger buckboard, and above it all, a hayloft that you got to up a ladder.

Beyond the barn, on the far side, was a large corral they could let the horses out into for exercise, and a little ways off from that, he discovered a smaller corral with a lean-to in place of a stall, and one lone gray pony in it. The pony snorted derisively as Buck approached, and reared briefly on his hind legs, as if to warn him away.

"No use looking at that horse, boy," Les said behind him, "Not if you are thinking about riding him."

He had come up without Buck hearing him. He looked well fed, now, and less taciturn than before, although Buck had long since decided that the foreman was not the chattering type, nor was he a man who smiled wherever he looked. That was fine with Buck, though. He could talk enough for two, if he had a mind for it. He liked a man that saved his breath for better things.

There was a little dab of red brown gravy on Les's upper lip, and seeing it, Buck had an urge to lick it clean and his tongue almost came out of his mouth of its own accord. As if he had read Buck's thoughts, Les ran his own tongue over it, and the spot disappeared. Watching him, the quick flick of his tongue, Buck's heart did a little dance inside his chest. Shit, but that man was something to feast your eyes on, he thought, and felt a warning movement in his trousers.

"What's wrong with him, then?" he asked, nodding toward the horse, deciding it was best to take his mind of the stir in his pants.

"Ain't no one on this ranch been able to ride him," Les said. "Can't even get a saddle on him. I'm just keeping him around to breed, if I can find a mare to his liking. And he don't scare her off. He's mean as cat piss."

"That there's an Indian horse," Buck said, as if that explained everything.

Les came up to stand close by Buck, so close that Buck actually thought he could feel the cowboy's body heat coming off of him. Damn, he had to stop thinking about that shit, or he would have himself a real boner in no time, and he felt pretty sure Les would not be pleased by that.

"What that horse is," Les said, "is the devil himself."

"Ah, he's just fooling with you," Buck said. "Testing you, like. Here, let me show you." He climbed the fence and jumped over it. "Come on," he said.

Les came up to the rail. "Damn it, boy," he said sharply, "I'm telling you, that pony liked to killed old Jack a while back, when he got too close."

"That's 'cause old Jack was afraid, most likely. They smell fear, horses do," Buck said. "You coming, or what?"

So there was nothing for Les to do but jump over the fence after him. Some of the boys had sauntered out of the bunkhouse by this time, washing at the trough, and one of them taking a noisy piss against the side of the barn. They saw Buck and Les in the corral with that wild horse and begin to drift over to see what was happening, the one fellow still hastily shaking himself off as he came, not wanting to miss anything.

"Someone's going to get himself hurt," old Jack muttered, remembering the day the pony had nearly killed him with its flying hooves, and a couple of the boys nodded; but they all were aware as well that the Nasoni knew his way around horses as good as anybody, and they waited to see what he had in mind.

The pony waited too. He watched the two men clear the fence, and as they approached him, he danced about skittishly and pawed at the ground and whickered his ears forward, but he kept his dark wet eyes on Buck in the lead and seemed to be waiting for him to do whatever it was he had in mind to do.

Buck came right up to him without pause, and taking hold of the pony's head, he said, "You got to breathe into his nostrils, like so." He snorted hard and loud up the horse's nostrils. To Les's surprise, the horse responded in kind, his nostrils flaring as he breathed a powerful stream of air into the Nasoni's face.

"It's the horse's way of greeting a friend," Buck said. "Now you do it."

Les approached, feeling a little foolish, but not wanting to be showed up. The horse whinnied but his large limpid eyes regarded Les with a steady appraisal, and he stood stock still, not a muscle moving. Les leaned forward till his nose almost touched the horse's, and breathed out hard, up the horse's nostrils the way Buck had showed him, and was rewarded with a blast of hot breath that all but choked him.

"Do it again," Buck said. Les repeated the ritual. "Now," Buck said, "he's your friend. You can ride that horse anywhere you choose."

By now the other cowboys had joined the watchers; the men crowded along the fence, staring, no one making a sound. The horse snorted, as if wondering what all the fuss was about, but when Les reached up to pet his muzzle, he rubbed gently against his hand.

"Well, I'll be a son of a bitch," Les said. "You really think he'd let me get on?"

"Won't neither one of us try to throw you if you was to want a ride," Buck said.

The men at the fence laughed loudly. Les blushed crimson, but when Buck put his hands down for a stirrup, Les stepped a size fourteen into them and swung his long leg over the pony's back. There was a moment of silence, everyone holding his breath. Les took hold of the pony's mane, and a minute later, the cowboys saw their boss riding the devil horse bareback around the corral, as polite as you please.

"How'd you know that?" Les asked Buck, riding over to where he was watching and looking mighty pleased with himself. "That he would let me ride so easy?"

"It was the way he whinnied," Buck said. "He acted nervous, but he sounded friendly."

Les had never thought to listen to how a horse whinnied. Blamed Indian might be a fool, but a man could learn a thing or two from him, it seemed like.

There was some lessons, of course, that he hadn't a mind to learn.

Chapter 5

On Saturday nights the boys usually rode into town to let off a little steam. Most Saturdays, Les let them go on their own, since they were likely to be more at their ease without their boss around. There was lots of drinking at the cantina and some poker games, and some of the boys visited one or the other of the whorehouses, Miz Yolanda's being the most popular.

Occasionally, after a few too many whiskies, one or the other of them would get into a shoot-em-up. Then Red, who usually went in Les's place, would have to take control of things until they got settled down. Once or twice, he'd had to go in the morning to bail a sheepish cowboy out of the local jail, where the sheriff had put him as much for his own good as anything. Mostly, though, it was all just harmless cutting up, and they came back to the ranch the better for a little fun, and ready to go back to their hard day's work.

It was a tradition, though, that on the Saturday after a roundup, Les took the boys into town himself, and he paid for everything, and if they were maybe just a little more subdued than they might have been on another Saturday, with their boss being around, they were always plenty grateful to him anyway for the gesture, and it meant they could drink their fill and have some fun with the girls at the whorehouses and, if they had a mind to, still come home with the same coins in their pockets as when they had left, and they counted themselves lucky to work for so generous a fellow.

This roundup was no exception, and their first Saturday night after they got back to the ranch, everyone saddled up and rode off in a group into town. Even Cookie and Big Joe went, the two of them in the buggy, leaving only Mama at home, sitting on her rocker in the kitchen with a pint jar of tequila on the table where she could reach it without much effort.

"She will be sitting in that rocker, still, when we get back," Red said when Buck asked if she would be all right there by herself, "except she will be dead to the world, and one of the boys will have to help Cookie carry her out to her shed. That's how it usually is."

They set out in the afternoon, and took their time riding into town, one of the boys occasionally larruping up his horse and galloping for a spell, and calling in a nasal twang, "Ah hah, San Antone." And then the others would take up the yell, "Ah, hah, San Antone," and toss their hats in the air, and some of them began to sing about a rose of old San Antone, which was a favorite among the local cowboys, who for all their tough hides could be a sentimental bunch.

In time, San Antonio appeared like a collection of fly specks on the horizon, specks that gradually grew to take the shape of houses and commercial buildings, and by early evening they were riding into a good-sized town of dusky beige houses and wide, dust-clouded streets that twisted and snaked around without any apparent pattern.

By this time, the men were laughing among themselves and making boasts of what they intended to do, the gist of many of them being the numbers of women they were going to make happy and the different ways in which they were going to do it. All of them enjoyed swapping the tales, and if some of them were unlikely, no one saw fit to point that out.

Even Les seemed to have unbent some from his usual grave demeanor, and riding just a little behind him, Buck found himself basking in the glow of the smiles Les flashed around from time to time at his cowhands. Once, he actually smiled straight at Buck, and Buck's heart leaped into his throat, so that he could hardly manage to smile back; but Les didn't notice that. He had looked away in an instant, smiling at another one of the boys. Still, Buck tucked the moment into his pocket, like a kind of magic charm that he could take out later and savor at leisure.

To everyone's surprise and puzzlement, however, they arrived at the outskirts of San Antonio to the accompaniment of a familiar sound. Somewhere nearby, cattle were bawling and lowing a chorus of complaints.

"Sounds like somebody's having a cattle drive right here in San Antone," Red said.

"Sounds like it," Les agreed, "but that makes no sense, does it?"

"Why would you want to herd cattle *into* a town?" Red said, mystified.

They had discovered on the ride in that it was Buck's first visit to San Antone. He had skirted the town on his way up from Galveston, but he hadn't stopped, wanting to find his way to the roundup he'd heard tell of, before it was over, and he looked around now with interest as they rode in. Red watched him with fond amusement. He was like a kid at Christmas, delighted with everything he saw, and even Les found himself enjoying the Nasoni's wide-eyed enthusiasm.

Most of the buildings where they passed were of adobe, low and pink-tinged and cool-looking. There were larger houses, too, several-storied wood structures with porches and gables and steep-pitched roofs. The sounds of music drifted out from an occasional cantina, as the local saloons were called, and the cooking smells—it being near the supper hour—were foreign and spicy, with that tang that Buck had come to associate with this part of Texas, which was still new to him.

"I expect this is different from where you grew up, ain't it?" Red asked.

"A lot different," Buck said. "I growed up mostly in Oklahoma and northeast Texas. And this is a big city, seems to me, bigger than Galveston even, and everything built up and modern like."

"What's so different about it?" Les asked.

"Well, you see more Indians where I was, and people come down from the French, when that was the Louisiana Territory." He looked around again. "And you hardly ever see any Mexicans up Oklahoma way."

He nodded in the direction of a Mexican youth, slim as a rapier, who sat atop a hitching post and idly tuned a guitar, discordant notes seeming to spill from his fingers and cascade to the dusty ground.

As they passed, women came to the front doors and porches to observe their progress, and occasionally one of them would call a greeting to a cowboy, and he would doff his hat and grin and nod, and then the others would tease him about it raucously.

The people were as varied as the sights and sounds and smells of the town, many of them dark-haired and dark-eyed, plainly of Mexican or Spanish descent, but others blond and Germanic, and every coloration in between. To Buck's surprise, a pigtailed Chinese darted across the street in front of their horses, incongruous and exotic in this rustic setting.

As they approached the commercial part of town, they found a large crowd of people collected at a plaza. A street that emptied into the plaza had been wired off with a funny kind of wire, with metal tufts every few inches apart. Les and his company paused to consider it.

"What is that stuff?" Les asked one of the men standing nearby.

"They call it barbed wire," the man called back, making two syllables of "barbed."

"Funny-looking stuff, ain't it?" Les said. "What's it for?"

"Fellow that strung it up, he says it'll stop cattle from going where they ain't supposed to. He's driving a herd of them down this way just now, for a demonstration."

Which explained the braying and lowing they had heard earlier. Les and his cowboys sat on their horses and watched, and a few minutes later, just as the man had said, a small herd of longhorns, maybe fifteen or twenty of them, came rushing down the side street at them, a passel of cowboys behind, driving them forward.

The wire barrier that had been strung across the street, no more than three strands above one another and spaced about a foot apart, looked too fragile to contain even this small herd.

On the prairie, a handful of cattle had been known to push their way right through the wire fences that the farmers strung up to protect their growing fields.

Sure enough, though, the cattle got to that barbed wire, and once the leaders encountered those funny metal tufts, they quickly decided they did not like them. They stopped in their tracks and began to mill around, puzzled and bawling their confusion at one another, and in no time, the flight of the herd had ground to a halt.

The men in the watching crowd, who looked to be mostly farmers, shouted and cheered, and several of them ran over to have a closer look at the wire and to talk excitedly among themselves.

"What'd he say that stuff was?" Red asked, astonished.

"The end of the open range, is what it is," Les said. "Let's go get us a drink, boys. You ask me, that is farmer kind of stuff." Which, to a cow herder, was disparaging indeed. The cowboys snickered among themselves and followed him on down the street, but Red looked back once, at the milling cattle and the wire that had stopped them, and found himself thinking, sadly, that Les was probably right. Some folks, farmers mostly, were already busy fencing up the land, seemed like everywhere you turned. The more land they fenced, the open range as he had always known it, the prairies that were the life of the cowhand, were sure to vanish.

The fact was, though, that the old Texas way of life had already largely disappeared in the boomtown that was modern-day San Antonio. Dogs and old men still dozed in the plaza as they had since the days of old, but the wide, winding streets were crowded with traffic, so that the cowboys were constantly dodging coaches and buggies, other horsemen and foot travelers, all the busy commerce of an important town. The Chisholm Trail, the most popular of the trails for the cattle drives northward, started near the Mexican border and came right past San Antone, almost the last town it reached in Texas, and it was here that cowmen stopped for supplies, and to rest, and to relieve pent-up energies.

The Double H boys visited one of the cantinas and Les bought everyone a round of Irish whiskies—poteen, Red called it, a word Buck had not heard before. Buck had never been much of a drinker. He had lived a hardscrabble life, on his own, and he had found long ago that it was best if he kept his wits about him, and that it did not take much whisky to rob him of them. Despite some good-natured ribbing from the others, he drank a sarsaparilla.

While he was there, Les made arrangements with the bartender to see that the hands were well supplied with whatever they wanted, and he would come back later to settle up, and as he was well known and respected, that suited everyone just fine.

He and Red left, Buck tagging along with them. They hadn't exactly invited him, but they hadn't shooed him away either, and it seemed to him like Les had never been more friendly in his presence, and he vowed to take advantage of it and to be on his best behavior—at least for a little while.

They visited a couple of the whorehouses favored by the boys—not, Buck quickly understood, so that they could satisfy themselves—here, too, Les arranged things with the women who ran them, Miz Yolanda at one and Miz

Annabelle at the other, to insure that any of the Double H boys who stopped by wanting to be pleasured, would be accommodated.

"You weren't planning on lingering a bit?" Miz Yolanda asked when they were getting ready to leave. Les and Red were both known to the girls and favored by them, and the good-looking foreman was particularly popular, especially since he was known to pay well, and several of the girls waited about and eyed him hopefully. But Miz Yolanda noticed, too, with her business-woman's eye, that the handsome young newcomer seemed to have caught everyone's fancy also.

"I got business to see to for the moment," Les said. "Thank you just the same, another time for me, I reckon. But the boys here can do as they wish."

"I reckon I might stop by a little later," Red said, and smiled at a little dark-haired girl, who giggled and smiled back at him. Red and Les both looked expectantly at Buck.

"Reckon I will just tag along with the two of you for a spell," Buck said, rubbing his hands down his pants legs. "If that is all right. I was hoping to see a little bit of the town before it got dark."

Les gave him a careful look, but the boy looked back at him all innocent-like. Seeing him like this, you could hardly even remember how he had been making a pest of himself since the day he had arrived. He seemed to have nothing peculiar on his mind, now, though, and Les shrugged. He had actually found himself enjoying Buck's excitement since they had arrived in town. Shit, when he wasn't acting up, it turned out the kid was pretty good company.

"Well, then," he said, "I guess me and Red might show you around the town some, if that's your fancy, and then you can do as you please, later. If you was thinking about a girl," and he raised an eyebrow almost hopefully, "Miz Yolanda's is where you will likely want to visit."

"You come on back," Miz Yolanda said, smiling warmly at Buck. "We will see you are proper taken care of."

From Miz Yolanda's whorehouse, they took him to see the San Antonio River that flowed in a leisurely and aimless course through the city and looked, Buck thought, more like a muddy stream than a river.

"Don't seem to know where it wants to go, does it?" Buck said.

"The Payaya name for it," Red explained, "meant drunken old man going home at night, on account of the way it twists and turns about," and Buck could see how it had gotten that name.

After that, they went for a stroll through the nearby Mercado, a sprawling marketplace of shops, lean-tos and open stalls where vendors, most of them Mexican, sold a seemingly endless variety of goods and services. There were workers in leather and tin and silver, and stalls that displayed brilliantly colored pottery, and flowers, toys and jewelry. And everywhere there was food, luscious displays in infinite variety. Baskets overflowed with mouthwatering berries and plums and a funny, rough-skinned fruit that Red told him were called "alligator pears." Other tables were laden with rich-looking baked goods: baked pies and fried pies, and cakes and sheets of pone. Elsewhere, great slabs of beef and goat hung to roast, dripping their savory juices on the fires beneath them.

"You see lots of Mexicans around here, don't you," Buck said. "Weren't there some kind of war between Texas and Mexico?"

"We can show you the mission where they fought, if you want to see it," Les said; "the Alamo it's called, which is the Mexican name for them cottonwood trees like we have got out to the ranch. That was a long time ago, course, when they fought there, though it seems like there's still some prejudice, on both sides."

"Reckon I know about that," Buck said, but without any self-pity. "There's some folks stick their noses up at me, being what I am."

It gave Les pause. With everything else, he forgot half the time that the kid was a half-breed. There were plenty who did not take kindly to them, either; but it seemed to Les that, aside from all those outrageous sex comments of his, at least half of which he was inclined to think were just a joke, but apart from that, surely Buck was as much a man as anybody else, and more than some, maybe, no matter of the nature of his blood.

"I reckon that most of these people just consider themselves Texans, though," Red said, "regardless of what they started out as."

Buck followed his nose to a stall where an enormous cauldron sat over a low burning bed of coals. In it simmered what appeared to be a cross between a thick, maroon-colored soup and a thin stew.

"Smells powerful good," Buck said, leaning down to sniff at the spicy aroma. "What is it?"

"It's a San Antone original," Red said. "Invented right here. Folks around here call it chili. I guess you could say it's the local favorite."

"I guess I will have to try me some of it, then," Buck said.

With a few words in English and a few in Mexican, and few more that Les thought must be Nasoni, Buck managed to negotiate the purchase of a bowl of the stew from a grinning Mexican girl, who took the proffered coins and ladled him a steaming bowlful. Several people at the nearby stalls seemed to take an interest in the purchase and grinned back and forth at one another, and a couple of young boys ran up to stand and watch, smiling.

"Must be big news when somebody tries this for the first time," Buck said, looking around at his suddenly amassed audience.

"It can be," Red said, looking oddly amused himself.

"Look, boy," Les said, "maybe before you start, I ought to tell you, about how to eat that . . . "

"I expect I can manage to feed myself okay," Buck said. He took a big spoonful of the stew into his mouth, chewed on a chunk of meat, and swallowed. "Say," he said, "this is delicious, and it is so . . . it is so . . . "

He suddenly felt as if he had eaten one of the embers from the cooking fire. Tears sprang to his eyes and he found himself literally gasping for air.

"So hot?" Les suggested, and laughed aloud with the watching Mexicans as Buck did a little dance in the dust of the street, hopping from one foot to the other, and saying, "God damn, God damn."

"No, wait," Les said when Buck reached for the dipper in a nearby pail, "not water. That'll only make it a river of fire all the way down your gut. Here, eat a piece of this." He took some bread from a basket next to the pot. "It'll soak some of it up. And then a beer, that suits it better than water. *Una cerveza*," he told the girl, and she quickly took a dark, stubby bottle from a tub of water, uncapped it and handed it across.

Buck took his advice, and found that a big mouthful of the bread and a sip of cold beer really did help. The burning sensation lingered, but it was much less than before, and now he could actually savor the taste of the stew, and found that he liked it.

Only, "Is it always that hot?" he asked, fanning his mouth.

"Or worse," Les said. "Folks around here like their food hot."

"It's the chilies," Red said, "the peppers. That's what it's named for. The Mexicans have a way of their own to tell if they have got it hot enough. They give some to a newcomer and if it makes him holler and hop around, why, then they figure they got it about right."

"Well, I guess they can figure this batch is fine," Buck said. "Tastes good, though. I can see how a fellow would get used to it."

"Shit, in a few months, you'll be complaining that batch is too tame," Red said. "You see if you don't."

"Say," Buck said, dropping his voice so the watching Mexicans could not hear and suddenly grinning that silly grin of his. He looked down at the front of Les's trousers, "I just got me a good idea of what would cool my mouth down better than any hunk of bread, if you was willing to help a fellow out, since he has burned his mouth bad."

"Shit," Les swore aloud. "I just got to thinking maybe you wasn't so damned crazy after all, and there you go again."

He shook his head in disgust and turned and walked quickly away. Buck and Red lingered where they were for a moment. Red looked at Buck, and followed his gaze, and saw that it was glued to Les's butt.

"What're you thinking now, boy?" Red asked.

"I'm thinking maybe the boss man says no a bit too loud," Buck said.

Red looked after Les again. He didn't say anything—Les was an old buddy as well as his boss, and he owed him some loyalty, it seemed like to him—but privately, he wondered if maybe Buck mightn't just have a point.

Funny thing was, though, that he had never noticed before, but his boss really did have a nicely shaped bottom on him, not little and pouty like Buck's but bigger, man-sized and firm and rounded like a pair of those low Texas hills, with a deep valley in between them. He realized for the first time what he had never even noticed before now: that it was a butt really did look like it was just made for a man to climb on it and ride for home.

Forget it, he told himself. "Forget it," he said aloud. "Ain't nobody ever rode that."

"Somebody's got to be the first one, don't they?" Buck said.

"If it was to get rode, somebody would have to be first," Red said, "but that don't mean anybody is ever going to get on it." He hurried after his boss.

Buck watched them go, and smiled to himself like a man who knew things others maybe didn't. Regardless, he thought, he felt pretty sure that Les's handsome butt was ready for a riding, even if Les didn't know that yet himself, and somebody was going to be the first one to ride it one of these days. He had in his mind, too, exactly who that somebody was going to be. He just had to convince somebody else of it, was all. Wouldn't be the first man he had convinced, either, that had thought he was dead set against it. You just had to find the right way to go about convincing him.

He hitched up his pants and went after the other two with his spurs a-jingle, admiring the pair of manly butts in front of him, Red's being a fair sight to see as well, and thinking that was just about his favorite kind of scenery. Especially Texas butts, he decided, which appeared to be just that much finer than any that he had seen elsewhere.

Must be chasing them longhorns, he thought, smiling to himself. Maybe over time them saddles pounded them into just the right shape for riding.

Chapter 6

Les's confidence that installing Buck in the bunkhouse, where whatever it was exactly that he needed doing could surely be seen to, proved to be overoptimistic. He should have guessed something when he sat down to breakfast the Sunday morning after their trip into San Antonio, and discovered Cookie's kitchen skills had miraculously improved.

Cookie had been with the ranch longer than Les himself had been. He was now almost blind, and except for cooking on the roundups, he took little part in the chores outside the house, but he seemed otherwise indestructible. The men were fond of him and content enough with his cooking, which was nothing to brag about but was always plentiful and sometimes surprisingly varied on the long weeks and months out on the prairie, when things could get tiresome on other roundups.

They joked about his coffee, tar black and bitter, but they drank it by the gallon about as fast as he could brew it, and they ate pot after pot of pinto beans, and biscuits that, as they sometimes said, you could break rocks with. There was jerky, of course, and plenty of hardtack. To a man, however, the boys were sharpshooters the same as Buck and there was no shortage of game to be found on the range, to supplement the stores Cookie brought along in his chuck wagon—big fat jackrabbits, sweet-fleshed, like the one Buck had shot, and antelope the color of smoky sunlight as they ran; and wild turkeys, scrawny, but whose dark-colored meat had a spicy tang to it; and peccaries, the wild pigs that could slice through a leather boot with one sweep of razor-sharp tusks; armadillos, which made for better eating than a man might expect; and even, when they ventured up into the mountains, bighorn sheep. They caught pheasants and partridges and quail, and occasionally, a bear, the roasts from it larded with so much fat that it made your hands greasy to eat it. The seemingly empty prairie abounded with provisions for the man with eyes to see and a gun to shoot.

All of these things Cookie cooked competently and sometimes with surprisingly good results. There was one thing, though, that nobody had ever praised him for, and that was his flapjacks, which had the look and consistency—and for all anyone was willing to say, the taste—of cow patties.

So that when Les sat down at the table the next morning, and asked, "Morning, Cookie, what's for breakfast?" and Cookie answered, "Flapjacks," Les groaned inwardly, and prepared to make a meal of coffee and those rocklike biscuits.

At least, he thought that, until Cookie set a big plate of flapjacks in front of him, and Les saw that they looked nothing at all like what Cookie had served up before in that vein. Even more surprising, his fork went right into them without the usual struggle. He cut off a piece of one, held it on the tines of his fork, and regarded it suspiciously, but when he took a bite, he found it tender and delicious. The best flapjack he had ever eaten.

When Cookie came back into the room, Les said, "These flapjacks are light as feathers," savoring a big mouthful. "What'd you do to make them so different, Cookie?"

"Weren't me," Cookie said. "It's that new boy. That boy is a natural-born cook."

Les almost choked on a swallow of coffee—it was better coffee, too, than Cookie's usual brew, though he hadn't thought about that before. "You talking about Buck? He is cooking now?"

"Sure is. Been teaching me all kinds of things," Cookie said. "You would be surprised what all."

"Maybe I wouldn't," Les said. He hesitated and regarded the plate of flapjacks, like there might be some trick to eating them. There were things, weren't there, that a body could slip into your food, to put starch in your pecker? At least he had heard stories about shit like that. He sure did not want to be sitting here with his dick lifting the table off the floor and Buck grinning that fool grin of his at it, but the damned flapjacks were just too good to ignore, and he dug in enthusiastically.

"I even told him, long as he was going to help out with the cooking, he could have my little room behind the kitchen there, to sleep in," Cookie said, "and I would move out to the shed with old Mama."

Which Les thought was even more astonishing than the flapjacks were, considering all the years when Cookie had resolutely resisted sharing Mama's sleeping arrangements.

"What does old Mama say about that?" Les asked, shoveling more flapjacks into his mouth.

Cookie gave a laugh like a chicken's cackle. "All that old woman said last night was, '*Gran Dios, el gas*,'" he said on his way out to the kitchen. "It was that last batch of beans, was what she was nattering about." He stuck his head back through the door to add, "Buck says he can fix that, too."

It was all mighty mysterious, it seemed like to Les, but it was Buck's move into Cookie's room behind the kitchen that puzzled him the most and that he felt most inclined to ask him about.

When he saw Buck after breakfast, Buck was all het up about his new cooking chores. Almost the first thing he said was, "How was them flapjacks you ate this morning?"

"They was okay," Les said.

"Okay, is all?" Buck asked, screwing up his face in a disappointed grimace. He looked, Les thought, like a rabbit with his pecker caught in a muskrat trap.

"Well, shit," Les said impatiently, "if you're going to start crying about it, they was delicious, I guess." He couldn't see making all kinds of fuss about a stack of flapjacks, even if they had been tasty. He had eaten them about as fast as Cookie could dish them out. Still, it wasn't seemly, in his mind, a man getting all worked up over how his food tasted.

Buck's face brightened again. "I am glad to hear it," he said. "I was the one that made them for you, case Cookie didn't tell you."

"He told me you fixed them," Les said, annoyed for some reason he couldn't quite get hold of. "I didn't reckon you fixed them especially for me."

"Well, sure, I made them for the boys, too," Buck said. "But it was mostly you I was thinking of when I whipped them up. Ain't nothing a cowboy likes better in the morning than a good stack of flapjacks, is my experience. I figured you would be the same."

"Well, I am grateful, I guess," Les said, feeling kind of embarrassed at being singled out, "but I don't see no need for you to be fixing things special, not for me, is what I mean."

"See, what it is, is I am teaching Cookie a few tricks, and he is teaching me how to make a chili," Buck said, and looked Les up and down. "Let me take a guess here, I would say you are a man likes things good and hot."

"Depends. Some things probably hotter than you could handle," Les said, and changed the conversation back to what was puzzling him. "Now, what's this business about you going to sleep in Cookie's room behind the kitchen? The way you talk all the time, I thought you'd be happy as a fly on dog poop, sleeping in the bunkhouse with all the boys. I figured maybe you would be getting what you been saying you wanted out there."

"Maybe what I'm wanting ain't out there in the bunkhouse," Buck said. "Maybe you never thought about that. You don't sleep out there yourself, do you?"

"Don't see what that's got to do with anything," Les said.

Buck lowered his voice to a conspiratorial level, although they were by themselves at one end of the barnyard and there was no one close enough to overhear. "Well, the way I see it," he said, "I figured you wasn't likely to stroll down to the bunkhouse at night, all them boys out there, like you said, and you being kind of shy about some things, I can see that for myself. But, hell, I reckon you could sleepwalk your way out to the kitchen of a night."

"Excepting, I ain't a one for no sleepwalking," Les said, and started to turn away, but he paused to ask, "Didn't you ever have yourself no women, boy?"

"Some," Buck said, like he thought the question was odd. "Now and again. Whores, mostly, but there was a pretty little gal down in Galveston liked to lay in the grass of a night and get her petticoats wet, and I accommodated her a time or two."

"You didn't like it?" Les asked.

Buck shrugged, his expression sort of puzzled. "Well, sure, who doesn't? You think I'm queer or somethin'?"

"I think you're something, that's for sure," Les said. "So how's come if you like putting your what's-it into women, you're always trying to get some fellow to, you know, like you talk about?"

"Well, see, when I was in Galveston," Buck said, "there was this lady, Miz Montgomery, she ran a boarding house I stayed at for a spell, and every Sunday Miz Montgomery fixed fried chicken, and that was some delicious chicken. I never could get my fill of it. I must have eat it by the skillet full. But the thing is, much as I loved that chicken of hers, it never stopped me enjoying a big old juicy hunk of meat when I could get my hands on one. 'Sides, if you want to know," he grinned slyly, "I can do things with a nice piece of beef that old lady couldn't ever dream of doing with her hens."

"Seems to me like the steer might have some say in that," Les said. No matter how he tried, it just didn't seem possible to get this damn fool to talk sensible, and he gave it up now as a lost cause. "We got work to do, boy, best get to it. Just don't let that cooking be interfering with your ranch work. That ain't what you was hired on for."

"Hell's bells, I can rope a steer with one hand and cook with the other, if I've got a mind to," Buck said. "You come on down to the kitchen some night, I'll show you some things I can cook up."

"Happens I don't have the appetite," Les said shortly. He walked away, but he knew without looking that Buck was staring at his ass, and it made him strangely self-conscious, as he practically never was.

The damnedest thing was, his butt had begun to itch for some reason, and he started to reach back to scratch it like he normally would, and then thought better of it, and shoved his hands into his pockets. For sure scratching his butt now would only put ideas in that half-breed's head, and he didn't need no encouraging.

With the days growing steadily longer, the boys were often finished with their chores now before night fell, and most evenings, they congregated in the barnyard and outside the bunkhouse. Some of them whittled, and Jack had taken up strumming on a banjo, and Matt played his harmonica, neither with much musical success. They played some cards, and told yarns, and found other ways to pass the time.

Les finished his chores that night and came out of the barn to find a group of them throwing knives at a crudely drawn bull's-eye they had tacked up on a fence post. As he watched, Buck took a throw and hit the target dead center. A couple of the men took turns, and then Buck again, for another bull's eye. It was clear that none of the others were as good as he was.

Jack saw Les standing a little apart and nodded in his direction. "Now there's the champeen knife thrower in these parts," he said.

"That right?" Buck gave Les a speculative look. "How's about a little friendly competition. Take turns, first one misses the target loses. And no fast draw."

"Ain't much of a target," Les said.

"Seems I been hitting it just fine," Buck said. The men chuckled, and waited to see if Les would rise to the challenge.

"Somebody give me a knife," Les said. He took Jack's, stepped to the line they had scratched in the dust, and threw. The knife hit the target just off the bull's eye.

Buck took a turn. His Bowie struck dead center again.

Les's next throw was dead center too, and then Buck threw one that just caught the edge of the target, the first time since he and the boys had been throwing that he had missed the bull's eye. He looked sheepish when he retrieved his knife.

Les threw another bull's eye, but Buck's next throw missed the target altogether and thudded into the wood of the fence post.

Les handed Jack back his knife and started away without a word. Buck came after him. "Let's make it three out of five," he said.

"I done beat you already, fair and square," Les said.

"Can't hurt nothing, having a rematch."

Les stopped dead still. "Your trouble, boy," he said, "is you just can't stand the idea of me topping you."

"Well, now, ain't that exactly what I've been talking about for days, is you topping me," Buck said. "Just 'cause you outdrew me and beat me at knife throwing, don't mean I lost my interest. I already figured you was a hard-driving man, I'm trying to figure out how to get you to drive the right thing where it's supposed to go."

"That ain't where it's supposed to go," Les said. "Where'd you ever get these damn fool notions of yours anyway?"

"If you ain't never tried it, you don't know nothing about it," Buck said.

"Shit fire," Les snapped, and stomped away. What really riled him was that he had been thinking, just now looking at Buck, and him grinning like he didn't have no sense, that the crazy half-breed sort of reminded him of a puppy, all rambunctious and jumping around and wagging his tail. If you thought about it, the little fucker was kind of cute, in a way.

Keep thinking that way, he warned himself, *next thing you'll be plugging that hot butt for him like he keeps talking about*. And that was never going to happen.

His damn fool dick took the idea seriously, though.

The feud between farmers and cattle ranchers had gone on just about as long as there was a Texas, and the antagonism and the resentments ran deep on both sides. For the cattleman, the very idea of the open range was sacred. On the other hand, the fences that were a sacrilege to the cowboy were an essential to the farmer, who could hardly grow crops if the cattle were free to tromp across them and feed on them at their pleasure.

The farmers strung their fences, though, and sometimes the cowboys came right along after them and took them down, and the disputes from time to time had flared up into actual battles. So far, no one had been killed, not in this part of Texas, anyway, but there had been shootings, and a couple of actual woundings, which only worsened the tensions between the two factions.

So, when Les's nearest neighbor, a German-American farmer by the name of Hansen, rode up the lane to the Double H the following day, accompanied by a half-dozen of his men, some of the Double H cowboys put their hands on their guns, and Ben went so far as to draw his rifle from the saddle holster.

"Put that damn thing away," Les said. "We don't welcome neighbors with firearms."

"They may be neighbors, but they are farmers first," Pete said, "and I don't see them wearing no neighborly smiles."

That part was true enough, at any rate. The farmers looked plenty grim as they rode into the barnyard where Les and the boys had congregated. Old man Hansen rode ahead with his oldest boy, Ron, on a big bay beside him. They stopped a few feet from where Les waited, the others fanning out behind them. Hansen was a big-jowled man, his face like a hound's, and it was doleful now, and angry-looking too.

"Howdy," Les greeted him, and came forward to offer a hand. Hansen leaned down from his saddle to shake it, but he did not dismount. "What brings you over our way?" Les asked.

"Like you didn't know," Ron said sarcastically. He was an ample fellow, almost as tall as Les, and built sturdy, with a repu-tation as a troublemaker, and he made no secret of his scorn for cowboys. Badness on the hoof, was how Les had once described him, and most cowboys thought the description a good one.

"No, I don't think I do," Les said evenly. Red came to stand alongside him and, uninvited, Buck drifted to the fore too.

"Them damned cowboys of yours wouldn't have done what they did without you put them up to it," Ron said, but before Les could reply, his father made a gesture to silence his son.

"Hush, boy," he said. "I'll take care of this."

Ron gave his father an angry scowl, and pushed his hat back from his head, and glowered down at Les.

"Appears we've had some trouble," Hansen said, and paused, looking uncomfortable with what he had to say.

"What kind of trouble would that be?" Les asked.

"Seems some of your cows got into my patch of corn. What they didn't eat, they trampled down all over the place. There's not much of it left that ain't been ruined."

"Could be it's not my cattle," Les said.

"Oh, it's yours, all right," Ron said, but his father gave him another look to silence him.

"They got the Double H brand on them," Hansen said. "I had a look see myself, to be sure, before I came to see you. Wouldn't have wanted to make no false accusations."

"Well, I appreciate that," Les said. "But cattle will sometimes push a fence down on their own."

"These cattle didn't push their way through no fence," Hansen said. "Someone took the fence down, a mile or more of it, posts pulled up and all. Whoever did it, did a full job of it. They might even have driven the cattle into the field while they were at it. I can't say about that, but those cattle wouldn't likely have gone in there if the fence hadn't been downed."

"And you are saying," Les said, "that it was some of my boys as did it?"

"Now, who in the hell else would it be?" Hansen's son said hotly.

"Damn it, Ron, I told you," his father said sharply. "You leave the talking to me and Les, here." He turned again back to Les. "I reckon he is right, though. It would just about have to be your boys, wouldn't it? Who else would have done it?"

Les thought for a minute. There wasn't another cattle ranch for the better part of a hundred miles. Cattle could drift that far, all right, but it was pretty far-fetched to imagine any cowpunchers had ridden that far just to cause mischief, or even out from San Antone, for whatever reason.

"I expect he is right, seems like," Les said. He turned to Red, standing beside him. "You know anything about this?"

"Not a damned thing," Red said, "but if it was from here, somebody sure as hell does." He looked around at the cowboys. Practically the whole Double H crew was there in the barnyard by this time. "I don't want no fiddle farting around now, boys. Anyone knows anything about this, I want him to step up right now, like a man, and own up to it."

There was a moment of silence, everybody looking from one to the other, and then Pete stepped forward, looking shamefaced and turning his hat around nervously in his hand, and couple of the others hands, Matt and Rex stepped out alongside him, Rex's arm still in the sling from the fall he had taken a while back.

"It was us, Red," Pete said. "We was just fooling around."

"We didn't drive the cattle in there, though, like he said," Matt said. "We just took the fence down and rode off."

"Don't matter about that," Les said. "Any fool would have known them cattle would find their ways there soon enough, get them a sniff of that corn."

"We didn't mean no harm," Pete said. The other two hung their heads. "We was just meaning to cause them farm boys some aggravation. Some extra work, like. Wasn't no harm meant."

"Well, mean it or not, the harm was done," Les said, his expression somber. "You boys can pick up your pay later, up to the house. I'll have it ready for you before supper. I expect you to be gone by sunup."

"You saying you are firing us?" Rex said, looking astonished. No one had ever heard of Les firing any of his hands.

"That's how it is," Les said. "Won't have no troublemakers working for me."

The three men looked at Red. "You got nothing to say, Red," Matt asked.

"Les is the boss," Red said, "What he says goes. But you might as well know, if it was me, I wouldn't have given you till morning. Best be getting your things together, boys. You ain't got no place here anymore, and the sooner you are gone, the better, as I see it."

The three miscreants exchanged glances. Matt looked at Les, half grinning, as if he thought maybe this was all a joke, but Les turned away from him.

"Fuck it," Matt swore. "Come on, boys, this place is smelling too much like a farm for me." He strode into the barn. After a minute, the other two followed him, heads down.

"I apologize most heartily," Les said, turning his attention back to his neighbor. "You figure up how much this has cost you, and I will see that you are paid every cent of it."

"I'll get it tallied up, then," Hansen said. He hesitated briefly. "I'm afraid it will be a bit. Lost just about all my corn, and it's late now to be planting new."

"Whatever it is, you just let me know," Les said. "Red, you take some of the boys out and get that fence repaired."

"No need for that," Hansen said. "I already set my boys to working on it. I appreciate how you handled this, though. I like a man is fair about things."

"I'm a cattleman," Les said, "And you are a farmer, but that don't mean we can't both handle things like men. I don't put up with that kind of foolishness, any more than I expect you would."

"No, I wouldn't," Hansen said. "And I reckon you are right, about that other." They looked at one another a minute longer. Hansen tipped his hat, and reined his horse around. "Guess we might as well head for home, then, boys," he told his men, but he paused to look back at Les.

"We're having us a barn dance this Saturday night, over at my place," he said. "You're welcome to come, if you would like, you and your Segundo there, anybody else feels so inclined."

A barn dance wasn't much to Les's liking, any more than he imagined it was to Red's, but he figured there was fences that needed mending, and not just the ones those boys had taken down.

"Red and me will be there," Les said, nodding. "And thank you for asking us."

Hansen tipped his hat again, and led his boys back down the lane.

Chapter 7

Buck had been thinking about the situation between him and Les, and it had occurred to him that even if Les were to feel inclined to try things out, he would probably be shy about having his cowhands know it. And, so far, the two of them had never really been alone together. Out on the roundup, and even here at the ranch since they had ridden back, the others were always close at hand. That was why he had moved into Cookie's little room behind the kitchen, but so far, Les had not made use of the proximity.

Buck had learned from Red, though, that Les did not ordinarily go into town on a Saturday night with the boys like he had the Saturday before, and he made up his mind that the following Saturday, when the other hands rode into San Antone, he would stay here at the ranch with Les. He had hopes that maybe with everybody else gone, and just the two of them with the place to themselves, why, who knew what might happen? He might find himself that unlocked door he was watching out for.

The fact that Les and Red were planning on going to the Hansen's barn dance on Saturday night, however, changed everything, and Buck found himself at loose ends, and feeling out of sorts because of it. He was of no mind to go into town with the boys, and it seemed like the only other choice for him was to stay at home by himself. He did not mind so much being on his own, that was the cowboy way, but he had his heart set on spending the evening in Les's company.

"Can't see why he would want to go to no barn dance, anyway," Buck complained to Red about it the day before. "Ain't that farmer kind of stuff?"

"It is, that's the truth," Red said. "But old man Hansen, him and Les shook hands a year or so ago. That was after some shots had been fired. It was a handful of hot heads on both sides, and one of Les's hands got wounded, wasn't no more than a scratch, mind you, but the boys they got all riled up and was for riding over there and having things out. Les, though, he made them stay where they were, and got everybody all calmed down, and he went to see Hansen himself. The two of them sat down together, and they agreed that they would try to patch things up between their two spreads, at least, and work out their differences in a more civilized manner, and that is what they have tried to do since. Besides, if you look at it right, Les is kind of a farmer himself. Not like the way Hansen farms, of course, but hell, we grow hay for the stock, and alfalfa, and there is some acreage in wheat, even. So it ain't like he don't have some sympathy for the farmer."

"I wondered about that," Buck said. "That planting, I mean, it seems an odd thing for a cattleman to do."

"There's some has complained about it, saying they don't care to do farmer's work, and some think a cowboy has no business planting crops, but Les just says that is how it is going to be, and he did the planting where the cattle couldn't easily get at it, so there was no fencing to be done except for piling up some mesquite good and thick in a couple places."

"Well, why did he do it, then, seeing as he is not a farmer?"

"It is Les's idea of being prepared for any rough patches," Red said. "It goes back to that time when we lost the herd, to hoof and mouth, that I told you about. Les had him this idea after that, which he talked to Miz Cameron about, that if we had some crops going in addition to the cattle, we could fall back on that if things got tough again. The way he put it was, if a man built a house up on one piling, and that came down, why, the house came down with it. But if it rested on a bunch of supports, and you lost one, then it was likely to remain standing till you could get the damage repaired. So, raising some crops was his way of seeing that the Double H remained solid if we were to have trouble again with the cattle. Besides which, we could make use of what we growed, the wheat and such. Not like we were planting it to sell. So that's what we did, and he keeps it up, not in any big way, but enough that it is there."

Which only made Buck's hero shine brighter in his eyes—but it still left him with no plans for a Saturday night.

The big surprise, though, was that as Saturday night drew close, Les sought Buck out and mentioned the barn dance to him.

"I was thinking," he said, "I reckon the other boys would rather spend their Saturday night in town, at Miz Yolanda's likely, and it might be that you was thinking about going with them. If you didn't exactly have your heart set on that, though, well, as you know, me and Red are going to this barn dance over at the Hansens' farm, and you are welcome to ride along with us if you have a mind to."

"I would like that aplenty," Buck said, nodding his head and his eyes flashing happily. He managed to contain his excitement until he had left them and gone into the barn, but once he was out of their sight, he jumped wildly into the air, clicking his heels together, and gave a loud yell.

"Yahoo," he shouted enthusiastically, and threw his hat toward the hayloft.

Les and Red heard him, of course, and Red grinned at Les and said, "I guess you just about made little Buck's day for him, Les. That was a right nice of you."

"I wasn't planning on holding hands with him on the ride over," Les said dryly. "What I had in mind is, well, I figure, him being as young as he is, he has got all that sap running, the way a young fellow does, and spending all his time here with nothing but men around him, I figure maybe that's how come he gets them damn fool notions stuck in his head. But I got to thinking about it, and I expect there is bound to be lots of young gals at that barn dance. Hansen's got himself a couple of daughters, as I recollect, but I reckon there will be some others there, too, hopefully some pretty ones. Even if Buck don't dance with anybody, I reckon just seeing some pretty young things up close might get him to thinking about some fried chicken for a change."

Red gave him a puzzled look. "Fried chicken?" he said.

"Just a way of talking," Les said. "You just wait and see, anyhow, I expect you will see a big change in his ideas once we been there."

"Might be," Red agreed, although privately he was not so sure. Not that he had any doubts that Buck could pleasure a woman well enough when he had a mind to, but as Buck himself had put it, a man liked what he liked, and he had a pretty good notion by now what it was that little Buck liked the most. He had a notion, too, that Buck could be powerful stubborn, and that once he got an idea in his head, he was not a one to let go of it easily; which only reminded Red of someone else that he could name, but he knew better than to express that opinion openly.

The Hansen farm was the next property over from the Double H, so they were the nearest of neighbors, but this was Texas, and neighbors did not mean close. It was a twenty-mile ride from house to house, and that was going directly across the prairie instead of by road.

The three of them set out in the gloaming, but it was night by the time they arrived there and hitched up their horses. There were other horses by the score, and buggies and wagons from around the county, and some had even ridden out from San Antonio in fancy carriages. Texans mostly lived a hard life, and they took their fun where and when they could find it.

The Hansen's enormous barn had been cleaned out for the occasion, bales of hay put around for the men to sit on, and chairs brought from the house for the ladies. The dirt floor was watered and packed down for dancing, and the glow of scores of lanterns made the inside of the barn as light as day.

The boys had dressed in their best, and Buck had washed and scrubbed until his hands were red and raw and his face just about glowed. He put some bear grease on his hair to try to hold it in place—with only modest success, since one or two shiny curls insisted on spilling across his brow, grease or no grease—and he picked his teeth clean with a sprig of wintergreen from the garden, to be sure that his breath was sweet.

One of the hands who was close to his size loaned him a fancy shirt that had come all the way from down Mexico way, embroidered across the front with red and white roses. Buck was rightly proud of the dungarees he had bought while he was in Galveston, which were the height of fashion just then, and he had gotten the attention of one or two of the hands earlier in the day while he knelt bare assed by the horse trough for the better part of an hour to scrub his trousers to a fare thee well, so that they were spotless now and nearly as good as the day he bought them. He had purchased a new bandana at the Mercado when he was in San Antone the week before, yellow as the eyes of a wildcat, and he wore that tied at his throat, and his white snakeskin boots were cleaned and polished, to where you could just about see your reflection in them.

Only his Stetson was old and shabby. He would like to have replaced that, but there hadn't been the time, and he hadn't wanted to ask any of the boys about borrowing one, since a cowboy's hat was a personal thing and something he was hardly ever without. Buck wore his own, old one instead, and though he felt somehow half naked without it, he hung it over the horn on his saddle and strode hatless with Les and Red toward the light that spilled out the barn door.

Glancing at him as they went in, Les thought that the boy looked right fine. It appeared to him, surveying the room, as if

Buck was the handsomest young fellow in the place, in fact. For some reason, it made him feel downright proud to have the boy alongside him like this, and his chest kind of puffed out, like. If there were any unattached girls present, he felt sure they would sit up and take notice.

Red looked at Buck, too, as they went into the barn, and found himself wishing after all that him and Buck were back at the ranch. Damned if the boy didn't look like he was good enough to eat. Well, it was hard to imagine that any little girl here wouldn't feel the same, seeing him, so maybe this idea of Les's had been a good one after all.

There was a moment of stillness as the three stopped in the barn doorway, and even the musicians at the far end of the barn let their music trail off as everyone turned to look. Old man Hansen himself, though, came quickly across to welcome them, his wife at his side, and after a moment, the hum of conversation started up again, and the fiddlers picked up their tune and began to scrape and saw again.

"Mighty glad you could come," Miz Hansen greeted the cowboys. She was near as tall as her husband, a big-boned woman with a sun-dried face like a prune, but her smile was friendly and her eyes shone warmly.

"Mighty good of you to have us," Les said, and introduced the two with him.

"There is some punch over there where the ladies are standing at that long table, if you are thirsty from your ride," she said, waving a hand in that direction, "and I expect that one or two of the fellows might have something stronger, if you were to ask around, but of course, I know nothing at all about that." She smiled, and her husband gave the boys a wink as if to say they would get to that later.

"Reckon you should meet the rest of my family," Hansen said. He led the way across the open floor, where a few couples had begun to dance together. His three sons stood with their friends off to one corner, all of them wearing the farmer kind of overalls that cowboys disdained.

"You know my oldest boy, Ron," Hansen said, "and this here is Brett, and the youngest, Tom." His oldest boy, Ron, ignored the hands that were offered, but the other two shook with the cowboys, although they did not look too enthusiastic about it, particularly when it came Buck's turn.

Buck did not much mind for himself. He was a half-breed, and he was used to the idea that some people didn't care to shake his hand, but he took offense at seeing Les and Red rebuffed, since he felt certain that they were the better of any man present. If either of them minded, though, it did not show on their faces. You might almost have thought they had not even noticed when Ron turned his back on them.

"And these are our daughters," Miz Hansen said, and led the cowboys to a pair of young ladies seated on wooden chairs nearby. "Emma is our oldest. She will be getting married in the fall." Emma was tall and willowy, plain of face, although she might have been pretty if her lips had not been set in such an icy line. She only nodded at them without saying a word, and quickly averted her eyes.

"And this is our baby, Margaret," Miz Hansen said, indicating the other girl.

• • •

"Maggie," the young lady corrected her. "Margaret makes me sound like an old maid, Mama."

"I don't reckon anybody would mistake you for that," Buck said, grinning, and she responded with a little giggle and bowed her head, blushing shyly, but not before she had favored him with a friendly smile. "Not as pretty as you are."

She was pretty, too, Les thought, with hair the color of corn silk, and cheeks that needed no rouge to paint flowers on them. He began to feel that maybe this had been the right idea, after all, to invite Buck to come along with them. If that little girl couldn't run the idea of butt fucking out of that Indian's head, he reckoned nothing could. After which, maybe he could have some peace back at his ranch, which was greatly to be desired.

The fiddlers launched into an energetic polka, and more couples joined the enthusiastic movement on the dance floor.

"Say," Buck said, "that music has my toes to tapping, Miz Maggie. What do you say, the two of us take a whirl?"

Maggie giggled again, but she held out her hand to him and got up from her chair. "If it's all right with Mama?" she said, and gave her mother a quick glance.

The pause in her mother's reply was no more than a heart-beat long. "No sense in wasting the music," she said, and turned to Les. "Would you care to try your luck with an old farm woman?" she asked.

"Thank you most kindly, ma'am," Les said, "but you'd be lucky to have the use of your feet by the time I got done stomping on them. I never did learn how it was done. Now, Red, here, he knows his way around a barn dance."

"If you would do me the honor, ma'am," Red said, taking his cue, and led her onto the floor.

Les and Hansen stood together and watched the couples twirling and jouncing energetically. The polka ended and was followed by a reel, the dancers lining up in facing rows. Les saw that several of them were looking sideways at Buck, like they were not quite sure that they ought to be on the floor with him, but he was with their host's daughter, and while one or two couples retired to the sidelines, most chose to wait and see.

If Buck noticed their reluctance, though, he paid it no mind. He gave a tap of his foot, and seemed to fly across the floor with his partner, dashing at the line of dancers before him as if he would run right into them, then spinning his partner about with graceful abandon, her skirt billowing in a cloud about her legs, and a swift promenade while the others clapped time. There was the rippling sensuality of a gamboling colt in the easy swing of Buck's hips and thighs, and the other dancers on the floor with him forgot entirely their reservations, and found themselves instead sharing his boyish delight, and threw themselves into the dance with renewed vigor, the men determined not to be outdanced, and the ladies thrilled to be whirled about with such manly enthusiasm.

It came as no surprise to Les to see that Buck was as light as a feather on his feet, and it seemed as if he and the girl were enjoying themselves mightily. She laughed at something he said, smiling up at him, and it was clear enough that she found him pleasing to look at.

Well, shit, who wouldn't, Les asked himself? The boy was truly a treat for the eyes, all fancied up the way he was tonight, as sweet-looking as an angel, if he *was* full of the devil inside, with them dark curls of his and that big grin, and built as lean and hard as an Indian pony—and he had a pretty impressive bulge himself in the front of them dungarees, now that Les's eyes happened to look down there by the merest chance.

Les was immediately embarrassed by that thought, though. A man wasn't supposed to notice that about another man, was he? Let alone think of a man being pretty. Hell's bells. What was happening to him? It seemed any more like he didn't hardly even know himself.

He dragged his eyes away from the dancers and turned to Hansen. "I guess I could use something to wet my whistle," he said, "if there was anything a little more interesting than that punch your wife mentioned."

"I think we can find the right thing," Hansen said, with a friendly smile. "Let's us stop over to the house for a minute."

Red escorted Miz Hansen back to her chair after their one dance and thanked her for it, and was relieved that she did not expect another one. He thought his dancing was about the same thing as watching a dog walk on his hind legs. You were so surprised to see him doing it at all, you just about didn't notice that he was doing it so badly.

He watched Buck and the girl, gliding about the floor now in a two-step, as elegant as his reel had been spirited, and he was happy to see how well Buck danced. He kind of wondered where and how he had learned it. However it had been, though, it was clear that the girl was enjoying herself, and the looks she was flashing up into Buck's face were plenty pleased.

For some odd reason, that gave Red a pang. But that was the way of it, wasn't it, he told himself quickly. A boy and a girl met, and fancied one another, and generally they did something about it, and maybe they even got hitched in time. That was not likely to happen in this case—he had seen the quick glances that Miz Hansen had given her daughter and Buck while they danced, and it was certain she would not welcome a half-breed Indian into her family, even if she did let her daughter dance with one.

More than likely, though, Buck would get himself hitched in time, if not with this filly, then with another one day. It saddened him to think that what he and Buck had going between them would most likely come to an end when that time came.

"Well, it ain't come yet, not over one little dance or two," he told himself. He took his tobacco pouch out of his pocket, and made to roll himself a cigarette, but then he looked around at all those bales of hay, and decided to do it outside after all.

Wouldn't do neighborly relations any good to burn the barn down in the middle of a dance.

Buck saw him go, and when he had escorted Maggie, laughing and with her yellow hair falling across her face, back to her chair, he excused himself and went in search of Red. He found him by the glow of his cigarette, in the shade of a live oak at the far edge of the farmyard. Red passed the cigarette to him as he walked up.

"Looks like you are enjoying yourself some," Red said.

"Been a while since I done any dancing," Buck said, laughing softly in the darkness. He took a puff off the cigarette and passed it back.

"She is a pretty little thing," Red said.

"That she is."

"You getting any ideas?"

"What kind of ideas?" Buck said, and looked at him in the darkness, just able to make out his face, and laughed again. "Well, I ain't no farmer, exactly, but I have never minded doing a little plowing now and again, when the opportunity presented itself."

He reached to put a hand on Red's shoulder and gave it a friendly squeeze. "Don't you be worrying none about that, though. Girls like that, they don't get themselves tangled up with half-breeds, except for some wrestling out behind the barn, which I got no objections to, but I can take it or leave it. I told you before, I like what I like, and I ain't forgetting who my friend is."

"That never even crossed my mind," Red said, but he felt better for hearing that said.

When they came back inside, Buck saw that Maggie's oldest brother, Ron, was engaged in some serious sort of conversation with her. They appeared to be having an argument. She tossed her head at something he said and gave him a fierce glower.

Buck walked over to them and, giving Ron a nod, he said to Maggie, "I was hoping you would favor me with another dance, Miz Hansen."

"The dancing is over," Ron said.

Buck glanced at the dance floor, where other couples were two stepping to the beat of the music. "Looks like some are still at it," he said.

"Let me make it plainer, then," Ron said. "We are done dancing with you."

"Ron," Maggie said, "I told you to leave it be."

"Well, now," Buck said, smiling at the young man, "I had in mind dancing with your sister, but I guess I could accommodate you, if you are wanting it badly enough. The thing is, I only know the man's part, by which I mean to say, you would have to be the girl of it."

"You come outside with me, half-breed," Ron said, looking nasty, "and I will give you a dance all right."

Buck took a moment to consider this in silence. Over Ron's shoulder, he saw Red hurry out the barn door—going, he supposed, to find Les. He knew exactly how Les would feel about his making any trouble. The last thing he wanted was to cause Les any aggravation—of that sort, anyway.

"I ain't of no mind to fight with you," he said.

Ron sneered. "I might've knowed you would be a chicken," he said.

Buck looked around. Others had begun to notice them and to listen to their exchange. Still seated in her chair, Maggie was red with mortification.

"Oh, Ron," she said. Beside her, her sister Emma smirked and looked hopefully from one to the other of the two young men.

"I guess I could teach you a step or two," Buck said with a sigh. "Whyn't you lead the way, then, seeing as this is your dance?"

"Come on, then," Ron said, and began to shoulder his way through the crowd that had gathered. They went out into the barnyard, a distance from the barn, so that they were mostly in shadows. Buck stripped off his shirt as he went, since it was borrowed and he would not want to give it back with no blood on it. His bandana went too, and he tossed them to the ground, and unlaced his holster, and the sheath for his Bowie, and put his weapons aside with his shirt.

Ron began to do the same, but seeing his opponent like this, he couldn't help having some second thoughts. Parading around on the dance floor the way he had been, Buck had looked more like a frolicsome boy than a man to be concerned about, but now that he was shirtless, flexing his muscles as he waited, he looked like someone to be reckoned with.

Ron looked at some of the boys crowding around the open door of the barn. "Someone go find Brett and Tom," he yelled. "Tell my brothers to get their asses out here."

One of the boys in the throng turned toward the barn and yelled, "Brett, Tom, Ron is fixing to kick the shit out of this half-breed."

A minute later, the two younger Hansens, neither as tall as their brother but both of them thickly built, rushed out and pushed their way through the crowd.

"Hang on, there, brother," Tom called, and Brett said, "I'm wanting to carve me a piece of that Indian's ass while you are at it." Tom already had a Bowie in his hand and Brett pulled his from the sheath strapped to his legs as he ran.

They stopped abruptly. A six-foot, three-inch cowboy had stepped directly into their path, his feet planted wide, his hands resting on the handles of his six-shooters. While the brothers blinked, trying to take this in, the big redheaded fellow came up to stand alongside him, hand on his gun as well.

"What you cowboys got on your mind?" Brett asked, making a show of bravado.

"We got on our mind that those two over yonder will have themselves a fair fight, one on one," Les said. "Without no help from you two and without no knives."

"Well, who says you got any right to say how things will be, here on our farm?" Tom asked, but he took a step back so that he was half behind his bigger brother.

"It ain't me saying it," Les said, running his fingers over the butts of his guns. "It is Mister Colt's idea."

"Maybe we could just tell you and Mister Colt to go somewhere and mind your own fucking business," Brett said.

"You could," Red said, speaking calmly, like a man without a care in the world, "but you wouldn't want to if you had good sense. Some people don't take kindly to being smart-mouthed."

Tom took another step behind his brother, and Brett swallowed hard and slipped the knife back into its sheath, but he put his hand on his gun instead.

"You ain't scaring me none with them damned guns," he said. "Hell, I got me a gun of my own, if you are looking for a shooting match, and I know how to use it, too," and he started to draw it, but it hadn't begun to clear its holster, before he saw that there were two six-shooters aimed right at his middle section. Damn, he hadn't even seen the fucking cowboy's hands move. The other one, the redhead, his gun was still holstered, but he was grinning from ear to ear like he had just heard a good story.

"Shit," Brett said, shoving his gun back down into his holster, "ain't got nothing to do with us anyway, that's between the two of them, seems like to me. Say, Tom, I hear some of the boys have got them some Pensacola rye down back of the house, and I reckon I am feeling a mite thirsty. Whyn't you and me go get ourselves some?"

"I could use a snort myself," Tom said. They began to move in the direction of the corner of the house, backing up at first, and then turning and moving quickly.

"Hey, where you guys going?" Ron called after his brothers, but they didn't answer, they just kept going, not quite running but not exactly walking either, until they reached the corner of the house and had disappeared around it.

"You come back here, Brett, Tom," Ron called after them, and got no reply. "Damn chickenshits," he said, and spit at his feet.

He turned back to the half-breed and took stock of his situation. Damn, what worried him the most was that the guy didn't look like he was scared at all, even though he stood a head shorter than Ron himself. Didn't even look nervous, in fact. What it was, actually, was he looked like he was fucking crazy, now that Ron took a good look at him. Shirtless, the half-breed stood kind of in a crouch, like a cougar getting ready to spring, his muscles still shiny with sweat from the dancing he had done earlier. His eyes glittered in the moonlight, it almost seemed like there were sparks coming out of them, and the way he grinned, his teeth showing, unnerved a fellow. There was something else too, that he did just then, that Ron had never seen nobody do before: the Indian's nostrils flared as he stood there waiting, like he was sniffing the air, or something—like an animal, looking for a scent.

Ron suddenly thought of when he was a boy, and older fellows had scared him with stories of Apaches, the things they did when they were in hand fights. He had heard of one, sprang on a man and ripped the fellow's throat wide open with nothing but his teeth. There was another tale, too, about a fellow, got into a hand fight with an Apache and had his balls clawed right off him while they was wrestling on the ground, the Apache just reached down and grabbed a hold of them fast as lightning and tore them loose before the other man knew what was happening.

Remembering, Ron felt a little shiver of fear zigzag its way up and down his spine, and all at once it felt like he was about to take a shit in his britches. Sure thing, this fucking Indian looked plenty crazy enough to have something like that in his mind. He did not much care for the idea of losing his balls, let alone having his throat ripped open.

"Shit, I ain't of a mind to fight with no half-breed Indian trash," he said, buttoning his shirt up again. "I got me more important things to do."

He turned his back and began to walk away, but you could see that he was listening for any movement behind him. Buck was motionless though, until Ron had disappeared after his brothers, walking a bit faster as he got farther away.

Buck looked at Les and Red then. "I didn't start it, Les," he said. "Don't be sore at me."

"I know you didn't," Les said, holstering his guns.

"And I appreciate your help, boys, really, I mean it," Buck said, donning his shirt and his bandana, and strapping his weapons on, "but I wasn't worried about that peckerhead. I could've took him on with one hand tied behind my back, him and his pissant brothers too."

"Sound mighty sure of yourself," Les said with a grin. "He is a pretty good-sized dude, appears to me."

"Reckon so, but he was scared shitless," Buck said. "I could smell it on him."

"Like them Indian horses do?" Les asked.

Buck grinned back at him. "Guess it just runs in the blood," he said. "Anyway, once you got a fellow scared, you got him half beat already."

"Reckon you could have whipped him, at that," Les said. "Didn't mean to say that you couldn't. Imagine you could have easy enough, as long as a fight stayed fair. We was just providing knife insurance. Ain't got no mind to see any of my cowhands carved up by a couple of polecats."

"I am much obliged to you for that." Buck stepped forward, and the three of them shook hands all around, in a strangely formal sort of acknowledgment of their comradeship.

"You planning on any more dancing?" Les asked.

Buck glanced at him, and toward the barn, and thought of little Maggie, but there wasn't much likelihood now of any trips behind the barn, and he knew well enough that nothing more than that was ever going to come of it.

He looked back at Les and shook his head. "I reckon it would just cause trouble for her with her brothers," he said. "They won't forget they was humiliated, and others to see it happen. And by a half-breed, that will make it worse."

"Then I expect we might as well be heading for home," Les said.

Red said, "Unless you want to wait and dance with old Ron there and his brothers when they come back, looked to me like they was pretty light on their feet," and they all three laughed.

When they were on the trail for home, Buck looked from one of his companions to the other. The night smelled of sage and dust, and the faint scent of something dead and decaying that came downwind at them, a stray steer, maybe, that the coyotes had brought down, but a long ways off. The air was warm and dry, and fine for riding.

He thought about the two of them backing him up the way they had, and he felt like his chest was about to bust with happiness. There wasn't anything in the world better, the way he saw it, than to have a couple of true friends, cowboy friends. He began to sing at the top of his lungs: "Oh, bury me not on the lone prairie . . ."

"If I had known you was going to howl like a wounded coyote," Les said, "reckon I would have let them boys cut you up back there."

He larruped his palomino up to a gallop, and after a moment Red and Buck spurred their horses and galloped alongside him, Buck between the other two, the three of them pounding across the plains, feeling free in the way that only a cowboy can feel free, on his horse, out on the range.

Out of nowhere Les, who was not as a rule a man to show excitement, yelled at the top of his lungs, "Yippee-i-o, cowboys."

Buck answered him by throwing back his head and giving a coyote howl, and they all three laughed, for the sheer joy of being cowboys and being alive, and riding through the summer night together, the hooves of their horses beating a steady thrumedy-thrumedy-thrum on the iron hard ground.

Chapter 8

Their raucous mood stayed with the cowboys for the rest of their ride home, and even when they dismounted in the barnyard, all three of them were still keyed up, making jokes and clapping one another on the shoulder. It was as good a time as Buck could ever remember having, and Red was surprised to see his old friend Les, who was generally a somber sort, so unwound and carefree-acting. It had been a long time since he had seen Les laughing and cutting up the way he was, and he was happy to see it.

And then, out of nowhere, something changed. Buck and Red had just taken friendly punches at one another, still laughing, and Buck turned toward Les, and found Les no longer smiling, but staring at him in a way that was hard to read. He almost looked as if he were suddenly angry about something—but what? Except for nearly getting into a fight with the Hansen boys, Buck had been on his good behavior the whole evening.

He and Red stopped laughing and exchanged a glance, and Red shrugged. "What," Buck started to say, but before he could form the question, Big Joe had come out of the house, by the kitchen door, and hurried across the barnyard toward them, hobbling on his crutches.

"It's old Mama," he shouted while he was still some distance away. "She has done passed on."

They found Cookie sitting by himself at the table in the kitchen, a bottle of tequila in front of him, and a pint jar in his hand, half full with amber liquid. Mama was in her shed, where Cookie had found her. She had died in her sleep, it appeared.

Les lit the oil lamps in the dining room and turned the wicks down low, and cleared off the table there. He and Red carried Mama in and laid her out on the table, and Les got a sheet, and spread that over her.

"I'll have to ride into town for the doctor," Les said. "He'll have to certify her death, to make it official. Best go ahead and do that now. We will want to get her into the ground pretty quick, the weather being warm and all."

"I can go, if you want," Red said.

"No. Miz Cameron will have to be told," Les said. "I reckon that is my job. When the boys get back from town, you set some of them to digging a grave, and then I guess you had better keep Cookie company. He complained about her all the time, but I expect he will be feeling pretty down just the same, seeing as the two of them go back a long ways."

He saddled up again, and rode for town, and Big Joe, who was never comfortable with any emotional demands, retreated to the bunkhouse, leaving Red and Buck to sit with Cookie in the kitchen.

"Might as well have yourselves a drink," Cookie told them, indicating the bottle of tequila. "It was hers, of course, but I don't imagine she will care much now."

Buck got a couple more jars from the cupboard, and half filled Red's, and poured a little bit into the other for himself, to be friendly. The three of them toasted one another, Buck just sipping his, and Cookie half draining his glass.

"It's a funny thing," Cookie said, looking down into his glass rather than at them, "somebody's in your life for a long time, you kind of forget all about whether you like them, or not, or stuff like that. It's kind of just like, well, like they have become a part of things, and the liking business don't have much to do with it, the same as with the weather. It just is, is all. You never think about your left thumb, and it wouldn't keep your life from moving along if you was to lose it, but you would miss it all the same."

"Reckon you would," Buck said, and asked a question that he had pondered before. "What was her real name, anyway?"

"Don't know that I ever knew it," Cookie said. "If I did, it has plumb escaped my memory." He wrinkled up his weather-beaten face, trying to recall. "Consuela, maybe? Conchita? A Mexican name anyway. Well, I guess it would've been, wouldn't it? Seems like I always just called her Mama."

"How'd you come to link up with her?" Red asked.

"Just plain bad luck, I guess," Cookie said, and laughed faintly, but without any amusement in it. "I was up north, in Ragtown, back in the buffalo hunting days. You'd know that as Amarillo, now, cause of all them yellow houses." He glanced at Buck. "Amarillo means yellow, in case you didn't know."

Buck nodded. He did know that, but he did not want to interrupt Cookie now that he seemed inclined to talk, thinking that the talking would be good for him.

"They called it Ragtown then, though, on account of, that's all there was in them days, the buffalo hunters and all them hide huts they lived in, buffalo hide, that was the one thing there was no shortage of. The buffalo is gone, now, and the hunters, too, course, but they was plenty of both in them days."

"Was you a buffalo hunter?" Buck asked. It was hard to look at this wizened old man and remember that he too had once been young and filled with energy and dreams. To the young, the old are just old.

Buck remembered tales from his own youth, tales passed around among the Indians, of the buffalo that once roamed the prairie in uncountable numbers and had provided many of the Indian tribes with their chief sustenance: food and hides for clothing and tepees, oil for lamps and bones that could be fashioned into tools and weapons. Even the dried manure of the buffalo had been used for fuel. The Indians had wasted nothing, found a use for everything.

"Nah," Cookie shook his head slowly. "I had no heart for it. To tell you the truth, it was a magnificent sight, to ride over a ridge and see one of them herds in the valley below, like looking at an ocean." He paused and looked at the two of them.

"I saw me the ocean, once," he said, smiling with the memory. "The Atlantic Ocean, they call it. I rode clear over to Mobile town on the coast of Alabama, just to have a look see. Took me nigh onto six months, there and back, but I reckoned it were worth it. I had never seen nothing like that in my life, all them waves washing up on that sand, and they had come all the way from Europe. China, even, I guess. I had it in my mind that one day I would ride out to California and see the other one, that Pacific Ocean, and I figured then I would have seen about as much of the world as a cowboy could want to see."

"Did you ever go?" Buck asked.

Cookie shook his head. "Nope, I never made it there. Don't guess I ever will, now, I'm too old for it, but if I was a young man, that's what I would do."

He swirled the tequila around in his jar and they waited for him to resume his story. In all the years that Red had known him, he had never known Cookie to talk at such length. Like Buck, though, he figured it would do the old man good.

"They was like an ocean of their own, they was, them buffalo," Cookie took up his story again. "Just them shaggy brown bodies, as far as the eye could look, moving slowly, unconcerned. They was peaceful critters, and not very bright, it seemed to me, but the Indians had always killed them no more than they needed. Why, a bull could weigh three thousand pounds, and measure twelve feet long. They didn't have to kill too many of them to get everything they needed. The Indians, see, they would cut them out of the herd one at a time and run them down, so that the herd almost didn't seem to notice, and the animals just had never felt especially threatened. You could shoot one down, and the others would see him fall, and look at him, and never even see it as any kind of threat to the rest of them. Thing was, they just didn't have any real enemies, so they didn't seem to know what danger was. Course, they had no idea what kind of mischief the white man could set loose on them."

"There was a bounty put on them, wasn't there?" Buck said.

Cookie nodded. "It weren't the buffalo, course, that the United States government wanted to get rid of, it was the Indians, but someone got the idea in their head, 'Say, if we was to kill off the buffalo, why, we would kill off the Indians with them.' So, yep, like you say, they offered a bounty, a dollar a head, and there is never a shortage of men looking for easy money, and in no time at all, you had herds of hunters, looking to line their pockets and with never a thought of where their actions was leading. It wasn't like you or me would hunt for food, mind you, or even like men hunting for the sport of it. They would drive the animals into a dead end ravine, and they set up them rapid repeaters, Gatlings, they called them, on the hillsides, and they would take out them buffalo by the thousands at a time. It wasn't any kind of sport, I tell you. It was just slaughter, is all it was.

"After a while, the buffalo herds were gone, and most of the Indians had gone with them. So the government was right, I reckon."

He paused again, looking down into his glass with a solemn expression. "I was just a drifter at the time, understand," he said finally. "I was a young man, then, looking for some excitement, and a way to make a few dollars. Matter of fact, if you want to know, that's where I started cooking, up in Ragtown, but first, I made some money in a poker game or two. I was pretty handy in them days with a deck of cards.

"There was lots of them fellers there, though, didn't much care to cook for themselves, and they wasn't so awful choosy about what they ate, as long as it was hot and there was lots of it. So, this one time, I won me this big haunch of buffalo in a poker game, and I cooked up a stew from it and kind of passed it around, and next thing you know, people was lining up for the meals I fixed, and paying me for them. Funny thing was, half the time I fed them buffalo. I would dry out the meat for jerky, or I would pound it up with berries and suet to make pemmican, just the way the Indians did it, but if I had told them it was Indian food, they'd have turned up their noses at it, for certain. So, I kept that to myself, and fed them with it, and for a while, there, the money was pouring in. There was plenty of money around in them days, and those boys were generous when it come to getting what they wanted."

An errant breeze blew through the kitchen, and the light from the kerosene lamp on the table danced nervously up and down the walls, and then got still again, as if it were waiting.

"Well, after a time," Cookie said, "I figured I had me all the money I needed, a cowboy don't never need much, and the way it was, I seen a few of them killings, and it didn't set right with me. I started feeling kind of funny like, making all that money off of something that just seemed wasteful. I began to think about moving on. I had heard about Santa Fe, out New Mexico way, and that it was a right pretty little town, and I had me a mind to head out there and see for myself.

"I guess maybe it sounds foolish to you boys, me having everything so nice like I did, and the money pouring in faster than I could spend it, and then just picking up and leaving it behind that way, I expect some would call that foolish."

"That's how it is with most cowboys, ain't it?" Red said. "Don't make no difference how far you ride, the horizon is always out there yonder. You can't never get to it."

"That's exactly right," Cookie said, shaking his head. "And, like I said, I began to think that maybe what they was doing was wrong. I expect you would see that clearer than some," he said, looking at Buck. "Being Indian yourself, or part way, anyhow."

"It was the end of plenty of the plains tribes, that is for sure," Buck said.

Cookie nodded and took a sip of his drink. "But, then, it happened," he said, "When I was about fixing up to leave, why, that was when I found her one night, old Mama, sitting out in the rain, half frozen and looking like she was starved to death. She wasn't much to look at it, I tell you, and that is no lie. She was old already, seemed like to me, although I wasn't but a young 'un myself at the time. She looked so pathetic, though, like some dog has been beat half to death, and it made me feel right sorry for her, so I stopped to talk to her. At first, she thought I was meaning to pay to bed her, which couldn't have been further from my mind, especially once I got a good look at her. I tell you the gospel truth, boys, that woman had a face on her like a bucket full of vomit. But when she saw that I wasn't interested in that, well, she began to talk to me. Seemed like she'd had this man, had treated her something fierce, it was him put her out to whoring, and he beat her awful, and stole every cent she made, till finally she had run off from him, only, even with all them horny buffalo hunters around that town, she couldn't find one that was interested in taking her in, her being so ugly, and all.

"Well, to make a long story short, I took pity on her. I figured nobody else would want her, and she was going to freeze to death laying out in the weather the way she was, so I took her back to my tent, and fed her, and nursed her back to health some, and then, nothing would do but I had to do her, seems like that was the only way she knew to thank a fellow for being kind. I wasn't much inclined, but she kept pestering me and pestering me, and, shit, I was young, I guess my nuts was as hot as anybody else's, and you know what they say about a pecker in the dark, so I finally up and crawled on top of her, and let her have it. Wasn't so bad, long as I kept my eyes tight closed. Pecker doesn't see nothing, anyway, once it's in there."

They all three nodded and grinned, and chuckled softly, and Cookie took another sip of his tequila.

"I reckon it did make her happy, all right, too. I had the knack for pleasuring a woman in them days, if I do say it myself. Only, after that, she wouldn't hardly leave me alone, she was after it all the time. Seemed like I had done too good a job of it that first time.

"I had told her all along, though, about riding to Santa Fe, and she kept crying and wailing and saying take her with me, take her with me, and I told her there was nothing doing, I wasn't a man to get hitched, and she wasn't who I would get hitched with if I was, but you know how a woman is when she gets something on her mind.

"Well, so, finally, the time come when I made up my mind to just go ahead and go, and I gave her my hide shack and a few dollars, I figured she would be all right till she found herself another man, mostly them boys wasn't particular what they stuck it into, and ugly as she was she was as pretty anyway as a buffalo cow, and that was good enough for some of them fellows. I loaded up my saddlebags then, and I rode out for Santa

Fe. Damned if she didn't follow me clear out to the edge of town, howling up a storm the whole way, and people coming out of their tents to see what was happening, like I was beating her or something. She plumb made a spectacle out of herself, and me too, but after a while, I kicked up my horse, and I left her behind, and, to tell you the truth, I was glad to see the last of her."

"Well, then, if you left her behind in Ragtown, how did she come to be here after all?" Buck asked. "At the Double H?"

"I am a coming to that," Cookie said, and drained his glass, and filled it again from the bottle. "Understand, I wasn't in no hurry to get where I was going. Santa Fe was just another place to ride to, and in between times, I had me a run in with some Comanche." He gave them a lopsided grin. "Now there is another story I can tell you sometime, I was pretty sure that I was in line to have my scalp lifted, but it never did happen, and I managed to ride on after all, and in one piece, which I counted myself lucky." He ran a hand through what was left of his hair, as if to confirm that it was still there.

"Anyway, what with one thing and another, it was three, maybe four months before I finally rode into Santa Fe. Either of you boys ever been there?"

They both shook their heads. "I hear tell it's a pretty town, though," Red said.

Buck said nothing, not wanting to distract Cookie from his memories. As long as he could remember, he had been thrilled by the yarns the old-timers could spin, of the old west, before it got all built up and civilized, when a man could take six months to go see an ocean, or be caught by the Comanche and live to tell the story. He took a little sip of his tequila, to be friendly, and waited patiently for Cookie to continue his tale.

"That it is," Cookie said, "least, it was back then. I ain't been there for many a year, not since that one time, is all. It's got this nice little plaza right in the middle of it, see, so when I rode in, I tied up my pony, and I started across that plaza, looking for a bite to eat and some place to put down my blanket, and God almighty, if she wasn't sitting right there in the middle of the damned plaza, looked like she was just waiting for me to come along.

"Well, I was so flabbergasted, at seeing her, that I let her take me back to this lean-to where she was living, and she commenced to crying and crawling at my feet and hanging on my legs and begging me, and finally I gave it up and climbed on top of her, and put it to her again, just to shut her up. Had to close my eyes again to do it, it still being daylight when we started. Later, though, when it got dark, and she went to sleep, then I got to thinking about her tricking me the way she had, and beating me to Santa Fe, I never did know how she had done that, and I made up my mind that I wasn't going to be hogtied that way by no crazy, fucking Mexican woman, and ugly as sin to boot. So I slipped out of bed while she was sleeping sound, and got my things, and my pony, and I rode out of town in the middle of the night, and it wasn't until I reached the open range that I began to breathe easy, and I swore that this time I had seen the last of her.

"Looking back on it, that is when I should have headed to California," Cookie said, "I reckon she couldn't never have gotten to me there. But, when I was back in Ragtown, I had heard some cowboys talk about El Paso, down along the Mexican border there, and everyone said that was a fine place to visit, and California was a long ways and there were Apaches between me and there, and I still had the memory of them Comanche and the narrow escape I had with them. So I made up my mind instead to ride down El Paso way, and I did, and I decided when I got there that I liked it well enough to stay for a spell. Besides, I hadn't been there but a couple of days before I got me a job, cooking again, in this cantina, and things were going along nicely. I was making money just like before, and El Paso was a right friendly town, and there was this little señorita, pretty as that red rose she wore pinned in her hair. Well, her and me, we got to flirting with one another, and I had made up my mind that pretty soon we would do something more than just making eyes, and I reckoned she was feeling agreeable.

"So there we was one night in that cantina, this fellow was pounding the tar out of this piano, and I was standing at the bar and my little señorita was sitting at one of the tables, and smiling at me, and then she would lower her eyes, the way a woman does when she wants to let a man know she is interested, and then she would look back at me and smile some more, and I was just about to walk over to that table of hers when she looked past me, and the fellow at the piano went still, and they both got these surprised looks on their faces, like they had just stepped in a fresh cow pie. Well, I looked over my shoulder to see what it was, and, shit, if it wasn't that damned woman again. She had somehow followed me there. I couldn't for the life of me figure out how she had even known where I had gone. I swear on a Bible I hadn't breathed a single word to her about El Paso. I hadn't even thought of it myself until I had ridden out of Santa Fe, but somehow she had known. I swear, I think the devil himself was in cahoots with that woman."

"I tell you, it got me plumb loco, her finding me like that, and I dashed out of that cantina like a ghost was after me, and I got my things together, and I sold my horse to the man who owned the stable, got almost nothing for her, but I didn't have but one thing on my mind then, and that was to get out of that town fast. I already knew there was a stagecoach leaving that same day for San Antone, and when it pulled out, I was on it, and I leaned out the window to look, and there was no sign of her.

"I thought for sure, then, that I had lost her this time, since I knew there wasn't another stage to San Antone till the following month, that's how often they run. By that time, I had found me a job here at the Double H, where I figured she would never find me even if she did make it to San Antone, and I had begun to breathe easier then, till one day, I was working in the kitchen, and the dogs started to put up a ruckus. I looked out the window and saw someone walking up the lane, and my heart sank. I knew right away, before she even got close enough to have a good look, that it was her, and that it wouldn't do me no good to try to go somewhere else, cause there wasn't any place that devil wasn't going to follow me. So, here I stayed, and here she stayed, and I reckon you know the rest." He went silent then, lost briefly in his own thoughts.

"Well, she is gone now," Red said after a time.

"Funny, ain't it?" Cookie said, staring into the bottom of his glass. "Looks like things is turned clear about, ain't they?"

"How is that?" Buck asked.

Cookie glanced in the direction of the dining room, where old Mama was laid out on the table. "Next time," he said, "It'll be me following her, won't it?"

He found that his glass was empty, and started to fill it again, and then changed his mind and took a long swig directly from the tequila bottle instead, and thought for a moment.

"Wasn't nothing but an ugly old Mexican whore," he said. "I reckon I was a good-enough-looking fellow in those days, although you might not guess it now, and there was lots of pretty girls made it clear that they fancied me. I always could pick and choose among them when I had me the urge. I never could for the life of me get my mind clear on how it was I got saddled with that woman."

He lifted the bottle again, and as quick as that, he had passed out. His chin dropped on his chest, and the bottle slipped from his fingers. Buck caught the bottle before it hit the floor, and Red took hold of Cookie before he slipped out of the chair, and laid his head down on the table, where he began immediately to snore loudly.

"Guess we will have to carry him out to the shack," Red said.

"I'm thinking he might not want to wake up out there," Buck said, "on account of that was where she slept. Whyn't we put him in his old room, here, and I'll take the shed for the night."

They carried Cookie into the little room off the kitchen, and settled him on Buck's pallet, with a blanket over him. He never opened his eyes the whole time, only farted once, loud and odiferous, and when they left him there he was sawing logs again, louder than before.

Buck paused in the doorway to look down at him, and he thought of the old woman dead in the dining room, and of Cookie, all alone now.

"It's kind of sad, ain't it," he said, "a fellow ending up all by himself, the way he has."

"Reckon everybody does," Red said. "Listen, I was thinking, if you didn't want to sleep out in that shed, on account of her dying there, you could come on down to the bunkhouse with me."

"No, I don't think I am of a mind for all the boys just at the moment," Buck said. "Guess I will sleep in the shack. Only, Red . . . ." He paused and looked at his friend.

"I'll go get me my bedroll," Red said, understanding what was on Buck's mind without its even being said, "and be back in a minute. I think maybe you ought to sleep with old Red for the night, just for the company, is all."

"I would be grateful," Buck said, glad again that he had Red for his friend, and he reckoned a man couldn't ask for a better one. "It don't have to be just for the company, though."

Red gave him a smile. "I reckon we will just see how that goes," he said. "It ain't necessary, is what I mean, but I wouldn't never turn down a chance, if you was of a mind."

"I reckon I am pretty much always of a mind, old buddy, where you are concerned," Buck said.

"Well, then," Red said, looking shy and pleased all at the same time. He slipped out through the kitchen door, and Buck checked once more on Cookie, and headed for the shed out back.

• • •

Chapter 9

The boys came back from town shortly, and Red put some of them to digging a grave, the way Les had said, and then he went to where Buck was already sound asleep on his pallet, and laid down gently beside him, and put an arm around him, and Buck turned and nestled up against him and murmured something too low to hear, still asleep.

The baying of the dogs woke Red during the night. He had been asleep with Buck cuddled in his arms like a child, and he extricated himself gently from Buck's embrace, so as not to wake him.

It was the doctor who had ridden up, having been sent by Les, who was still in town. He examined Mama's body, to make everything official, but there wasn't much to see. Red had left the coffee pot to keep warm at the back of the stove, and they drank a cup of coffee together, not talking much, before the doctor left for the ride back to town.

It was near morning by then, and despite the fact that he had gone to bed late and drunk, Cookie came into the room just after the doctor had gone. He said nothing. It seemed as if he had talked himself out the night before, and he only nodded briefly in Red's direction and began to stir about the kitchen.

Les was there by mid morning, with Miz Cameron, him driving her buggy for her, with his palomino hitched behind them.

It was the first Buck had seen the owner of the ranch. She was a little dumpling of a woman, dressed all in black, and holding a parasol to protect her from the Texas sun. Her skin was pale white and delicate-looking, and belied her years, and behind her gold-rimmed spectacles, her eyes were bright and as blue as the bluebonnets on the prairie. She smiled freely, and greeted most of the old timers by name, remembering them even though she hardly ever came to the ranch any-more. The boys, used to their own rough and tumble way, were shy with her, but they looked glad to be acknowledged, and all of them were on their best behavior the whole time she was there.

The hands had dug the fresh grave out in the family grave-yard behind the house, which surprised Buck a little, since old Mama had not been a part of the family, and he would have expected them to dig it somewhere on the open plain.

"Seems like Miz Cameron, she thinks of every one of us here at the Double H as family," Red said. "Always has done, her and Les too. Everyone that dies here at the ranch, gets buried out there, same as if they was kin. Reckon I will, too, one day, and I am glad to know I will have a resting place, to tell you the truth. There's cowboys just turn into dust and bones out there on the prairie, but I believe I will sleep better knowing where I have been planted."

It struck Buck as mighty kind, that Miz Cameron would think of her hands in that way, and he found himself inclined to like her before he ever actually met her. If, he added, he actually did meet her, since he considered it unlikely that she would concern herself with a new man she didn't know, and a half-breed at that.

They gathered at the gravesite, Les and Miz Cameron at its head, and Cookie standing by himself alongside it. Old Mama was already tucked into a plain pine box that had been nailed together hastily. In the heat of the summer, here on the range, it wouldn't do to keep a body lying around for too long. Someone, Miz Cameron, maybe, or one of the cowhands, had gathered a bunch of bluebonnets and scattered them atop the box. They had begun to wilt already, but their color was still a vibrant blue against the white of the pine.

The boys, all of them, stood behind Cookie in a double row, everyone dressed in their Sunday clothes, hair slicked down, and their hands folded in front of them. It was the first time Buck had seen most of them without their guns strapped on, and with that and their hats off—cowboys liked to say that they only took their hats off to pray or to sleep, and it was more true than not—it seemed to him that it made them look somehow younger and more innocent, like a bunch of boys just playing at cowboys, and not like the tough hombres he knew them to be.

Les read a bit from a big old leather Bible. Buck's Ma had not known how to read, and Buck wasn't much more skilled at it, and it impressed him to see that Les had the knack. When he had been a boy, Buck's Ma had told him stories that came from the

Bible, of Daniel holding off a whole den of lions, and of the baby Moses who was born in a basket in the water, but aside from that, he hardly knew his Bible at all. Les read a piece about walking beside still waters, and the Valley of Death, which conjured up a vivid picture in Buck's mind, of a deep, purple-shadowed mountain valley he had once ridden through, with Apaches trailing him the whole time. Les's voice as he read was strong and surprisingly musical-sounding, for a rough cowboy, or so it seemed to Buck.

When Les was done, and had closed the Bible solemnly, Miz Cameron commenced to sing, in a clear, sweet soprano: "Bringing in the sheaves, bringing in the sheaves . . ."

After a couple of notes, Les began to sing with her, and then, one by one, the other cowboys joined in too, all rag tag and tripping over one another, and some of them humming where they did not know the words, but singing it out lustily, with their hearts in it.

It was like nothing Buck had ever experienced before, to see these grizzled cowboys singing this old hymn by the grave of a dead Mexican woman. A passing breeze paused as if to listen, and carried the voices off and scattered them like seeds across the vast Texas prairie. Cookie stood alone by the grave with his back to the others, and Buck thought he saw his frail shoulders tremble slightly, or it might just have been his shirt billowing in the wind, you couldn't say.

There was a moment of silence when they had finished the hymn, and then a mockingbird in one of the cottonwoods took up the song, and for a few seconds he echoed the melody. Miz Cameron looked in the bird's direction, and smiled, and listened until he had tired of the song and flew away.

At a motion from Les, a quartet of the boys stepped forward and took the pine box and lowered it on ropes into the hole, and Cookie walked to its brink and tossed a handful of dirt inside, and Miz Cameron and Les followed suit.

It was the first real funeral that Buck had ever attended. His own Ma had been buried in the night in an empty field, with no one but a ten-year-old boy to mourn her. There was a lump in his throat as he thought about her now, and though that had been years ago, and he had lived the hard life of a drifter since then, he saw her face as clearly as if she were standing before him, and he had to quick blink his eyes to keep tears from forming in them.

They went into the house for a bit. Despite passing out the way he had the night before, Cookie had been up before Buck was, preparing an elaborate spread that he had laid out in the front room. Buck had offered to help him, but Cookie declined, and thinking that the work was probably the best medicine for him, Buck left him to do it on his own.

He had fried up a couple of old Mama's hens, and baked some pies with last year's dried apples, and some of the boys must have gone hunting early, as there were roast quail as well, stuffed with pecans from the trees in the yard and glistening with the bacon fat he had basted them with. Beans steamed in big pots, and there were plates of fresh biscuits, better ones now that Buck had showed him the trick of it, slathered with honey, and fried potatoes shiny with grease, and, of course, gallons of coffee, everything spread out for people to help themselves.

It was the most food Buck had ever known Cookie to fix, and the best, too. Somehow, he had seemed to take inspiration from the occasion, and he had outdone himself. Everyone kind of milled about for a while, the boys uncomfortable being inside the house, where they almost never ventured, but he noted that their shyness did not interfere in the least with their appetites, which were as hearty as usual, and in no time at all the bowls and platters were mostly clean.

After a while, Les gave the boys the signal, and they went gratefully back outside, unloosening the collar buttons of their shirts as they went and beginning to relax once again. It seemed that Miz Cameron would not be staying, but meant to return to town right off, and a few of boys, Buck among them, lingered on the porch for a last look at her before she left. Red had already brought the buggy around to drive her back into town, and tied his own sorrel behind it for the ride home.

Miz Cameron came down from the house and climbed into the buggy with Red's help. She opened her parasol and looked around and saw Buck on the porch steps. She had noticed him when she first arrived—had, in fact, had an eye out for him, but he had kind of hung back, and she had not until now had an opportunity to speak directly with him. Seeing him on the steps, she crooked a finger at him, and Buck came obediently down and stood politely by the buggy, his battered Stetson in his hands.

"You're the new man," she said, looking down at his face.

"Yes, ma'am," he said, a little nervous, knowing that she was really the boss, even though Les ran things for her. Not everyone was comfortable about half-breeds. He hadn't had any trouble with the boys, who seemed to accept him just fine from the beginning, but women could be different.

"I hear you stopped a stampede, a little while ago, out on the roundup."

"Well, course, it weren't just me, ma'am," he said, blushing, and wondering who had told her the story; but it must have been Les, mustn't it, he was the one who had fetched her from town. "It was like it was all the hands together. But I did my part, yes."

"They tell me you were very brave."

"Or plumb loco. Sometimes it is hard to tell the two apart." He smiled, showing a flash of white teeth in his tawny face.

His smile seemed to warm her. "My, you are a handsome thing," she said. "They didn't tell me that."

He blushed again, and said, "That's mighty kind of you, ma'am. Though there is some wouldn't call a half-breed hand-some." He paused slightly. "Some who wouldn't favor a half-breed working on their ranch, as it happens."

She tossed her head. "I am sure Les would not have kept you on if you weren't a good worker," she said. "And Red speaks very favorably of you, and he is no fool when it comes to judging people."

He smiled back, and glanced at Red, who was checking the horses just at the minute. "Reckon he ain't. I wouldn't say old Red was a fool in any way."

"No, I think you are right about that."

"They told me about you, too," Buck said. "Only thing is, they didn't tell me how pretty you are."

She gave a pleased little laugh, for a moment looking and sounding like a young girl, and turned to where Les stood on the porch, watching them with a wary expression on his face. "Now,

Les," she called to him. "I feel maybe you ought to think about keeping this young man. He seems to know a thing or two."

Les had been watching them together. He had avoided Buck throughout the day, and even more unusual, he had avoided Red too. His thoughts were all awhirl since the night before, when they came back from the barn dance. Everything had been just fine. He had, in fact, found himself enjoying the Nasoni's company greatly. Of course, for once, he had made none of those fool remarks of his that never failed to rile Les. Plus, he once again showed he wasn't afraid of things, the way he stood up to the Hansen boy, who was considerably bigger than he was, and the three of them had ridden home laughing and fooling like a bunch of kids. He couldn't remember when he had last been so happy.

And then came that odd moment in the barnyard, before Big Joe came out to tell them about Mama. They were joking around together still, and Buck and Red had just exchanged punches, playful like, not meaning anything by them, and Les looked at Buck, and the damnedest thing came over him, out of nowhere. He suddenly had the urge, it almost overpowered him, to take Buck in his arms. Not the way they had been horsing around, not just the kind of bear hugs exuberant cowboys sometimes gave one another. He wanted, well, just to embrace him, like, to hold him in his arms and to feel Buck's arms around him. This peculiar vision came into his head, of Buck's dark curls nestled in the golden hair of his own chest, of Buck cuddled against him, all tender like, the way he imagined you would hold a sweetheart, though he had no actual experience of that, never having had a sweetheart.

He had never felt anything like it. He hadn't embraced anyone since his Ma, when he was a boy. Even with the girls in town, at Miz Yolanda's, it was just a matter of climbing on top and poking at them until everyone was happy, but he had surely never thought about hugging any of them, not embracing them and just holding them to him.

It was only Big Joe's shout as he came across the barnyard last night that had saved him from where that vision might have gone, and broken whatever strange spell had come over him.

He had found himself glancing sideways at Buck throughout the morning. It had not come back, that feeling, but it worried at him all the same. Where had it come from? What did it mean?

He was a cowboy, plain and simple. Always had been, and always would be, and nothing more nor less. He ran a ranch and bossed a bunch of cowhands, he broke horses and herded cattle, and plowed the land, and plowed a woman now and again as well. It was his nature to control his world. A cowboy could not afford to let his world control him. So it fretted him, and it angered him, too, to think that someone might have planted ideas in his head that were contrary to his nature.

Maybe that Indian did have magic tricks. Folks said a time or two that they did, that they could conjure up spirits, even. Because that was all it could have been, surely, some spirit sneaking into his head, and not his own thoughts.

Miz Cameron was looking at him now from the carriage. She was waiting for him to reply, smiling and looking altogether pleased with the Nasoni, who was standing there so polite and like he was nothing but an innocent little boy.

Innocent, hell, Les thought, half sore again. "That he does," Les called back to her. "That boy knows a thing or two, all right."

Miz Cameron saw the scowl on his face, and wondered what on earth that was about.

Les shoved his hat on his head and came down the steps. "Reckon I will get back to work, with your permission, Miz Cameron," he said. "Red will see you get safely home." He nodded at her, and strode across the yard.

She puzzled at his strange mood, and looked back at Buck, waiting patiently. He was such a polite young man. She had forgotten the drift of their conversation. "They tell me that you are a good worker," she said.

"I mean to earn my keep," he said.

"Of course, there are some cowboys, they get the urge to travel on every few months, can't seem to stay any one place for long. You're not one of those, are you, stays a spell and then flies away like the wild goose?"

"I might have been, at one time," he said honestly. "But now, I kind of feel like I would like to stay around here, if things work out right for me."

He was not looking at her, however, when he said that, and she followed his gaze and saw that he was staring at Les's departing back. All at once, something came clear as crystal to her. When Buck looked at her, he seemed embarrassed to have been caught watching Les go.

She smiled again. "Such a good man, our Les," she said.

"Reckon he is that," Buck said enthusiastically, forgetting his embarrassment in his happiness at her endorsement. "A mighty good man."

"Of course, it is sad to see a man so lonesome," she said thoughtfully.

"You think he is?" Buck asked, kind of surprised. "Lonesome, I mean? Les?" He had never thought of Les that way. He always seemed so comfortable just with his own self, a man who didn't need anything or anyone.

"Oh, my yes, more lonesome, I suspect, than he even realizes himself." Her head bobbed up and down. "It's not good for a man to be so completely alone, in my opinion. Everybody needs someone to belong to, someone who belongs to them."

Buck's face, so serious a moment before, suddenly broke into that wide grin that was so dazzling, it fair took the breath out of you.

"Yes, ma'am, I think you are right," he said, as delighted as if someone had just handed him a bag full of money. "I surely do."

"Well." She looked around. Red waited patiently in the driver's seat beside her. She hadn't even noticed when he got into the buggy. He looked from her to Buck, and back to her again, and she had a notion that he was just managing to suppress a smile. So he knew too, did he, the old devil?

You never could exactly know about these cowboys, she thought. After all these years, they did still surprise her from time to time. She had never thought about Les in anything near that way. She had always just supposed that he liked his women well enough, and probably, in that she was right.

She had never quite been able, however, to picture him settling down with one. She had no doubt that he would find plenty of willing candidates. Heavens, what girl wouldn't fancy that good-looking cowboy, and he was, as she had said, truly a good man, in every sense that mattered. No one knew that better than she did.

But how could either of them be happy for long, whichever woman he picked, or who picked him? The time would come, and when it did, it would come more and more often, when he would have to ride off, and she would be left alone at home, with the babies that a lusty man like him was certain to give her.

She thought of her own dear Henry. Henry had been a cowboy in his heart, too. He had loved her, she had no doubts of that, and she loved him, with all her being, but she had always halfway suspected that when he had left her, it was as much about him and his lifelong friend, Ray, going off together as it had been about going to the war. She supposed if she had argued and cried, she could have convinced him to stay behind when Ray went; but the result would have been the same. He would have died as surely that way as he had the other, only more slowly. No, some men just couldn't be tied down. She had known that instinctively, and she had watched them ride off with no feeling of resentment for the man at Henry's side, who could be something for him that she knew she could never be, their love notwithstanding.

There had been no children for them except for a son she lost in birth. She'd had Les, though. He had been little more than a child when he came here, and he had grown up as much her son as he had been his birth mother's. He had been for her, all these years, the son she and Henry had never had, and she could think of nothing that would give her more happiness than knowing that he had found his happiness, however and wherever he found it.

She truly believed what she had said to Buck, that everyone needed someone of his own. She had just never imagined that kind of someone for Les. Still, if one were to put aside her prejudices, and she probably had fewer of them than most, having lived nearly all her life among cowboys, she could see that in many ways that solution might be more suitable for a man like Les than the other.

Well, if that was the way things went, she thought, he could certainly do worse for himself than that polite—and handsome—young man standing beside the buggy, who wore his heart so plain to see on his sleeve. *And what a beautiful smile,* she thought. How could anyone resist that for long?

"Tell you what," she said, "if the time should ever come when you start to think of moving on, whatever the reason may be, you come and talk to me first, before you do it. Promise me, now?"

"Yes, ma'am, I promise," he said, all serious and polite.

She gave Red a little nod, and said, "I guess we should go," and smiled down again at Buck. "Good luck," she said, "with everything."

Chapter 10

The Double H cowhands were not, for the most part, the sort to think over much about things, but if any of them had paused to think about it, they would have said that they were glad Buck had joined up with them. Some of them, in fact, wondered how they had ever gotten along without him.

Certainly they ate better than they ever had before. Buck had turned out to be, as Cookie had said, a born cook. No one quite knew when Buck found the time for it, with everything else, but his hand was evident now in nearly every meal that was served. Those rocklike biscuits of Cookie's had been replaced with ones that threatened to float off your plate into the air if you didn't keep your fork in them, and rolls studded with pecans and sweet, sticky syrup thick on top of them. Meats that had been tough and a challenge to chew were so tender that they melted in a man's mouth when he bit into a chunk, and there were fried pies rich with the dried fruits that they had mostly just eaten plain in the past. One time he had treated them to something that he called "a pot-ay," a kind of soft sausage mixture in a bowl that you spread on bread like butter. They joked about it, and about cowboys eating frenchified food, which was what he had told them it was, from Louisiana, but when they were done, the bowl had been scraped so clean it hardly needed washing.

The time that Buck put into cooking did not come, though, at the expense of the other chores about the ranch. Buck worked as hard as anyone. There was no job too arduous or too dirty, and he never shirked and never complained. It seemed as if he was just as happy shoveling horseshit as he was riding and roping.

Oddly, the boys found that they liked working alongside him, and often they would vie to be given him as a partner in whatever task Red set them. There was something about him that they would have found even harder to explain to themselves, but to a man, they had grown uncommonly fond of the young Nasoni. He had a way about him, always laughing and full of spirits. He sang lots of the time, badly off key.

"That boy couldn't carry a tune in a wooden bucket," Jake said.

"Don't you know any Indian songs?" Ben asked him one day, thinking maybe he would be better at them.

"Why, sure I do," Buck said, "I know the Nasoni rain chant," and he began to intone something in what might have been Nasoni or, for all any of them knew, might have been nothing but gibberish, since none of them would put it past him to pull their legs like that. Ben looked at Red, who just grinned and shook his head, and when he was done with that, Buck went back to his usual cowboy songs and nobody asked for Indian songs again, since that one hadn't been any more tuneful anyway.

No one really minded, though. Everyone agreed that it was more like the braying of a mule than singing, but they grew accustomed to the sound of it and somehow found that they enjoyed hearing it, and his whistling too. When he threw back his head and begin to yowl at the top of his lungs, the boys smiled to themselves and one another, and felt that, somehow, all was right with their world. The boy just seemed to bubble over with some mysterious joy, and gradually they became infected with it as well, so that this bunch of old cowhands, who had been dour and slow to smile in the past were now as playful together and as spirited as a bunch of colts in a springtime pasture.

When it came to the rest of it, the boys minded Buck's peculiarities not at all. If anything, they respected his openness about how he was, and they watched his continuing pursuit of Les with amusement. Now that Buck had called their attention to it, several of them had themselves taken note of the way Les filled out his trousers, which they thought was very nice, indeed, though none of them had any expectations of doing anything about that.

As for Buck, more than a few of the hands thought their little half-breed—for they had begun to think of him in a possessive way—was plenty cute, and there were those who would happily have accommodated him in his appetites, but for all their wild ways, there was a code of honor among them, and none of them were inclined to poach on what had clearly become, for the present, at least, Red's private preserve.

In all fairness, Les had to admit himself that the Nasoni was a good ranch hand, damned good. Like the cowhands, he could see that there wasn't much about the ranch that Buck didn't already know, or if he didn't, he took to it naturally. He worked hard and he never complained.

As outrageous as he often was, it was clear that the other hands respected him, and Les halfway suspicioned that Red wasn't the only one who had taken a ride in that little saddle of his, which did not concern him at all in one way or another. It was nothing to him, he told himself repeatedly and firmly, what they did that way, and he hoped none of them thought otherwise.

'Course, he did think it was just a little peculiar, them being cowboys and all, and a tough bunch of hombres, and he couldn't help being just a little bit surprised how interested some of them seemed to be in a little twitchy-tail when it happened along—even if it was a shapely little one, which he could see as well as the next man, not being blind. Only he kept that thought to himself, and he probably would not have been aware of it at all if his pecker didn't take notice from time to time. You couldn't trust a pecker to have any sense, though. He just plain did not care in the least, however, about anything like that, and he would have told any one of them who asked him, in no uncertain terms. Which nobody did, lucky for them.

None of which he would have minded at all, if Buck hadn't continued pestering at him the way he did, all the time making his crazy little remarks and looking him over like he wanted to eat him up on the spot, and which it was plain the boys saw too, and he caught them more than once exchanging grins or winking at one another like it was some kind of joke they was sharing. It seemed to Les like he couldn't hardly even take a crap in the privy without fearing Buck would want to wipe it for him.

It just plain got on Les's nerves, who had never had any nerves before, till where he was self-conscious about it all the time, and even when he was in bed at night, he would find himself thinking about things Buck said and getting himself so steamed up that the only way he could get to sleep was to take himself in hand and work off a good load. Even at that, sometimes he would wake up later with his damn prick once more hard as a rock and grinding against mattress like it hadn't been taken care of an hour or two earlier, and he would have to satisfy it all over again before he could go back to sleep, and then he would wake up in the morning on the wrong side of the bed, and feeling testy for the whole day, and ready to bite heads off.

And the more all this worried at him, and the more frustrated he felt to do anything about it, the more that fed his anger, like spring rains feeding Bantam Creek. It began to feel to him like his whole life, which had been going along all smooth and serene like, before, had somehow been turned clear upside down, and he didn't exactly know when or how it had happened.

The only thing he knew for sure was who had done it.

Which was how they happened to come to blows, though afterward he couldn't remember just which remark of Buck's had finally made him explode—he was always saying something or another, with them looks of his, and they were all down the same trail.

"Damnation," he snapped one afternoon, "I don't want to hear no more of them remarks of yours, and I don't want you looking at me any more like you have been."

"What way is that?" Buck asked, with that innocent look he put on as easy as his Stetson.

"Like you was a tomcat eyeing a barn mouse," Les said.

Instead of looking worried, Buck laughed. "Well, I reckon I got some tomcat in me all right," he said, "but what I have been eyeing ain't no mouse, unless they are growing them lots bigger than they used to."

Which really got Les steamed, especially when the boys laughed at the joke, because he halfway feared they might think Buck had gotten himself a real look, and he said, "Now that just tears it. I got me half a mind to pound some sense into that fool head of yours. And I don't expect you'd find that so damned funny, fucking filthy half-breed."

Buck continued to laugh, and the boys standing around laughed with him, but Red, at least, saw that his eyes had gone blacker than coal.

"Never shied away from a fight," Buck said. "I got me a couple of fists myself."

"Well maybe you'd better just show me if you know how to use them," Les said.

"Anytime you feel like a jackrabbit," Buck said, "you just go ahead and jump."

The mood among the cowboys had grown sober. Red stepped forward and put a hand on Les's arm. "Les," he started to say, but Les shook his hand off.

"No, let's just get us this party started," Les said. He took off his bandana and his shirt, and tossed his Stetson on the ground, and raised his clenched fists.

Buck looked him over and seemed to be considering for a moment, and the boys watched to see if he was going to take the dare or not. Les was big and strong, and tough as they were, none of the boys had ever had a mind to tangle with him.

After a moment, Buck shrugged and stripped to the waist as well. Les stood six foot, three inches tall, his hairy chest and long arms thickly muscled. Buck was shorter by a good six inches, and you could see at a glance that he must weigh fifty pounds less, but his slender body was hard and chiseled. When he stood like this, his half-naked body gleaming bronze with sweat in the afternoon sunlight, it was easy to see his Indian heritage. If he had traded his dungarees and boots for a loin-cloth and leggings, he could have been one of the fierce Apache braves that had once struck fear into the hearts of the early settlers—except for the grin that never left his face.

"Now, I ain't really wanting to hit you," he said, although he raised his fists defensively. "Seems to me there's things we could do we'd both like that's lots better, as I think you could find out for yourself if you was to ask around."

"Ain't no damned concern of mine who's been plowing your back field for you, since it ain't me," Les said.

"Well, that ain't cause I ain't tried," Buck said, and got another laugh out of the boys, who had formed a circle about them.

"And as for what I would like," Les said, "it will suit me just fine to take that damned grin off your face."

He took a powerful swing with his right fist. Buck ducked it and backed up a couple of quick little steps, and the momentum of his swing was so great that it caused Les to stagger a step or two before he regained his balance.

"I sure think there's better ways the two of us could spend our energy," Buck said, and dodged another blow.

"I might've knowed you would turn out to be a sissy, for all your hot air," Les said.

"Now, nobody never called me a sissy before," Buck said angrily, his grin finally fading. "You take that back, you son of a bitch." He danced in close, fists up.

Watching him, Red groaned inwardly. If he could have coached Buck on what he should do, he would have told him to keep out of Les's reach. Les had long arms and massive fists, they looked like a pair of hams when he clenched them like this, and he was as strong as an ox.

Les's temper was like lightning on the prairie, though, it came on him fast, and it left him almost as quick. Red figured that, given a minute or two, he would have thought better of what he was doing, and, nimble as Buck was on his feet, if he could just keep himself out of the way of those fists for a while, this whole fight could be over shortly with nobody landing a blow.

But rushing in at Les the way he had, Buck had put himself in harm's way, where Les could get at him, and if Les wasn't as quick on his feet as the Nasoni, he was no slowpoke either.

Buck landed a glancing blow on Les's chin, to distract him, and hit him hard in the gut, the kind of blow with which he had knocked many a man's supper clean out of him. Only, it felt to Buck like he had just punched his fist against a fucking rock, and Les didn't even grunt or flinch.

Worrying, Buck tried to dance back again out of range, but he was bewildered by what had happened and he wasn't quite quick enough, and Les's long reach gave him an advantage. The next thing Buck knew, somebody had hit him in the belly with a sledgehammer, and before he had time for that even to register fully, another sledgehammer caught him on his chin. He staggered backward, his arms wind milling, and just like that, he was sitting on his backside in the dust.

He shook his head, completely flummoxed. He had been in a fight or two in his time, and nobody had ever seated him, and he had a hard time comprehending that it had been done.

If he had stayed where he was, which was what Red was hoping for, that would mostly likely have been the end of it, but Buck was too sore now to think. He swore and scrambled to his feet and ran at Les so fast and so suddenly, that again he was able to land a blow on Les's chin, this one hard enough to make Les's head snap and remind him that the kid was no feather duster.

The result was the same as it had been before, though. Les smacked him hard on the chin again, and when he went down this time, Buck sprawled flat on his back, his eyes glazed over.

"I think that's enough, Les," Red said, and this time when he put his hand on Les's arm, Les did not shake it off.

The anger went out of Les all at once, and he unclenched his fists and dropped them to his sides, suddenly ashamed of himself for picking on someone half his size. Sprawled out in the dust like that, Buck looked more like a little boy than a tough cowboy. Hell, he *weren't* nothing more than just a kid, either, Les told himself, and just being fresh the way kids did. Damn little fool ought to have learned to keep his fucking mouth shut, that was the trouble.

Les learned in that very instant, though, what many a man had learned before him, that sometimes when you got what you thought you wanted, it turned out that you didn't want it after all. He had taken that grin off Buck's face just the way he said he would, and now that it was gone, damned if he didn't wish it was back again.

"You okay?" he asked, and stepped forward to offer Buck a hand up. Buck's lip was bleeding where Les's fist had caught him. He wiped the blood off with the back of his hand and shook his head, ignoring the hand Les offered. A couple of the boys came over to help him too, but he shoved their hands away as well and got up on his own and began to slap the dust off his dungarees.

"I reckon I'll live," he said. He looked around for his shirt. Jake picked it up wordlessly and handed it to him, and Buck put that on without once looking at any of the others or meeting anybody's eyes, buttoning it quickly, and retied the bandana that Jack handed him, and got his Stetson out of the dust before Red could pick that up, and clapped it down firmly on his head.

"Seems like I was getting ready to clean some stalls," he said, and strode into the barn, walking with something less than his usual swagger.

Everyone looked after him, and looked wordlessly at one another, and nobody looked at Les. Finally some of the boys began to drift back to what they had been doing.

"Damnation," Les said aloud, staring at Buck as he went and wanting to run after him and do, he didn't know what, just do something, to undo what had happened. He wiped the sweat from his brow, and sucked the blood off a scrape on his knuckles where they had connected with Buck's chin.

After a moment, he snatched up his own shirt and bandana and hat, and stomped away toward the ranch house. The boys parted to make room for him, but nobody met his eyes.

Les had to beat off three times that night before he got any real sleep. He had a hard time thinking of gals he had been with in the past, which was usually how he got himself going. Instead, he kept seeing Buck sitting on his butt in the dust, looking surprised and hurt, like he would have cried only of course he was too much a man for crying. Shit, Les knew that. The boy wasn't no sissy, regardless of how crazy he talked.

Les felt like a field after a brush fire had swept over it, seared, exhausted, with an aching emptiness. Somewhere inside himself he seemed to understand that something new would come of it in time, the way the field grew over eventually, but shit, right now he just felt all hollow inside.

The goddam fool, was all Les could think, and began to work on his stubborn prick again.

Buck was leading his pinto out of his stall when Red found him in the barn that night.

"What're you fixing to do, boy?" Red asked.

"Reckon it is time I was riding out," Buck said, not looking at him. "There's lots of Texas I ain't seen yet."

"Don't go being no damn fool, Buck," Red said. "Who do you think old Les was fighting with out there?"

"Well, I don't know who else was in it, but it was my jaw he was punching on, that is for sure," Buck said, rubbing his hand across it where it still ached.

"Shit, Buck, he wasn't fighting with you, he was fighting with himself," Red said. "And I got me a notion he has just about lost himself that fight."

Buck took a minute to consider that. "Damn it, Red," he said, his voice close to breaking, "fucking varmint knows how I feel. He's got to."

"'Course he does, Buck. He's just being ornery. Shit, he's just being Les. I told you he was as stubborn as a goddam long-horn," Red said. "He can be as mean as donkey piss, too, but he ain't like that, not really. I'm telling you, he'll get up tomorrow morning feeling lower than a rattlesnake's belly, and wishing he could make it up to you."

"Well he sure enough knows how that would be done, and it don't appear to me as if he is likely to be doing it."

"I wouldn't be too sure of that, if I was you," Red said. "You give him a little more time, is all. If I was a betting man, I would bet you a month's pay, that tree of his is about ripe for the picking, and it won't be no time at all before you are getting the harvest of it. You ain't going to get nothing off it, though, if you go riding off with your tail between your legs. 'Sides, if you do, one thing I know is, he ain't going to be any happier about that than you will be once't you are gone. Or me either, I reckon, case you didn't know that."

"Reckon I would miss you, too, Red," Buck said. "Miss you plenty, if I was to tell you the truth."

"Well, then," Red said, and shrugged and managed a half smile. "I am telling you, boy, ain't nobody knows that old sidewinder any better than I do. You just give him a little time to get used to the idea, see if I ain't right."

They were silent for a long moment. The pinto whinnied, like he was wondering what they were up to, disturbing his sleep like this, just to listen to them jabber.

"Shit," Buck said giving his head a shake. "It hurts, Red. I never thought it would hurt like this."

"Course it does," Red said. "I know exactly how it feels, boy. But it's a sweet kind of hurt, ain't it? Once't a man feels that inside him, why, he wouldn't never want to be without it again. I expect a fellow wouldn't never feel alive after that if he lost it. Especially if he just threw it away, like."

Buck looked over his shoulder at him and gave him a measuring look. Red came closer to him and put one big leathery hand on the back of Buck's neck and gave it a gentle squeeze.

"Whyn't you come along with old Red for a spell, little buckaroo," he said in a soft voice, coaxing like. "I reckon I got me some medicine might make you feel a mite better, if you was of a mind."

"Reckon it might, at that," Buck said with a sigh, and he gave him a little smile, but it wasn't *Buck's smile*, and it made Red's tender heart ache. "Guess I best put this pony to bed first, though."

Red watched him go. He was still surprised at what a thrill of pleasure it was just to look at that slim-hipped youth, leading his pony back to its stall. Red was not a wise man, nor a sophisticated one, certainly not in matters of the heart. He had never spoken of love with anyone, had never imagined that it was something he would ever even know, leading the life he did, and if he had imagined it, he would never have expected it like this.

He was wise enough to know, though, what it was that had come, named or unnamed, to settle inside him.

The boy was right, he thought, swallowing. It sure could hurt, when you got somebody in your craw that way.

Chapter 11

Les wasn't much of a one for saying he was sorry, but he walked up to Buck first thing the next morning and said, "I been meaning to ride out to take a look at one of the watering holes. Last time I was out by Little Bantam Creek, the pond there was in the way of getting fouled. I was thinking maybe you would want to ride along with me."

"If you was wanting the company," Buck said, not looking directly at him.

"Well, I ain't fancying riding out alone," Les said, "and I reckon there is lots of the spread you ain't seen yet. If you are going to be working here, looks like maybe I ought to show some of it to you. Unless you would rather not. What I mean to say, I ain't ordering you, if that's what you are thinking. I was just asking, is all. If you was of a mind to ride along for a spell."

Buck nodded wordlessly, but by the time Les had saddled up his palomino and ridden into the yard, Buck was waiting for him astride his pinto.

They rode out in silence. It was a splendid morning in the early summer, the sun hot above and the ground below the horse's hooves thick with blue flowers. Buck felt all confused. He had been so sore yesterday, he had been ready to leave, and brokenhearted as well because he was convinced that Les did not like him at all, and if that was the case, what was the point in him staying around?

And now, here they were riding out together, just the two of them, and it was Les who asked him to come along, and he did it in a way that left no doubt of his sincerity. He even seemed to be comfortable enough with the company, though he could surely not have known what gladness he had set off in Buck's heart. Things could sure be confusing, Buck thought. He would just about think he knew what was going on in that handsome head of the foreman's, and then Les would go and turn everything upside down on him.

Living the life he had, though, he learned early on not to stew greatly over yesterday's pains. One thing was for sure: they were out here together today, all alone, and he did not mean to waste the time pouting over what had happened the day before.

"Look at them bluebonnets," he said aloud, shattering the silence.

Les looked around, surprised, wondering who had come along, but there was nobody out there that he could see but the two of them.

"You seeing ghosts, boy?" he said. "I don't see no bonnets nowhere, 'less that's what you call that old Stetson of yours."

"Them flowers everywhere," Buck said, gesturing with a hand. "Them's called bluebonnets."

Les looked down. The earth they were riding over was covered with a blanket of little blue flowers, like a sea of them. You could hardly see the ground for their blossoms.

"Is that what they are?" Les said. He had been riding this range pretty much all his life, and had never actually paid any attention to the flowers, although now that he looked he knew that he had seen them time and time again, without ever noticing.

"They are pretty, ain't they," Buck said.

"Reckon they are, now that you mention it," Les said.

"The Nasoni have a legend," Buck said. "There was this really bad drought one time, went on forever, seemed like, and everyone was afraid they were going to starve, and they was making all kinds of sacrifices to the rain gods, and the rain still didn't come. Well, it seems there was a little girl in the village, she had this favorite doll, had a blue dress on it and a blue bonnet, and she got this idea that she would burn the doll as a sacrifice to the rain gods. So she threw in it the fire, and it burned all up, and a wind came along and carried the ashes off and scattered them all over the plains, and that very same night, a rain began to fall, and everybody come running out of their teepees laughing and shouting, and the little girl went to the fire and thanked the rain gods. Come the morning, they saw that everywhere the doll's ashes had blown, the earth was covered with little blue flowers. Bluebonnets. That's where the name come from."

"Is that so?" Les said, looking down again at the flowers through which they were riding. He felt kind of foolish, that he had never noticed them before, and oddly grateful to Buck for making him aware of them. They were pretty, too, now that he saw them. Their brilliant blue fair shamed the washed-out dome of the sky above them.

They came upon some cattle grazing in a wide valley and rode clear of them, not wanting to spook them. The cows took notice, but without any alarm, watching with only mild interest as the two cowboys rode past them.

"Ours?" Buck asked.

"Yep," Les said. "Double H brand."

"They look different," Buck said, staring at the cows. It came to him all at once. "They got short horns. Hardly got any horns on them at all."

"What else do you see different about them?" Les asked.

Buck looked at them more closely. "They're fatter than longhorns," he said. "Don't look as tough, either."

"They ain't," Les said. "The Texas Longhorn is tough— tough living, and tough eating. And there's people back east who want a steak they can eat without a hacksaw. These cattle are cross-breeds. We've been mixing the longhorns with other strains. Hereford, mostly, and some Aberdeen. What you get is a lot more meat off each cow—the longhorn is pretty scrawny, too, even fattened up—and the meat off these cows is lots juicier and tenderer. You want my opinion, those cows you are looking at there are the future of cattle farming."

"Well, if these are so much better, why were we out there herding longhorns?" Buck asked.

"Haven't got enough of these yet to make it worth while," Les said. "Anyway, these cattle wouldn't survive a drive like the one we will make with the longhorns. We'd probably lose half of them, maybe more, by the time we reached Kansas."

"So what is the point of raising them, then?" Buck asked, "if you can't do nothing with them?"

"It's the railroads, boy, that will change everything," Les said. "They are talking about running them railroads everywhere over the next few years. They have already got them clear across the United States, all the way from New York City clear to San Francisco, out in California, and now they are talking about running them through Texas as well. If they are going to cross Texas with railroads, the way I see it, they have to run them through San Antone, which is just about the center of everything. Which means, a few years from now, San Antone will be as important a railhead as Wichita is now. When it is, why, we will have cattle ready to ship by rail, won't have to drive them across the plains. By that time, I plan that the Double H will have the best beef cattle in the country."

"Damn," Buck said, looking admiringly at his companion, "when I thought about cattle and cattle ranching, all I ever thought about was what we have been doing since I got here. I would never have thought about preparing for things to be different."

"Things is always different," Les said, telling himself once again that the boy wasn't half the fool he pretended to be some times. "Everything changes. Best if a man makes his mind up to that."

Which, when he thought about it, restored Buck's spirits somewhat. Things changed. So did men. Maybe Red was right: maybe Les was due for a change, too, a change in his thinking. He smiled to himself at that idea, and forgot that his jaw was still sore from the day before. Hell, if a man couldn't take a sock in the jaw, he wasn't no real man, if you thought about it.

"I hear we do some farming too, on the Double H."

"That bother you?" Les asked, glancing over at him. He knew that some of the boys didn't cotton to a cattle ranch that had crops growing in the ground.

"Can't say it does," Buck said. "The way Red explained it. Seems like it makes good sense."

Les nodded. "We do some. Not a lot, not like real farmers, I mean to say. Don't take much work, though, for what we get out of it. Hell, this dirt is so rich, you could plant a crowbar and grow ten-penny nails. But I reckon cattle will always be king in Texas."

They rode without talking for a spell, but the silence between them was a comfortable one now, and Les felt more at ease with his companion, and after a bit he struck up some more conversation. "Texas ain't the only place you been, though," he said.

"No, I been all kinds of places, seems like," Buck said. "Oklahoma, of course. Arkansas, Louisiana. Been down into Mexico a time or two."

"You never thought about settling?" Les asked.

"Well, sure, I thought about it," Buck said. "Thought about it plenty. Only home I ever knowed has been my saddle. Like I told you, I started drifting when I wasn't but a boy, been riding the range pretty much ever since. Can't say I wouldn't like to settle, but it ain't where a fellow settles, the way I see it, it's about who he settles with. I just never found me the right feller. Yet," he added.

Les was thoughtful for a spell, thinking about the young boy Buck had been, all on his own at a tender age. He had made the best of the hand he was dealt. There was no doubt of that. Probably, that was what had made such a tough little bantie rooster of him. The boy *was* tough, too, Les knew that, even if he had knocked him on his butt the day before. The fact was, Les had never been in a fight with anyone that he hadn't knocked them on their ass. That was just how it was, but Buck had landed a couple of pretty good punches himself before he got there, and there was lots hadn't ever managed that much, even.

"Most fellows, when they talk about settling down, they are thinking about women," he said aloud.

"A little belle amie?" Buck said, smiling across at him. "That's French. See, you got the Spanish influence down the south part of Texas, but up where my people were, the Nasoni, you had the French up there. Like in Louisiana."

"What's that mean, that bell thing, what you said?"

"Belle amie? Just like it sounds, a girlfriend."

"And you never found you one? A good-looking boy like you?"

"Well, I found me a few, sort of, I guess so, but most of them that I've known, the women, I mean, were whores. That ain't who a man wants to settle with. And most of the nice women I have known, well, I found there was plenty who was willing to take a boy in for a spell and see he was fed, and you would be surprised the way some of them fine ladies will act when it's just them and a randy young fellow, even if he is a half-breed and they wouldn't be caught talking to him in public. Mind you, that don't stop some of them from spreading their legs none for some stiff Indian pecker, in my experience, but they wasn't interested in settling down none. Same with men too, if a boy ain't too particular about things. Like I said before, I guess I got me the juices running earlier than some do, and I soon enough figured out that most of them who was willing to take me in, they was just looking for something they wanted in return, and I reckoned I had it to give without losing much, but I didn't figure any of them was the ones to settle down with, if you follow me. Anyway, the main thing is, I'm a cowboy."

"Shit, I reckon you are, I've seen that for myself a time or two," Les said, "but what's being a cowboy got to do with what we was talking about?"

"It's just, it seems to me that cowboys are way more comfortable in the company of another cowboy than they ever would be with a woman, except for the fucking part of it. So I figure the best thing for me is to find myself another cowboy, likes to be free same as I do, is just wanting himself a partner. When I find him, well, then, that's where I will settle. I guess I just don't reckon I'm rigged for a wife and a houseful of little ones. Any more than you are, seems like to me, seeing you ain't married either, and you are forty-one years old. Most men, the marrying ones, are already married by then, and have got them kids."

"That's the truth. I guess maybe you're right, about that cowboy part of it, I never thought about it that way. I ain't much of a thinking kind of man, to be honest, but now that you put it into words, I never fancied that kind of life much either, getting myself hogtied with a wife, I mean to say, and a bunch of little ones. I favor my freedom too much. I guess maybe that is the cowboy way, like you said." Les said. He rode for a few minutes, thinking over their conversation. "What is so different, then," he said, "about settling down with a fellow instead of a gal?"

"Well, I wasn't talking about hanging curtains and stuff like that, that wasn't what I meant when I said settling down with another fellow. What I meant was, see, with another cowboy, you got yourself somebody to ride the range with, and fool around together with, and just be partners. Kind of like the way you and old Red are, only I would want the fucking thrown in, too. Couldn't see myself settling down with nobody I couldn't fuck, that wouldn't do no good, would it? A fellow wants taking care of, don't he?"

"Reckon he does," Les said, "One way or the other."

Les had to think about all that. Like he had said, he was not a thinking kind of man. He was a cowboy, and he saw things the cowboy way. He was used to life on the range, and he doubted if there were few cowboys, if any, who hadn't done some of them things together that Buck talked about, especially the butt fucking from time to time. A man lived much of his life out on the range, there weren't so many choices available to him. It was mostly butt fuck, or do without a large part of the time. Most of them, he knew, chose the first one. That was just one of them things cowboys did for one another—except for him, and that plain wasn't his way—but that shit didn't mean anything to most of them either, except to their peckers, the way he saw it.

He had never even thought, though, about a couple of cowboys making something steady of it, being partners, as Buck put it, and the sex figuring into it too, although the way Buck described it, he had to admit it kind of made sense, considering the way things was. Hell, Buck was right about one thing, he was never at ease either around a woman the way he was with the men, didn't seem to him like most men were. Most cowboys, anyway. Shit, except for the sex part of it, everything else suited him just fine with a man, though there was other men, he knew, who saw it differently. They just hadn't grown up herding cattle, and spending all their time with cowboys, he supposed.

There was that sex part of it to consider, though, since even without trying it, he was just sure as shit that fucking a man wouldn't never satisfy him. Didn't see how it could, since a man didn't have on him what a woman did—although, he had to admit, just to his own self, that if a man was of a mind to fuck another man, Buck surely did have the butt for it. If he was honest, he would have to say that he hadn't never seen a prettier one.

He wasn't about to tell Buck that, though. The fucker never would stop pestering him if he was to hear him say that.

"It's beautiful country, Texas, I got to say me that," Buck said, as if that other stuff could not be further from his mind just at the moment. "Finer than any place else I ever been. God's country, the way some put it. Room enough, anyway, for a man to turn around in."

Les pointed to where some old wagon tracks were just visible in the grass beneath them. "Thing is," he said, "People keep coming and coming, and there is so much Texas, it just soaks them up the way the prairie does after a spring rain, till there is no more sign of them than that track there, and the land is still as big and open and wild as it ever was."

"Will it always be, do you reckon?" Buck wondered.

"I like to think so. If God had anything on his mind when he made Texas, I reckon it was to let a man know what it feels like to live free."

"I can see why you would love it," Buck said.

The funny thing was, Les had never talked about Texas that way before. He never even thought about it in that way, although looking around him now, seeing it through Buck's eyes, in a way of speaking, he could see that it was beautiful, the way Back had said, and he realized all of a sudden, too, that he did love it, always had; he had just never put it in those words.

He thought as they rode about all his years here, at the ranch, and riding this range. He had never given a thought to how many of them there had been. It might have been just yesterday when he come here as a boy. Where had they all flown to, the years? Like the hawk that hovered lazily overhead. He looked so permanent against the white blue sky, and then, just like that, he was gone. The days, too, like the flash of the sunlight on the hawk's wings before he disappeared. He might almost have dreamed them.

Buck remained silent, waiting patiently for Les to think through whatever ideas were circling in his mind, happy enough just to be riding beside him.

"I heard one time of another Indian legend," Les said after a long silence, almost like he was thinking aloud. "I don't rightly know what tribe it was, but it seems there was this Indian brave, he walked into the forest one day and he heard a mockingbird begin to sing on the branch of a cottonwood tree, so he stops to listen, just to hear the song all the way through, and when the bird is finished, he walks back to his village. Only when he gets there, there is nobody in it he knows or who knows him, until finally, one old squaw comes up to him, and she recognizes him from years ago, when he was a young fellow and disappeared into the forest."

He thought for a moment, and said, "I guess it's sort of like that for me. I come to Texas years ago, and I heard the mockingbird sing, and here I am. I don't guess he has finished that song yet."

He was silent after that. *Shit,* he wondered, *where had all that come from? Maybe that damned Indian was witching him again.* He looked aside, and saw that Buck's grin was back in all its glory, and he was glad to see it, and sore about it, too, at the same time.

"What're you laughing at?" he asked, peevish.

"Wasn't laughing none, I was just enjoying your story, is all. I never would have took you for a poetic kind of fellow, you want to know the truth."

"I ain't no damned poet," Les said sharply. Man, the fucking kid had a knack for just rubbing you the wrong way, didn't he? And things had been going so good, it had felt so pleasurable, just being with the boy.

"Didn't mean no offense," Buck said, looking and sounding sorry. "I kind of liked it, you want to know. It's nice, a man appreciating things like that. There's lots as don't. Shows you ain't just some dumb old cowhand, don't know nothing but wrangling. I like a man's got more to him than that."

"It just some old Indian hogwash somebody told me once," Les muttered, embarrassed. "I figured you might like hearing it, you being an Apache."

"Nasoni," Buck said.

"Well, they is all Indians, ain't they?"

The funny thing was, though, that except for all them crazy notions of his, and the way he was all the time talking about them, Les had begun to realize how much he actually enjoyed riding out with the Indian, just being with him, the two of them like this. There was something about him, about his enthusiasm for things. The damned kid had some kind of fire in him; he just about glowed with it. At times, you felt like you could put your hands up to him to warm them, like you would reach toward a stove in the winter.

He thought again of a puppy, jumping around and playing, full of piss and vinegar. Buck was like that, and when he was with him, Les felt as if he had been infected with it as well. Like, seeing them flowers for the first time, and talking about Indian stories. He had never talked that way with anybody in his life, or noticed stuff like that, or even thought the kind of things he had been thinking. Hawks in the sky, and mockingbirds, it was a lot of foolishness for a man to be pondering over, wasn't it? And yet, he didn't know how to put it, even to himself. It was just, well, shit, he felt alive in some way that he had never felt before, riding with the boy, talking the way they had been. His blood just seemed to run a little faster with Buck alongside him.

But what the hell was that all about? What did it mean, exactly? Where had he ever gotten such ideas in his head, that had never been there before? What the Sam Hill was it about this boy that made him feel so different when he was with him? The question worried at him. How some other man felt about things was up to him, the way Les saw it, but as for himself, he sure wasn't about to get himself tangled up with no fellow, not the way Buck talked about, and him a half-breed Indian to boot. Shit. Settling down. What kind of thinking was that for a cowboy?

"There's our watering hole, over yonder," he said aloud, glad that they had gotten where they were going. He indicated a stand of alamos in the near distance, looking oddly misplaced in the vast expanse of the prairie, and giving his palomino a flick of the reins, he began to gallop, and after a moment, Buck galloped alongside him, the two of them riding together through the sea of bluebonnets, the wrinkled plain unrolling behind their horses' hooves.

It was cool and sweet-aired in the shade of the cottonwoods. The Little Bantam Creek that twisted its way over the rangeland made an oxbow here and widened into a good sized pool, the water green-brown and still except for the ripples made by a pair of teals that quickly swam for the cover of the cattails on the bank, their feathers glinting blue in the variegated light. There were more trees, a thick grove of them, on the opposite bank, singing that faint song that cottonwoods did in the prairie breeze. The grasses whispered back to them, deep and lush, and greenish near the water, fading to brown further away.

"Looks clean enough now, I reckon," Les said, dismounting. "Have to keep an eye on these holes, ain't that many of them and the last thing you want is your cattle dying from thirst."

They were on a little knoll, looking down. The pond didn't appear to Buck like it could ever have been fouled, as deep as it was and as strong as the current was, although the recent storm had no doubt swelled it some. It looked cool and inviting after the hot sun.

"I've a good mind to take a dip," Buck said, and glanced at Les. "If you ain't got no objections."

"Go ahead," Les said.

"You ain't coming in?"

"Ain't much of a swimmer," Les said with a shake of his head.

"Me neither, but that don't stop me none," Buck said.

"You go ahead. I'll just lay up here in the grass and rest a spell."

Buck shrugged, and quickly undressed. Les was surprised to see that he wore no long johns under his pants the way most of the fellows did. No wonder them dungarees fit him they way they did. He held his breath as Buck's naked body came into view, and especially when he bared that rounded butt of his. It gave Les some kind of a funny feeling, seeing it naked like this for the first time, white as snow in contrast to the leathered tan of his back. He turned it in Les's direction as he bent down to pull his pants off, like he was modest about Les seeing him in front, and taking his time about getting out of those dungarees, so that instead Les had this unobstructed view of his bottom with its downfringed crack.

'Course Les's dick had to right off go and take notice of it, like it didn't have no better sense. Les made himself look away before the boy caught him staring. *Damnation, it was just a butt, was all,* he told himself, disgusted 'cause of the way his dick had gotten all excited over it. A man's butt, even. Wasn't nothing special about that. Everybody had one, and he had never noticed any of them before. He took his Stetson off and held it in front of himself, so that his half-hard wouldn't be noticeable.

Buck stood then and started down the hill toward the water. There were some bushes in his path, between him and the creek, and he pushed them noisily out of his way and smiled back over his shoulder at Les. Les tore his eyes away from that pale backside, embarrassed that Buck might have thought that he was staring at it, and all at once, out of the corner of his eye, he caught a glimpse of something moving in the grass.

"Boy, don't move a muscle," he said sharply.

Buck froze where he was, and when he did, he heard what the rustle of the brush had masked from his hearing: an ominous rattle, sounding like it was just at his bare feet. He stood, scarcely breathing, his smile fading, and watched Les draw his six-shooter, not his quick draw way, but moving slowly, so as not to startle the rattlesnake into striking. Les lifted his Colt and sighted carefully along the barrel. If someone had come along, it would have looked at a glance as if it was Buck he was drawing a bead on.

He fired, once, and there was a violent thrashing in the grass at Buck's feet. He jumped aside and looked down at the rattler, headless now, tossing about in the grass in its death throes.

"Jesus, that was some shooting, Les," Buck said, letting out the breath he had been holding, his grin bursting across his face once more.

"Didn't figure he would give me a second shot," Les said, and grinned back. They looked at one another for a minute. It made Les powerful happy, seeing the kid smiling like that again. It was stupid, but he surely had missed that dumb smile of his once it had disappeared.

"Anyway," Les said, embarrassed all at once, "I doubt that snake could have killed you. Way I see it, ornery as you are, you little fucker, the Lord wouldn't want you, and I doubt the devil would want the competition."

Buck whooped with laughter, like he had been paid a compliment, and even Les had to laugh with him. Damn, if that kid couldn't put a smile on a man's face when he looked like that.

"Maybe I will take a dip myself," he said. He felt strangely all keyed up, like that rattler had taken a shot at him instead of the other way around.

Buck grinned up at him and turned and jumped feet first into the dark water of the pool, vanishing under the surface and then bobbing up a minute later. He tossed his head, droplets spraying from his shiny black curls.

"Come on, then," he yelled. "It feels great."

Les undressed more slowly than Buck had, removing his shirt to reveal his bare chest with its tangle of red gold hair, and stripping off his trousers, and his boots, but he left his long johns on out of modesty. He climbed down to the water, aware that Buck was looking up at him and self-conscious of the way his dick swung back and forth in the loose confinement of the union suit. He looked carefully where he put his feet down, in case that rattler had some company nearby.

He paused on the bank of the creek. Buck gave a shout and dived under the water, his butt in the air for a minute, glistening wetly, looking like it was carved out of that shiny rock, they called it quartz. Les stared at it and swallowed, and hesitated. Maybe after all this wasn't the best idea he'd ever had, he thought.

Buck surfaced, and seeing Les standing there indecisively, he suddenly splashed water all over Les's hairy chest and his long johns.

"You chicken?" Buck said.

"You goddamn fool," Les said, but he was more tickled than sore, him standing there dripping wet, and Buck in the water below him, head back, laughing. Les laughed too, then, like a schoolboy on a lark, and he did a sudden cannonball into the pool, catching Buck by surprise and splashing the water all over his head.

Something funny happened then. They stopped being two cowboys and for the next several minutes, they were just two fellows, horsing around together in a swimming hole, laughing and cussing and splashing, trying to duck one another, and wrestling in the water.

It ended as abruptly as it had begun. Suddenly, Les was a cowboy again, and this wasn't no little boy in the water with him, but a man, with everything a man had on him, and in him. He had Buck's shoulders in his hands, in a firm grip. He had been about to dunk him, both of them laughing like fools; and their eyes met, and something like summer lightning passed between them, and they were both of them aware of who they were, and where, and that Buck was stark naked and Les not far from it.

Just like that, it came over Les again, that strange spell that had hit him before. He desperately wanted to . . . but he didn't actually know what it was that he wanted. Something, that was for sure, he could feel it rise up inside him, but it seemed to get stuck in his craw, and wouldn't come out. It couldn't be sex, he was sure of that, being as he had no interest in that with another man, but it was *something*.

Oddly, it was not Buck's eyes that held Les in thrall, as if time had been suspended. It was his mouth. Buck was breathing hard, panting almost, like he had just run a race. His lips were wet, and parted. His tongue flicked nervously over them. Lips as red as if they had been colored. Les felt as if he were falling toward them, as if a magnet were pulling him down, so that he could . . . .

"Time we was getting back to the ranch," he said abruptly, letting go of Buck's shoulders and splashing toward the creek bank.

His breath coming in little gasps, Buck stared after him, watched him climb out of the water. Les might as well have been naked, the way the wet long johns clung to his ass, and they were all but transparent now, too, so that you could see the pale pink flesh right through them. They concealed nothing, revealed everything as he scrambled up the bank: the flexing of the powerful muscles in those full rounded mounds, and the deep cleft between them, even the faint shadow far down the cleft that was his hole, and lower still, the pendulous sway of his balls.

Under the water, Buck grew instantly rigid. Jesus, he wanted that, bad as he'd ever wanted anything his whole life. And for the smallest minute there, he had thought Les was about to . . . but, no, he must surely have imagined that. There was lots of things he thought, hoped, that Les might be persuaded to try, but he could not even dream that Les was ever going to kiss him. That was something that had never happened before, with any of the cowboys he had fooled around with. Hadn't ever happened to him before, period. Nobody had ever kissed him, not since his Ma, and her not on the mouth.

"You coming?" Les said, climbing up the hill to where he had left his clothes. "We need to get moving, boy." He did not look back, or take time to dry himself off, but began to dress like a man in a hurry, putting everything on over his wet body and his wet long johns.

"In a minute," Buck said, willing his erection to go down, knowing instinctively that Les would just be sore if he got out of the water with that standing up the way it was. "I'm taking me a piss."

"Grateful you waited till I was out," Les said, "but there is no need to poison the cattle."

They spoke hardly at all on the way back to the ranch. Les acted like he was angry, and Buck just smiled to himself and whistled one of those tuneless songs of his, and pretended not to notice when Les glanced sideways at him out of the corner of his eye from time to time, like he was puzzling over something.

Red was in the barnyard when they rode in. Les tossed him the reins to the palomino and said, "Take care of him for me, okay? I got things to do inside."

"Sure," Red said. "How was the water hole?"

"Fine," Les said, and walked quickly away.

Buck dismounted and came to stand beside Red. They watched Les stroll across the barnyard, his long legs curved outward, his spurs jangling.

"You made a man of him yet?" Red asked out of the side of his mouth.

"Not yet," Buck said. "But I'm a going to.'Fore too long."

"You know," Red said, "I'm thinking you just might at that."

Les disappeared around the corner of the barn. "You never thought about riding him yourself?" Buck asked.

"Well, now, I never had, till you put the idea in my mind," Red said. "Once't you have, though, I have to say, you are surely right about one thing."

"What's that?" Buck asked.

"Old Les has got one hell of a sweet-looking butt on him, don't he?"

Buck smacked his lips noisily. "Don't he just," he said.

They looked at one another, and after a minute, they both laughed, and Red put his arms around Buck and gave him a little hug, and Buck hugged him back.

"I was just a thinking," Red said, "if you can get your mind off Les's tail end for a spell, I don't imagine anybody'll be coming out to the woodshed over yonder, not for a while, anyway."

"The woodshed? Well, now ain't that some coincidence," Buck said, "I was just kind of thinking of that big old log of yours, and that sounds like a right good place to see what we could do with that."

"I heard tell the Indians could get a fire going by rubbing sticks together," Red said.

"Reckon we could. If we rub 'em hard enough," Buck said, and they started off together toward the woodshed.

Chapter 12

Privately, the other cowhands were happy to see that Buck's grin was back now, although he was less rambunctious than he had been, and made fewer of his sly remarks. He sang less, too. They missed it, and they didn't. One or two of them wondered if maybe he had gotten his way with Les while they were out riding, but no one wanted to be the one to ask Buck.

For certain, none would have dared to ask Les. If Buck seemed happier, despite the fact that he was more subdued, now, Les went around most of the time with a ferocious scowl on his face, looking like a grizzly bear with a thorn in his paw. Which didn't fit either with the idea that the two of them had gotten something going finally.

No one knew what to make of it.

Les was surprised, when the boys rode off to town the following Saturday afternoon, to find that Buck had stayed behind.

"I thought maybe you wouldn't be so shy if it was just the two of us here," Buck said, grinning that grin of his, when Les questioned him. "Nobody would know, is what I mean."

"Afraid it's going to be just the one of you here, then. I got to go into town too, but I'm taking the buckboard so I can load up on supplies." He started to walk away, and paused and thought for a minute, and looked back. "Tell you what, boy, whyn't you come along with me, and we'll make a stop at Miz Yolanda's place. That is, if you really can handle a woman, like you say."

"Sounds like fun," Buck agreed enthusiastically. "Something for the two of us to do together, sort of like."

"It ain't going to be us doing nothing together," Les said. "But I reckon we'll have us fun enough, with them little gals of Miz Yolanda's."

Trouble was, it wasn't fun, though, at least not for Les, though it surely sounded like it was for Buck.

Les had begun to feel out of sorts almost from the first minute they walked in the door at Yolanda's. Usually, when he came to Yolanda's, the girls all made a big fuss over him, which he figured was on account of him being the boss man out at the Double H, although he sort of thought that it might have something to do also with what he had in his drawers, which in all modesty he knew was something more than the usual.

Tonight, though, from the moment they walked in the door, the girls was all over Buck like they had never even seen a man before, vying for his attention and chattering like magpies about how cute he was and what was that he had hanging down there in his trousers, and who was going to be the lucky girl, and everybody saying, "Pick me," and "I am the one you want, you sweet thing, you," and "I can show you the best time."

And of course, wasn't that damn fool Indian just eating it all up, laughing and teasing them back, and chucking them under the chin, and taking little pinches at their titties? Damned if he wasn't downright making himself look silly, in Les's opinion.

It seemed like it took him forever to choose, with Les chomping impatiently at the bit while he waited, but Buck finally decided on a little girl by the name of Celia, who didn't hardly look any older than he was. Claudine, a new girl who was plump with enormous tits and a loud laugh, and who had been among the ones clamoring for his attention, sat on the divan and gave them a pouty look.

"I sure had my heart set on you, cowboy," she said.

"Well, now, you sweet little thing you, if I was to be honest, you please me just fine, too."

"Well, then," she said, "why don't I just come along with the two of you. If you think you could handle us both," she added with a flirty grin.

"Oh, I could surely handle the both of you," Buck said. "Nothing to worry about on that score. Only, I'm just a working cowpuncher. I ain't got enough money on me to pay for two girls."

"I'm paying for this visit," Les said, "since it was me who invited you."

"You paying for two?" Buck asked, and three pair of eyes settled on him.

"If you think you can handle two, I reckon I can pay for two," Les said in a grumpy voice.

"Well, then, in that case." Buck grinned at Claudine, and she jumped up from the divan with a squeal. He took a girl on each arm and went off through the curtained doorway that led to the girls' rooms, pausing just long enough to give Les a leer and a big wink, that made the other girls and Miz Yolanda titter.

"If that boy isn't just something," Miz Yolanda said adoringly.

"He is that," Les agreed with a lack of enthusiasm. He looked around the parlor to make his own selection.

He had kind of been favoring the plump one himself, that Claudine, thinking she looked like she would be fun to be with, and with them big titties of hers, and all. He glanced around the room at what was left. Dora gave him a hopeful look, but he'd had her once and she had bad teeth, which made her breath sour; and Imogene was bony as a rail and had practically no titties at all, which might not have bothered him another time, but which he felt sure he would miss now, having had his mind set on that Claudine till Buck had up and snatched her from under his nose, the way he had. For himself, Les had never much favored a man who was greedy. And Belle looked like she had been rode hard and put away wet once or twice too often.

He settled finally on Rosita, who he'd had before and who he remembered as giving him a pretty good time. He paid Yolanda for his girl and Buck's two, thinking that this was surely the most expensive piece of ass he had ever got for himself, and he certainly hoped the results was worth it, in every way. They went through the curtained doorway to Rosita's room.

The girls' "rooms" were nothing but cubicles, big enough to hold a bed and a little wardrobe for their clothes, and not much else. The dirty curtains that hung across the doors did not quite meet in the middle and flimsy unpainted partitions of plywood separated the cubicles. Rosita had tacked up an unframed picture that Les did not remember seeing there before, of a beseeching Jesus with his hands outspread.

The set up didn't make for much privacy, which Les had never given a thought to on his previous visits, since every man there was about the same business and there wasn't anything particularly secretive about it.

When he came in with Rosita, the bedsprings next door were already creaking and squeaking something fierce, and a woman's voice moaned and groaned with steadily mounting volume, but you heard that kind of goings on just about every time you visited, and at first he hardly even noticed.

"Son of a bitch, that is sweet," Buck's voice said all at once, loudly, and Les realized that Buck and his two women were in the very next cubicle. He frowned and stood for a minute listening.

Rosita had already slipped off the dingy cotton dress she wore, and her bloomers that looked none too clean, which, again, Les had never noticed before, and she was naked on the bed, smiling and waiting for him to get to it. Les left his clothes on, which was how he usually did, and just opened his fly and hung his pecker out. It was still limp, which was a little surprising, considering the way it had been taking on, lately. He stretched out on his back on the bed beside Rosita.

"I'll just wait till they're finished over yonder," he said. "Hard to keep my mind on things, all the commotion they are making." She gave him a kind of surprised look, but she said nothing.

After a minute, the racket from next door reached a crescendo, and the moans became shrieks, and finally, contented sighs. Les began to stroke Rosita's naked thighs with one of his big, rough hands, realizing he had forgotten that her legs were skinny as matchsticks. His dick was still limp. He took hold of it with his other hand and began to work it.

The three next door were talking now, their voices an indistinct murmur through the wall, and laughing and giggling, like damn fool kids instead of a couple of whores and a horny cowboy. What in the hell could they have to chatter about, was what Les wondered? He found it distracting as hell, trying to hear through the plywood what they were saying. His dick got about half hard, and didn't seem to want to go no further.

"You put that little baldheaded feller right here," a girlish voice said clearly through the partitions. A minute later, the bedsprings started up again next door, louder than before, the bed banging up and down so hard Les half expected it to bounce right through the wall.

"Hot damn," Buck cried loudly, "that is really something, little honey."

Les suppressed an exasperated sigh. He just couldn't seem to get going. He climbed atop Rosita and tried to put it in, but it was still too limber, and it just kept slipping aside. Next door, the bedsprings had gone quiet, and the three of them were laughing and chatting, and then, just when Les thought he had finally gotten something started, those damned bedsprings commenced their racket again. *Shit, you would think with what Miz Yolanda charged, she could afford better beds, couldn't she?*

The noise got faster and louder, and there was more of their moaning and groaning, and throughout everything else, Buck revealed a considerable knowledge of words with which to describe their doings, one or two of them new to Les. Then there was some more fooling, before the bed started up again. Christ, didn't that damned Indian ever get tired?

Les tried a couple times, with no more success than before. He blamed it on that damned racket from next door. He worked on himself some more and got it up, and tried again while he kept his ear cocked to the wall, and it still wouldn't stay up long enough to get it in right. The problem was, he was just too big, and to work all that into a hole, even a well-used one like Rosita's, it had to be stiff as a poker, or it plain would not go.

He looked around the room to try to distract himself, and found his gaze on that picture of Jesus, who looked at him with sorrowful eyes, like he would rather be someplace else and not having to see what he was seeing.

Finally, totally disgusted, Les decided it wasn't going to happen on this visit. He got up from the bed and put his pecker back in his trousers. Despite the fact that he had already paid Yolanda, he took a dollar out of his pocket and tossed the coin to the girl on the bed.

"I guess we don't have to tell anybody," he said. He nodded down to where his pecker hung dispiritedly down his pants leg, "About, you know."

Rosita smiled, revealing a missing tooth in the front of her mouth, and clenched the dollar tightly in her little fist. "I won't tell a soul, señor, I promise," she said, shaking her head.

Which he figured to mean that by tomorrow, everybody at Yolanda's would know, if not half the population of San Antone.

He gave a loud thump on the wall of the cubicle. "Time we was heading back to the ranch, cowboy, if you are about finished over there" he called. "With your nattering, and all," he added, as they had taken up talking and laughing again.

Even getting out of the place, though, turned out to be a pain in the backside, to Les's way of thinking. Despite all that creaking and squeaking of the bedsprings, those two girls did not seem to want to let Buck go. They were still hanging on him and giggling and talking about what a sweet young thing he was, and how he was the best thing ever to come through the front door, and even the other girls got in the act and hung around him like flies around a watermelon. Only little Rosita hung back, probably out of some kind of loyalty to Les, but he noted that she had her eyes on the half-breed same as the others.

It was not just the girls, either. Miz Yolanda stood next to Les by the door and watched all the fussing going on, and said, "My, that boy is really special, isn't he? I have never seen those girls so worked up over anybody before."

"Yeah, he is something, ain't he?" Les said dryly.

"I am surely glad that you brought him along, Les honey."

"Yep, me too," he said glumly, but she did not seem to notice his lack of enthusiasm.

When Buck finally got himself untangled and started out the door, Miz Yolanda put a hand on his arm and, looking up him coyly, fluttered her eyelashes and said, "I don't know how you feel about older women, young man, but if you've a mind to, I think we could maybe work out something on your next visit. On the house, is what I mean."

"Well, now, that is mighty sweet of you," Buck said, and looked around the room with mock innocence, "but who is this older woman you are talking about?"

"Oh, you," she said with a giggle, and gave his cheek a playful smack. "Next time you are in town," she said, "you come on by and see me, you hear?"

When they were finally outside and walking along the dusty street to the stable where they had left the buckboard, Buck gave his crotch a squeeze and said, "Hoo-eee, that was some fun, wasn't it?"

"Yep," Les said.

"I am much obliged to you, for paying everything, I mean."

"Don't mention it," Les said.

"Well, I surely do appreciate . . ."

"I said, don't mention it," Les said.

Buck gave him a sideways glance, and seeing his grim expression, decided not to pursue the subject. He stuffed his hands in his pockets and began to whistle some of his unrecognizable music instead.

They reached the stable and hitched up the team without either of them speaking a word, and climbed on the buckboard, and started the drive back to the ranch. The silence continued, except for Buck's tuneless whistling, which had quickly begun to grate on Les's nerves.

Not until they were out of town and had reached the open country did Buck ask, "How'd you do back there with that little Rosita gal? She looked like she knew her way around a pasture."

"Just fine," Les said in a hearty voice. His pecker rose right up at that and called him a liar. "I pleasured her twice." He paused. "You managed to take care of both those gals single-handed?"

"Well, it wasn't my hand they was getting," Buck said with a chuckle. "But, hell, I did the little one three times and the other one twice. I could've easily evened up the score between them, too, if you hadn't been wanting to go."

"That sounds to me like you're bragging some," Les said, trying to remember exactly how many times that bed had banged around over there.

Buck laughed. "No, I swear, no matter how much I pump it, that well never goes dry."

The silence descended again, the deep silence of the prairie, like a cathedral, with the moon, full and bright, for an altar, and the stars like stained glass. Les was aware of Buck looking sideways at him. He hoped his hard on didn't show. Damned thing had surely developed a mind of its own of late, seemed like. Wouldn't cooperate at all a little bit ago, and now it was doing its damnedest to make a fool of him, trying to stand up when it ought to be laying down.

"You still randy?" Buck asked.

"Not hardly," Les said. He swallowed hard. "Not after that workout Rosita gave me."

"Well, *he* don't look tired." Buck reached across and gave Les's erection a friendly squeeze.

Les was so surprised, he couldn't think straight. His impulse was to shove Buck's hand away, and he would have too, in a heartbeat, but somehow his own hands wouldn't do it, and his dick was seriously threatening now to burst some buttons off his britches. He tried to say something, and opened his mouth, but all that came out was a kind of sputter.

Apparently Buck took that for some kind of agreement, and he began to fumble with those buttons on Les's fly. Like it was entirely of its own accord, Les's butt scooted forward a little on the seat, to make the buttons easier to manage, and a minute later, his fly was open. His dick jumped out into the moonlight, looking mighty pleased with itself and happy to be set free.

"Jesus," Buck said, taking hold of it. "You got you a pecker and a half there. I ain't never seen nothing like that on a fellow before. Damn thing is near a foot long."

Despite himself, Les felt a flush of pride. He almost corrected him: it was not a foot long, it was just shy of ten inches, as he knew, having measured it a time or two, just out of curiosity, but he decided not to share that information. The point was, he was big, and he knew it, and had always been secretly pleased with the fact; but it did not seem to him like something a man ought to talk about with other fellows. He guessed he had never actually talked about it with anyone. The gals, the ones he fucked, they found out soon enough for themselves, and there wasn't any reason that he could see to tell another cowboy about it, since it wasn't something that ought to have interested them any, as he saw it.

On the other hand, it surely did interest Buck mightily, now that he had a hold of it. Les swallowed again as Buck's hand began to slide up and down. Les had never had nobody else's hand stroke his cock. Even the girls at Yolanda's didn't take time for that kind of fooling around. With them, it was put it in, get it off, take it out. He'd always just figured another hand on it would feel the same as his own, but it didn't, it felt different somehow. Felt good, actually. That kind of worried him.

That wasn't but the beginning, though. To Les's astonishment, Buck leaned across the seat, lowered his head, and put his mouth right on it. Les near jumped out of his seat when those lips closed about the head of it.

"You oughtn't to do that," he said, his voice shaky like. "What if someone was to see us?"

"Out here?" Buck laughed. "Ain't nobody out here to see us but that coyote we passed a half mile back. Who's he gonna tell?"

He took it in his mouth again. Les wanted to object, he had no mind to let any fellow do what Buck was doing down there, but he couldn't, the words just wouldn't come out of his mouth. He had heard fellows talk about blowjobs plenty of times, seemed like it was something a lot of them favored, and he had always wondered what it must be like, but he had never gotten up the courage to ask one of Yolanda's girls to do it, afraid they would think he was queer or something, wanting that done. Now, here he was with Buck down there instead, slobbering all over him, and that hot, wet mouth slipping up and down, and the tongue flicking around under the flange till he was about to burn up. He gasped as Buck took the whole thing down his throat in one deep swallow. Where'd he put it all, he wondered?

Between unfinished business at Yolanda's, and what Buck was doing, Les was hotter than he remembered ever being in his life, and he came all too quick. When he did, his whole body seemed to erupt out of him, into that hungry mouth, shot after shot. Buck rode it out, all the way down on it and sucking it all down greedily. He gagged once but he never let go until he had it drained dry.

"Hoo-ee!" Buck said, finally letting it slip from his mouth, although he continued to hold it tight between his fingers. He lifted his head and smacked his lips, grinning at Les all happy like. "I can't believe you had all that left in there, after that Rosita. Felt like there was a gallon or more came out of it."

"I got me a pretty good well, too," Les said somberly.

"Well, we got us miles to go," Buck said, "and Mister Peter, he don't look like he is anywhere near finished yet, don't seem like to me." Despite the load Les had just fired off, his dick was hardly any softer than it had been before. Buck lowered his head again and would have resumed his sucking, but Les put his hand down and pushed his head away.

"I'm fine," he said, "And so is he. Don't need no more, thanks." He tucked his dick back into his trousers, not without some difficulty—damned thing had gotten stiff as a board all over again the minute Buck's mouth had touched him, and he wanted to stay outside and play a bit longer. Les got him put to bed finally, but he continued to pout in there and make his unhappiness known.

Buck shrugged and sat up on his side of the seat, pushing with his hand at his own lap, which was swollen mightily, although Les took no more than the quickest glance in that direction, kind of accidental like.

"Suit yourself," Buck said. "That sure was something great, though, I guess that was about the best I ever had."

"Well, that is over and done with now," Les said sharply. "Let's not be talking about it, if it's all the same."

"Fine with me, if you would rather not," Buck said, sounding not at all concerned.

"I would rather not," Les said.

"Got to say, though," Buck said, smacking his lips again, "That is sure a sweet piece of meat you got on you."

"I said," Les began angrily, and Buck put his hands up and said, "Okay, okay, I understand, I won't say a word, I swear."

Les glowered at him, and Buck shrugged and looked off across the prairie. They rode for a time in silence broken only by more of Buck's infernal whistling.

Les found himself wondering how in the hell that had happened anyway. Here he had been, minding his own business, just driving the buckboard home, and that damn Indian had tricked him into doing something he hadn't a mind to do at all. Only, he wasn't exactly clear how he had done it.

"How's come you to do that?" he asked out of nowhere. "What you did on me down there?"

"How's come?" Buck asked, puzzled.

"What I mean is, here I been saying no, over and over, that I didn't want that, and then you just go right ahead and up and take hold of it that way. How'd you know I wouldn't just haul off and sock you one, anyway, for trying it?"

"It was the way he whinnied," Buck said, grinning. "He sounded friendly."

Les was thinking that he *ought* to have socked him one. He still ought, knock those ideas out of his head, before he got to expecting anything—only, he didn't exactly feel like socking him. Anyway, he could have stopped him right at the beginning, couldn't he, and he hadn't. But why hadn't he? It wasn't like he was queer, or nothing.

He would be a liar, though, if he tried to say it hadn't felt good while he was doing it. Mighty good. Maybe the next time he went to Yolanda's, he would ask one of the girls to do that for him, and to hell with what they thought.

'Course, he would have to pay for that, and if you looked at it another way, he could have it for free when he wanted it, and with someone who surely did seem to be an expert at it, and gave every indication of enjoying doing it, too, which was even more puzzling to him.

That did not make it right, though, not because it felt good, and not just 'cause somebody could do it really good, either. It was not right for a fellow to do that with another fellow, he was convinced of it—but his pecker had damn sure enjoyed it.

Well, shit, what did a pecker know?

He whinnied friendly?

"In the future," he said aloud, in the voice he used with the hands when he was issuing orders that he meant to be obeyed, no two ways about it, and he pointed a finger down at his lap, still tented up all stubborn, "don't you be paying no mind to what he says. Damn thing is a liar."

Buck looked off to the side, so that Les would not see his smile.

Chapter 13

They arrived back at the ranch house still without talking. It was clear that the boys had not made it back yet from town, and the place had a deserted air about it. Les stopped the buckboard by the kitchen door. "I'll say good night here, then" he said.

"I'll help you with the supplies," Buck said. "Get stuff unloaded, like."

"No need," Les said, "I'll unload everything myself."

"Hell, now," Buck said, "I figured after what we just did, you would know I am powerful happy to help you with your loads anytime."

"Listen," Les said—he had been thinking the rest of the trip home about what to say. He had to say something, lest this fool get all kinds of notions in his head, and make something more out of what had happened than what it was, which was just some kind of accident, like. "What happened back there," he said, "well, hell, I was curious, that's all. I never had nobody do that before, but don't you be getting ideas off of it. I ain't queer, neither."

"Shit, I know you're not," Buck said, "I never thought you was. But, a man likes what he likes, the way I see things."

"You can like all you like," Les said, "just don't expect it to happen again, what you did to me out there. I just let it happen because I was curious, I had heard about having that done on you, and I kind of wondered about it a time or two, what it would feel like."

"So, then," Buck said, "how did it feel, that being your first time for it?"

"It don't matter none, how it felt," Les said firmly. "All it was is, I was still randy on account of that little Rosita back at Miz Yolanda's, 'cause she gave me such a good time, and when you started on it, you just caught me by surprise, and I would have put a stop to it right off, only, I figured I might as well see what it was like. I reckon most fellows wonder about that, if they have never had it done, but it don't mean nothing if they try it that one time."

"What I am saying is, you ain't said what it was like, though," Buck insisted.

"What *I* am saying," Les said getting angry because he thought what he said ought to be the end of it, "is there ain't no point in you wondering what it felt like for me, 'cause it ain't never going to happen again anyway, so just you get it out of your head, you hear me? I'm telling you straight out, that's all there was to it, I was just curious."

Buck jumped down to the ground and grinned up at him. "Well, you get curious about anything else, you know where I sleep," he said. "Maybe I'll just go ahead and oil up my back porch, in case. Reckon it's gonna need a good greasing if it was to accommodate that old foot-long of yours."

Even in the moonlight, Les's blush was obvious. "You have

a good night's sleep," he said with a curt nod. "Don't be waiting up for me." He whipped up the horses and drove toward the barn.

It was a good hour or more before Les got everything put away and the horses settled in their stalls. He came into the house through the kitchen and saw that Buck's door was ajar and a faint glow of light spilling out through the opening. He had intended that he would ignore it and go straight through to his own room, only he thought just then he heard something outside and went to the window to look. There was nothing to be seen out there, but the window was directly beside the door to Buck's room, and without even planning to, by the purest chance, he happened to look in.

Buck was naked on his pallet, lying on his side with his back turned toward the door. His curvy little butt was bare and ghost white, and it looked as soft and downy as a baby's in the lantern's glow, those little cheeks as round as apples. Damned if Les's pecker didn't just go and get excited all over again. That thing had been hopping up and down all night like a jackrabbit—only it did seem like it had been up more than down, the last hour or two, anyway.

"Well, hell," he told himself, "no sense only going halfway to town if the horse ain't tired yet."

Buck hadn't moved, and Les thought he was asleep. He freed his already rigid pecker from his trousers, and it gave a little nod of appreciation, and pointed to show where it would like to go.

Les had no sooner laid down on the pallet next to Buck, than Buck reached behind him and took hold of Les's hard on, just about made him drop a load right there and then. Les kind of froze up, just lying there without moving, but Buck scooted back toward him, and guided his dick where he wanted it to go. Les felt a shudder of excitement go through him. Damned if it wasn't greased, too, he thought. The little fucker. Les had thought sure he was just joking about doing that.

The hole that Buck steered him to seemed awful tiny, though, and Les's pole was plenty big. Grease or no grease, he had to push hard to force it in, and when he did, Buck gave a little groan and a grunt, like he was in pain.

"Don't you be doing no fucking complaining, you hear," Les hissed into his ear, "the way you been begging for it since you come here, boy Well, you are getting it now, and you can just fucking take it and like it, God damn it, till I finish what you started."

"Don't hear me begging you to pull it out now, do you?" Buck said sharply. He shoved back hard. All Les could think was, *Jesus, that is tight*. He had never stuck it in any hole felt like that. He hesitated, aware of how big he was, and afraid he must surely be paining his partner.

"I never done this before," he said.

"Me neither."

"You never took it up the ass before?" Les was astonished to hear that.

"Not no fence post," Buck said. He grunted again and twisted his little butt around, and almost made Les shoot a load right off, before he even got all the way in there. "You going to fuck, or you going to lay there jabbering?"

That did it, Les thought, really pissed now. He shoved Buck roughly over on his belly, rolling over on top of him, and drove it clear home in one mighty thrust. He began to fuck him hard with it, showing no mercy. Damn it to hell, he didn't care now if it did hurt him, the little fucker had it coming.

Only, if Buck minded any, he sure had a peculiar way of showing it. He could've made butter with it, the way his butt had commenced to churn.

"Well, how's that feel?" Buck asked breathlessly over his shoulder.

"It's okay," Les said after a moment, panting and pumping him steadily.

Buck snorted. "You liar. You saying it's just okay, is all?"

"Son of a bitch," Les swore, "all right, it feels fuckin' great, you stupid bastard, does that make you happy?"

"Powerful happy," Buck said with a throaty chuckle, and wriggled his butt some more.

For revenge, since it made him sore that he had been forced into saying that he liked it, Les began to ramrod him with it, so hard that Buck gave a little woof of breath at the impact, but he seemed to love it that way too, he twisted all the harder and arched his back to get every last bit of it inside him.

Les's arms were around him and Buck took hold of Les's hand and put it on his dick. Les had never had hold of any cock but his own. He hesitated for a moment and then tentatively slid his fingers up and down, surprised at how slick it felt. Hell, maybe he had greased that, too. Nothing the damn fool kid did would surprise him anymore. It was hard as rock, though, not as big as his was, but nothing to be ashamed of either.

Buck moaned with pleasure. It gave Les an odd thrill to know his dick could make somebody that happy. Yolanda's girls all moaned and groaned when you fucked them, but he had always figured that was mostly for show. He somehow knew instinctively that Buck's pleasure was real, and that it was him who was creating it, and he felt a surge of sexual power and pride he had never known, to discover he could do that with his cock. He had never thought of himself, or fucking, in that way. It had always just been what led up to shooting a load, and strictly for his own pleasure, but this, this was different. It wasn't just that he was giving somebody else pleasure at the same time he took his, which he had never before experienced. What was most different of all was that he could feel Buck's pleasure, too, like an echo of his own, and adding to it, and his dick inside Buck's ass seemed to send his own excitement right into the boy as well. It was like the two of them had melted together, had become one in some mysterious way.

He was only dimly aware of these thoughts, though, because what he was doing was so completely new to him and so unbelievably intense, that his conscious attention was focused down there at that hot little hole he was poking—which all of a sudden spasmed tightly, and he felt something wet squirting over his hand at the same moment. He realized belatedly that Buck had come. The discovery brought him off an instant later, his dick jumping and throbbing and pumping a powerful eruption inside Buck's ass. Christ, he knew for certain that he hadn't ever shot so much come in one night.

They lay locked together for several minutes, getting their breath back. Les scooted away after a bit and slipped his dick free, even though it hadn't yet gone down any. Now that it was over, and the fires had burned down some, Les felt guilty and embarrassed at how carried away he had gotten. He hoped Buck was not aware how much it had pleasured him.

"I guess that'll satisfy my curiosity," he said.

"I still got me plenty in the well," Buck said. "Maybe you ought to try taking turnabout, if you ain't too tired yet. Finish your education."

"School's over," Les said. He got up and tucked his unhappy prick back in his trousers. Hell, it would have started in all over again in a minute if he would let it. "Busy day tomorrow, boy. Best get yourself some sleep."

For the most part, Les made it a point to avoid Buck's presence in the days that followed. When they did meet, though, Buck was strangely subdued. In place of his usual sassiness, he would just smile and look down kind of shy-like, and scuff his boots in the dust. Even the other cowhands noticed something, though they weren't sure what it was they were seeing. One or two of them exchanged looks, and wondered if something might have happened. Les saw them looking at him and Buck a little curiously, and he would scowl at them until they looked away, and ceased to smile. So, they thought, maybe not, but no one knew for sure.

Only once, when it was just the two of them alone, did Les even mention Buck to his friend, Red. This was when they came out of the house together one morning and Buck and Jack were horsing around by the trough, making whips out of their shirts and snapping them at one another's butts.

Even Les could not help but notice the change that had come over his hands, and he commented on it to Red. "What do you suppose he has done to them?" he asked. "It is like he has put some kind of spell on the whole bunch of them."

Red thought about it for a minute. They were at kitchen door, and in the barnyard, the boys were playing like schoolboys, shouting and teasing one another.

"I think it's just the way he is," Red said. "Seems to me like, he got a bad deal when he was a boy, being left on his own as young as he was, and no one to look after him and all, and instead of cussing about it, or crying the way some would, it's like he just took hold of life by the balls and let it take him for a ride."

After a moment, Les said, "I reckon them's not the only balls he has took hold of."

He glanced at Red and saw a funny kind of look in his eyes. "What?" he demanded.

"I didn't say nothing," Red said, his expression one of studied innocence.

"You thinking he's had a hold of my balls, is that what you are thinking?"

"Ain't none of my business if he has, Les," Red said. "Reckon it would make him plenty happy if he did, though."

"Well, I ain't interested in making him happy, not that way, at least," Les said loudly. "Damn. That little fucker is going to drive me plumb loco before he is done."

"Shit, Les," Red said, "what're you getting yourself all worked up for, anyway? He ain't but a kid."

"He's old enough to be pestering cowboys to plug his asshole, he ain't no young 'un anymore, the way I see it."

Red shifted his chaw to his cheek and spit out of one corner of his mouth. "Happens I been plugging it a time or two," he said, "if you didn't know."

"Well, it don't make me jealous none if you do," Les said sharply. "Except, I don't want to hear nothing about it, and it ain't no goddam business of mine what the two of you have been getting up to out in that fucking woodshed."

With that, he stomped off, leaving Red to wonder how he had known about the woodshed anyway, and exactly why it had got him so riled up.

It was that same night, in the middle of the night, when three men rode up to the Double H. They paused in the dark shadows under a cottonwood tree and dismounted, and led their horses quietly, stealthily, toward the corral.

"What exactly are we fixing to do here?" Tom Hansen asked his two older brothers.

"We are just going to teach somebody a lesson," Ron said. He froze briefly at a nearby sound, but it was only a burrowing owl looking for its supper. "And have ourselves some fun."

"What kind of fun?" Brett asked. "There must be two dozen cowboys in that bunkhouse over yonder. They catch us up to anything, they will shoot all three of us full of holes. That don't sound like a lot of fun to me."

"Their horses ain't in the bunkhouse, are they? Unless I'm a fool, they are in the barn," Ron said. "And I don't reckon them horses got no guns on them. Come on." He pulled his bandana up over the lower half of his face, and the other two did likewise, and followed him across the corral toward the stables.

"Horses?" Tom said in an anxious whisper. "Damn it, Ron, they hang horse thieves."

"Hush up, you keep nattering, them dogs of theirs will hear us for sure, and rouse the whole place up."

They came into the barn. The well-oiled door opened silently. A couple of the horses muttered nervously at being disturbed in the middle of the night like this. Ron looked around, and spotted the half-breed's pinto. He had been mad as a wet rooster since his run in with the half-breed at the barn dance. The little son of a bitch had made him look a fool, and he had stewed ever since over how he could even the score.

"That's the one," he said in a whisper, grinning. "That's the half-breed's horse."

"What are we going to do?" Brett asked. He was thinking that his little brother was right—Ron was putting them into a pretty touchy fix. Still, they both knew how Ron was, and neither of them had ever stood up to his temper. He was the oldest, besides. He had always been their leader.

"We're just going to give someone a good scare," Ron said. He opened the stable door. He had brought a rope with him, and he looped it and put it over the pinto's head and led him out of the stall. At first, the pinto resisted, and hung back, neighing in protest, but Ron gave a sharp tug on the rope, and the pinto came reluctantly with him.

"They hang horse thieves," Tom said again.

"We ain't stealing him," Ron said. "We're just borrowing him, like, for a spell."

"What's going on here?" a voice asked out of the darkness of the barn, and a minute later, someone limped into view, walking on crutches. "What are you doing with that pony? You're fixing to steal him, ain't you?" He turned around and went as fast as he could toward the barn door, yelling as he went, "Hey, boys, wake up, come here, quick."

"Get him," Ron said, "Don't let that old fool get outside."

Brett ran after Big Joe and caught him, and knocked him off his crutches. Joe had managed to draw his gun, and he fired twice, the first bullet grazing Brett's shoulder and the other, as Brett kicked his gun hand, going wild into the rafters. Brett wrestled the gun out of his hand, and stood over him with it. A couple of the horses whinnied loudly, alarmed by the shouting and shooting.

"Go on, plug him," Ron hissed. But Brett hadn't a mind for shooting a helpless old man, and he threw the gun aside into the shadows instead, and kicked the crutches to where Joe could not reach them easily.

Ron and Tom were outside by this time, already scrambling into their saddles, Ron still leading the pinto by the rope. Brett ran to join them, holding his hand over the scratch at his shoulder, and a minute later, they were riding hard out of there.

In the barnyard, the dogs had begun to raise a fierce racket.

Red was the first one to reach the barn, a couple of the boys right behind him. As they ran inside, there was a sound of horses from out by the corral, riding off fast.

What they found was Big Joe crawling across the floor of the barn, trying to reach his crutches. "Horse thieves," he said as the boys helped him up. "I caught them trying to steal Buck's pinto, and they jumped me. I took a shot at one of them, Red, might have winged him, I ain't sure."

Buck had come in by this time, his long Winchester already in his hand. He went straight to the stall where his pinto was stabled. The door hung open, the stall yawned empty. He stood staring in bewilderment and grief. That pony had been with him for years, so long that it had learned to read his mind, it seemed. They were like friends. How could this have happened? A great ball of anger flared in him, and he kicked the stall door hard, making it slam against the wall with a loud bang that echoed around the barn and up into the rafters. The others watched him without speaking, no one having any words that would help.

Les ran in then from the house, still in his long johns, and took stock of the situation, seeing at once what must have happened. He turned to Big Joe. "Did you get a look at them?" he asked.

Joe shook his head. "There was three of them, was all I saw, but they had their bandanas over their faces. I didn't even get a good look at their horses, except that one of them was a big old bay. They rode off due west, took the pinto with them."

Buck was remembering the day the Hansens had ridden up to report the downed fence. The oldest boy, Ron, the one he had tangled with at the barn dance, had been astride a big bay on that occasion.

"I reckon I know where they were headed," he said in a bitter voice.

There was one thing that a cowboy regarded as just about the lowest of life forms, and the worst insult that a man could brand another with, and that was "horse thief." To take a man's horse was to render him all but helpless on the wide Texas prairie.

That it was Buck's horse, who they all knew he had loved as a friend, only poured salt on the wound. To a man, they were mad as the devil, and ready to plug someone full of holes.

"Saddle up, boys," Les said. "Someone find Buck a horse."

"What are we going to do with this fool horse?" Brett Hansen asked his brother. "We can't take him home, that's for sure. Pa would string us up himself if he knew we had stole it."

They slowed, and Ron screwed up his face in doubt and cursed silently. He hadn't really had a clear idea of what he meant to do once he had taken the pinto out of the stable. He had thought maybe they would just to tie him up somewhere out on the prairie, where the half-breed would surely find him in due time, and after a good scare, but as he sat there debating what he should do, he heard the distant sound of horses riding in their direction, the noise carrying clearly on the still night air. A lot of horses, and not so far behind—and there was no place right around here to tie up the pinto. If they were caught with it . . .

As if reading his thoughts, Tom said yet again, "They hang horse thieves, boys." His eyes were wide with fear, and his young face looked white as a sheet in the moonlight."

"You quit saying that, goddam it," Ron ordered. He was all confused now, angry and scared, his thoughts running around frantic like in his head.

"Well, what are we going to do?" Tom persisted.

"This," Ron said, drawing his six-shooter almost without thinking about it. He slipped the rope from the pinto's head, aimed at him and fired. He meant to shoot him between the eyes, kill him quick like, but with the rope gone, the pony danced back and to the side, and the bullet caught him in the neck instead. He neighed loudly, and sank to his knees on the ground, blood beginning to spurt from the wound.

In the distance, but not far enough distant, someone fired an answering shot, and another one right after that. "Come on," Ron said, "We got to get out of here."

"He ain't dead, Ron," Brett said. "You didn't kill him. You can't leave a horse bleeding like that."

"Well, you want to stick around and wait for company, that is your privilege," Ron said, and lit out as fast as his bay would go. Brett and Tom looked unhappily at one another, and at the horse, sprawled now on the ground and muttering to himself in his pain. Then they whipped up their horses and rode after their brother.

"Jesus," Brett said as they rode, as much to himself as to Tom, "we are in some deep trouble now."

"That ain't no fucking lie," Tom said.

It was no more than minutes before the entire Double H gang was riding hard west, in the direction of the Hansen's farm. Everyone had the same thought, without the need of voicing their opinions: it was the Hansens who had taken the pinto.

They had gone no more than a couple of miles, though, before they heard a gunshot ahead of them. A couple of the boys raised their rifles and fired in answer.

"Hold your fire, boys," Les said. "Till we see what's what." He had a sinking feeling, though, that he knew what that gunshot meant, and he was not surprised when, a short distance later, they spotted something lying on the ground ahead of them.

When they got closer, they saw that it was the pinto. He had been shot, once, but he was still alive. He kicked his foreleg and whinnied faintly as they rode up. Buck dismounted and ran to his pony, kneeling beside him and lifting the horse's head into his lap. He stroked his head gently and murmured something the others couldn't hear. The pony whinnied faintly and his limpid eyes regarded Buck with pain and confusion. He tried to rise, but his legs failed him and he snorted red foam out his nostrils, and sank back down. The ground around him was dark where the blood had spilled out of him.

Red walked up beside them, and took his Colt from his holster. When Buck looked plaintively up at him, Red said, "It will have to be done, Buck. He's in pain."

Buck swallowed hard and nodded. "Will you do it for me, Red?" he asked.

Red knelt wordlessly beside him, stroking the pinto's lean neck fondly, and put his gun to the horse's head, directly between his eyes, and fired once. The horse gave one final kick of his foreleg and died on the instant.

"The next bullet out of this gun will be for the man that shot him," Red said, standing and holstering his shooter. "Let's ride, boys." He swung into his saddle again, the boys barely restraining themselves, just waiting for Buck to mount again.

"Wait, now, boys," Les surprised them by saying. "I reckon that we all feel the same, and I mean to see that those varmints pay for what they have done, but they have got a good lead on us, a better one now, even, and they got the devil himself on their tail, which makes a man ride mighty fast. And it can be hard to follow a trail in the dark, too easy to read the wrong trail, especially if it leads where we expect it to lead. But it will be light shortly. What I say is, we wait until morning, when we can track these bastards right, and be sure there is no mistake. I want to see somebody strung up for this. I reckon we all do, but we wouldn't want to string up the wrong ones in the heat of things, though, and let the right ones get away with it. Wouldn't be no justice in that."

Buck got up from his knees and brushed his trousers off. The others watched him and waited for him to give them the word. For once, it was not Les who they would take their orders from. This was Buck's decision.

Les understood that, though, the same as the rest of them. "It's for you to say, boy," he said.

"Les is right. We'll ride in the morning," Buck said. "Come daylight, I will see their tracks plain enough, you can count on that, and I will follow them clear to hell, if I have to. We won't hang the wrong ones, I guarantee it. There is no way you can hide from a Nasoni, when he is after you."

Chapter 14

No one slept that night. Back at the ranch, Cookie had already made coffee. They sat around together in the kitchen, nobody saying much, except for the occasional "God damn," and "filthy bastards."

Red sat next to Buck at the table, and occasionally he would pat Buck's knee gently with one of his big, rough hands, but he spoke not a word. Les paced restlessly back and forth, glancing in Buck's direction from time to time, and then he would shake his head angrily and stride to the window to glare out at the lingering darkness.

Buck sat without speaking, staring down at his boots and hardly seeming to notice when one or the other of the boys would rest a hand briefly on his shoulder. The fury that had blazed in him earlier had burned itself down. He was not a man to dwell on anger. He had learned early that life could be hard, and that it was wise to understand that some things could not be changed, and that you just had to live with them, or they would eat at you until they had devoured your soul.

His pinto was gone, and that was just how it was, and it was not going to be any different no matter what he did now. He would see the men caught who had done it, that was only right, but to hold on to the hating of them for it would do him more harm than it would them, like drinking poison and hoping it killed the other fellow.

He did not reason this out all at once, though, but struggled throughout the rest of the night with the feelings that tore at one another within him, and he hardly heard the words that were spoken by the others, was scarcely even aware of their presence. He knew when Red would put his hand on his knee, and he was glad for it, for the warmth that it sent through him.

The simple truth was, though, he was not sitting in the kitchen with the others. He was out on the prairie again, him and his pinto, riding through the soft veil of a sunset, alive to one another, in that way that a cowboy and his horse could seem to share the same heartbeat sometimes.

How could he have spoken of that? What could he have told?

He sat and kept his silence, and waited for the morning.

As it turned out, they had no need to track down the horse thieves. The sun had barely begun to lighten the sky, and the cowhands were just in the act of saddling up, when a group of riders approached across the prairie. As they got closer, the men saw that they were from the Hansen's farm. This time, when the boys drew their guns, Les did not order them holstered.

"You won't need them guns," Hansen said, riding again to the fore. Behind him, his three sons rode with their heads down and their hands tied behind their backs, surrounded by the other farmhands who held their horses' reins.

"I overheard them, during the night, arguing amongst themselves, and when I confronted them, they admitted to what they had done," Hansen said. "I didn't raise my sons to be horse thieves. That is a thing than I cannot abide, not in another man, and not in my sons, blood be damned. I would have taken them straight to the Sheriff myself, but I thought that ought to be for you to deal with. You can take them to the Sheriff yourselves if you so choose. I reckon he will see that they are strung up plenty quick. I ask only one favor of you, who has no right to ask. If you are going to string them up yourselves, I would humbly beg you to wait until I have ridden away before you do it. They have a Ma, though they do not deserve her, and I would not want her to know that I had watched it done."

All eyes turned to Buck. "Boy?" Les asked. "Seems to me like it is up to you."

Buck regarded the three bound men for a long moment. Only the youngest of them, Tom, looked hopefully back at him. Brett's eyes were closed, he might have been asleep, so still did he sit on his horse, and Ron stared expressionless at the ground in front of his horse, looking more angry than sorry.

"Stringing them up won't bring my pinto back," Buck said at last. He felt more weary than he had ever felt in his young life. "Let them go."

There was a murmur of surprise that spread through both groups of men, and everyone's eyes were on him. Hansen studied his face for a moment, giving him time to change his mind if he chose. Finally, when Buck remained resolute, he turned to his hands. "You heard him, boys, untie them. And give them back their guns."

The farm hands did as he told them. His three sons belted on their guns and rubbed their wrists where the ropes had chafed them, and looked back and forth between themselves, uncertain what would come next.

"I won't have you back to my farm, though," Hansen said. "When you ride out from here, I never want to see any of your faces again."

"Shit," Tom said, and wiped the back of his hand across his eyes, but when he looked at his father, the older man turned his horse so that his back was to them.

"Pa," Brett said, but his father interrupted him.

"I ain't your Pa no longer," Hansen said. "And you ain't no sons of mine."

The boys exchanged looks again. Les stepped toward them, his hands on his six shooters. He had no doubt that it was the oldest boy who had set all this in motion, and a part of him could feel sorry for the other two, but they had been there, and a part of it, and they were both of them old enough to have done what was right.

"I'm not as generous a man as Buck, here," he said. "If you are wise, you won't show your faces around these parts again. Next time, Buck might not be around to spare your hides, and if someone was to plug you for what you had done, I doubt that the law would take much notice of it."

There was a muttering of assent from behind him, and one or two of the cowboys looked as if they would not wait for that time to come. Tom and Brett nodded sorrowfully, but Ron glared and spit out of the corner of his mouth. Then the three of them turned and rode off down the lane, slowly at first, and breaking into a gallop halfway along, stirring up a cloud of dust that hung in the air after they were gone.

Hansen walked his horse over to where Buck stood. "I thank you for that," he said. "Maybe they will live long enough to regret what they did, and be better for it. I will pay for your pony, of course."

Buck shook his head. "I wouldn't take no money for that horse," he said. "Ain't no price anyone could pay for him anyway."

"Well, then," Hansen said after a long pause, "I will settle for saying I wish you was my son, and I would be honored if I could call you my friend."

"I reckon the honor is mine," Buck said, "you doing what you did this morning, and I know it must have been hard."

"A man has to do what is right, the way Les said last time I was over here," Hansen said. "I ain't much of a religious man, hardly ever go to church, but I believe that every man has a book to his life, and whatever he does or says, gets wrote in it, and one day, it gets read."

"That sounds like religion enough for me," Buck said.

Hansen leaned down from his horse to shake Buck's hand. Then he was gone, leading his fellows away, his shoulders bent and looking all at once many years older than he had looked just a few evenings before.

"I thought sure you would want to see those boys strung up," Red said to Buck when the others had left them alone a bit later.

"If I could have strung up one of them without the others, I would have been glad enough to see that done," Buck said. "It was that oldest one, that Ron, he is the one who was to blame, that was plain enough to see. The way I figure it, though, is, he is a no-account varmint, he will never be up to any good. Sooner or later, someone else is going to plug him for us, you can bet money on that, and it won't be on our shoulders when they do. As for the other two, I have me a notion that they will punish themselves for what they did, just living with it, and far worse than we could by stringing them up. Shit, that youngest one, he ain't much more than a boy. Same age as me, looks like."

"That might be, in years," Red said. "But he ain't the man you are, and that is for certain."

"Thanks, Red," Buck said, and smiled wanly. He looked around, like he didn't quite know where he was, or why. "If it is all the same to you, though, I think I will just kind of mosey off by myself for a while. Nothing against you, you understand."

"I understand," Red said.

Once again he watched his young friend stroll away, but he had no medicine this time that could make things right, and he could only watch him go, and grieve for him.

Buck was just sitting on the fence of the corral later in that same day when Les came up to him, leading the gray devil horse on a rope. He handed the rope to Buck.

"Reckon this horse ought to be yours," he said, "being as you are the one who broke him."

"He is a fine pony, all right, I guess," Buck said, "but I ain't got the money to pay for no horse like that."

"Wasn't fixing to charge you for him," Les said.

"I ain't a one for charity," Buck said, his chin jutting.

"Well, shit, it ain't no charity. If it was my horse, now, I would out and out give him to you, but happens he is Miz Cameron's property, and the bank probably owes a piece of him too, since we had that corn of Hansen's to pay for. So even if she was willing, I don't imagine the bank would fancy my giving the stock away. But Red and the boys, they have been talking, see, and they have decided that they will pay a half dollar each of them out of their wages every month, to pay for the horse. And I will do the same, of course." Buck looked like he was about to argue, but Les cut him off quick. "It wouldn't set right with the boys if you was to turn them down, seeing as how they've got their hearts set on this. They all of them think a lot of you, case you didn't know."

Buck looked hard at him. Like he was waiting to hear something more, Les thought, but he didn't know what it was.

"'Course," Les said, "I reckon he would still be hard to ride, seeing as he ain't been proper tamed yet. Nobody's been able to get a saddle on him, even. If you was worrying about that . . ."

"I ain't worrying about riding him," Buck said. "Ain't never seen a horse I couldn't ride."

"So, then?" Les said, and when Buck still hesitated, he added, "See here, now, you are all the time jawing about how you would like to do this or that to make me happy. Well, what if I was to tell you that it would make me powerful happy if you would take this blamed horse off my hands for me, seeing as he ain't no good to anyone the way he is?"

Buck sighed. "I guess that's how it will be, then," he said, "Only, you got to take the half dollar out of my pay too, same as everybody else. Course, that means I will have to stick around here for a pretty good while, though, till this pony is paid for, anyway."

"Hell, I don't see nothing wrong about that," Les said. "Seems to me like you earn your pay and then some. And them boys will sure enough be glad to have you around. Like I say, there's some of them seems to like you well enough."

Bucked sighed and waited a minute again, expectant-like, and again Les had the feeling that there was something more Buck expected of him—but he still did not know what that was.

Finally, Buck nodded. "If we can settle it like that," he said.

"It's settled, then," Les said. He reached out and put his hand on Buck's shoulder, meaning just to give it a squeeze, the way fellows did, but, somehow, his hand kind of lingered, his fingers kneading the muscles of Buck's shoulder, and they found their way to the nape of his neck, soft as silk under the curly hair that hung down to protect it from the sun, and they massaged there, too, astonishingly gentle for a man so strong, with hands so big.

Buck let out a ragged breath that he hadn't even realized he had been holding, and leaned back at the hand on his neck, and rubbed to and fro against it.

As quick as that, the hand was gone. "The horse is yours, then," Les said, and walked away, leaving Buck with the gray.

The cowboys were glad to hear that Buck had accepted the pony, and, embarrassed, they shrugged off his thanks when he offered them, saying that it was nothing to make a fuss about, and anyway, they were only looking out for their own skins, since if Buck had no horse it meant just that much more work for the rest of them.

When Buck began to talk to his new pony in the little corral the next morning, however, whispering secret words in his ear, they all took notice, although they were careful not to intrude. No one would have asked what it was that he said, but the pony seemed to understand him well enough. The gray was skittish at first, but over the next few days, they all of them concluded again what they had known on Buck's first day with them: no one had the knack for horses like Buck did. When he mounted in the saddle, there seemed almost to be some sort of spiritual communication between horse and rider.

By the end of their first day, the gray, which no one could saddle in the past, was wearing a saddle as if he had been born with it on his back, and the second, Buck was working him in the pen with the longhorns, getting him used to them. By the third day, man and horse had become one in that mysterious way that the best riders had.

No one expected the new pony to be the equal of the pinto that had been lost, of course, or that it would take the pinto's place in Buck's heart—but they were relieved nonetheless to see him in the saddle again, and with a horse that looked to be worthy of his skills.

To a cowboy, though, a horse is more than just a ride. The pinto and Buck had been friends, and they knew that he ached still for his loss, and they ached with him. These were not men accustomed to showing affection and even had they thought to do so, they would not have known how to go about that. For all of that, though, and in their cowboy way, they were fond of their "little Buck," as they now thought of him. They missed his ear-piercing songs and tuneless whistles, and the smiles that broke over them like the sun rising all at once the way it sometimes did over the far Texas horizon, and they watched him now with concerned eyes and hovered close as if to encircle him and protect him from some enemy or danger.

Not a day went by and not a one of them who did not find some excuse to reach to him—a hand on his arm, a pat on the back, an arm draped carelessly about his young shoulders—even, occasionally, a quick slap at his butt. They made gifts of doing things for him. Sometimes Buck would interrupt himself at some chore, and return to it later, to find that it had been finished for him. He discovered one morning that his saddle had been oiled until it was almost like new, and he could find none who confessed to doing it. No one rolled a cigarette without rolling one for him as well. Whatever they had, little though it might be, they shared with him and, even when he sat wordless, they included him in their every conversation, and took care to see that he was seldom alone.

In these little ways, crude but heartfelt, his companions sought to nurture him back to wellness, and when, finally, they heard him whistle softly to himself one evening as he settled his pony for the night, they each and all of them felt as if a great weight had begun to lift from their own shoulders, and their hearts felt gladdened.

When Saturday night came around, and the boys prepared to ride into town as usual, they took it for granted that Buck would be going with them, and they were surprised, and even dismayed, to learn that he was not.

"Well, now," Ben said, almost belligerently, "I had a mind that I was going to buy you a drink at the cantina," and Little Joe expressed the very same idea.

"I thank you kindly for the sentiment," Buck told them, "but I am not of a mind to go, just the same."

Red, however, thought he understood, and when Buck had walked away, he told the others, "Now, boys, let it rest. It might be that Buck has things on his mind that he wants to see to here at the ranch, that he would rather do without us underfoot."

When he said this, he gave a significant glance in the direction of Les's palomino, standing unsaddled in its stall. The others saw, and got the message, and there were lots of winks and grins exchanged as they saddled up, but they kept their faces straight when they parted from Buck a short while later in the barnyard, since what they suspected he was about, they saw as his own business—and Les's, too, of course.

Red was the last to go, and he walked his sorrel over to where Buck was standing near the trough, and said, "The boys was just being friendly, you know."

"I know that, and I am grateful," Buck said, and looked after them fondly as they walked their horses down the lane, glancing back occasionally and one or two of them waving their Stetsons at him. Even Cookie and Big Joe were going in the buggy. It seemed to Buck like the bunch of them had gotten themselves in a playful mood all of a sudden, over something. He waved back, and turned to the man beside him. "You have fun now, Red," he said.

"You too," Red said, and managed a smile, although Buck could see that it was not as gladsome as Red's smiles sometimes were.

Red clicked his tongue to his horse, then, and rode after the boys, and Buck strolled into the barn, to see that his new pony was settled and fed.

Les thought about Yolanda's on that Saturday afternoon, but he would be embarrassed if the girls all knew about his failure the last time he was there, as he imagined they probably did. He decided that maybe he would go and look for a poker game at the cantina instead, and went out to the trough by the barn to wash up. He was only half surprised when Buck came out of the barn.

"You might as well have gone with the boys," Les said, stripping off his shirt. "I'm fixing to ride into town shortly. By myself." He emphasized the latter.

"What about, you know?" Buck said. "Saturday night's our night, ain't it?"

"Our night?" Les said. "What are you talking about, our night? We ain't got no night."

"Well, seems like Saturday is when we generally get together. That was when we rode over to that barn dance together, was a Saturday, you and me and Red, and it was a Saturday night when we, you know, that time in the buckboard. We was coming back from town when we did it, and later on, back in my room. That was a Saturday."

"They ain't nothing wrong with my memory," Les said. "And I reckon I told you to forget all about that shit, as I remember."

"I was just thinking, is all, seems like that is the best time for us. As I recall, you was worried that time in the buckboard about someone might see us. Well, everybody being gone, we don't have to worry about anybody would be seeing us tonight, or interrupting, or anything."

"Dammit, they ain't no *us*," Les said vehemently. "And they ain't nothing for nobody to interrupt. You get that shit out of your head, boy. Just 'cause I fucked you once, 'cause I was curious, is all that was, I told you that already, besides, the way you kept going on about it, and seeing as how you seemed to need it so bad, I figured that was the only way I was ever going to get any peace and quiet. But that don't mean I'm going to do it for you again. You done had all my pecker you're going to get, cowboy, so you might as well get that into your head." He took a bucket and began to splash water from the trough over his back and chest.

"Well, you gave me that pony, didn't you?"

"It wasn't just me. It was all the boys. I told you."

"Yeah, but you was in on it, wasn't you?" Buck said.

"So?"

"So, what's that supposed to mean, Les, if you don't like me none? How am I supposed to read that?"

"Damn it," Les said in an aggravated voice, "It ain't that I don't like you, Buck, I reckon I do, well enough. Hell, I reckon I like you just fine, if you want to know, only when you ain't worrying the piss out of me the way you do. It just means, well, shit, it don't mean nothing."

"It means something to me, Les. You ought to know that."

Les gave a sigh, weary-like. "Well, shit, course it does, I didn't mean that. What I mean is, well, oh hell." He took his head in both his hands like he wanted to squeeze something out of it.

"Shit, boy, you get me all tangled up in my head, half the time I don't know what I think anymore. That's the God's truth."

"Maybe . . . " Buck started to say.

"No, you listen now, what I want to say is, we are just a couple of cowboys, kid, we ride together, and . . ."

"Well, happens *you* had a ride," Buck said, "A pretty good one, seemed like to me, but I ain't been in your saddle yet."

"My saddle ain't for riding," Les said sharply. "And it ain't my saddle, damn it, it's my butt you're talking about."

"I reckon I know what your butt is," Buck said.

"I'm glad you do, but you ain't going to ride it."

"Well, if it ain't me, then who is, is what I would like to know?"

"Nobody," Les practically shouted. He took a deep breath, and calmed himself down, and said, blushing and kind of stammering to get the words out, "To tell the truth, I guess if it was to be anybody, hell, maybe it would be you, Buck, on account of . . . well, just on account. But I ain't going to do it, I tell you."

"Why, then?"

"Because . . . because, I don't feel like I ought to. Two grown men, doing stuff like that to one another, it don't seem right, somehow, don't matter how good it feels."

"Well, you don't know how good that feels, 'cause you ain't never tried it," Buck said.

"And I ain't going to, I am telling you, don't matter how many of them tricks of yours you get yourself up to, you ain't sticking nothing up my ass." Les leaned back down to the trough and splashed some more water over himself.

"The trouble with you, *cowboy*," Buck said, spitting the word at him, "is you are too goddamned stupid to see what we got going here."

Les turned on him. "All we got going here is a hot-assed half-breed Indian had to get himself fucked, and now he thinks that gives him the right to stick something up my ass in return, only, I told you and I done told you, that ain't never gonna happen, you dumb Apache, and you can put that in your peace pipe and smoke it."

"Well, you keep saying that ain't never going to happen," Buck said, speaking each word crisply and distinctly, "but I been around some, and I know what I know, and I don't need you or nobody to tell me when a fellow is wanting it, I can tell that from a mile away, and I ain't never been wrong about it, either, and I knowed that you was the first time I laid eyes on you, that you was all primed for it." He paused, and added sharply, "And I ain't no fucking Apache besides, and you damn well know it."

"I ain't primed for nothing," Les said, his voice rising again.

"All is making you sore," Buck said, stepping up close to him and jabbing a finger hard in Les's hairy chest, "is your asshole's been twitching for it since I got here, and that is the gospel truth, only you just ain't man enough to admit it."

Which really riled Les, because he *had* been feeling this funny kind of itching back there, all a-tingle like, of late, that he hadn't yet put any name to. That hot temper of his went off like a firecracker.

"You stupid bastard," he swore, and charged at Buck, not swinging his fist like he had that other time, but just grabbing him and dancing him around like a grizzly bear, too steamed up to think straight. Only, somehow their feet got all tangled together, and they fell to the ground. They rolled back and forth in the dirt, punching half-heartedly at one another with not much result and grunting and snarling. "Son of a bitch," someone said, and "Cocksucker."

After the first minute, though, it was evident that their hearts were not in it. They fell apart and lay side by side, breathing heavy.

"Don't much feel like fighting with you, boy," Les said. Truth was, he was remembering how bad he had felt that last time, after punching the boy the way he had. Besides, their bodies rolling around together, all twisted up the way they was, had made him start thinking about some other ideas. And that made him nervous-like.

"Me neither," Buck said.

"'Sides, it don't look like nobody is winning."

"That is the truth," Buck said. He wasn't any more enthusiastic than Les about continuing their fight.

Les got up and gave Buck a hand, and he took it and got up too. They dusted themselves off, taking longer than it might have needed, and both of them feeling a little foolish.

"Nasoni," Les said in a mumble. "I know that. I was just talking stupid. 'Cause I was pissed off."

"You're bleeding," Buck said. "On your chest, there."

"I rolled on some rock, is all," Les said.

"I'll wash you off." Buck took off his bandana and dipped it into the trough.

"I can wash my own self," Les said stubbornly.

"Let me," Buck said, and when Les looked like he was about to argue the matter, he added, softly, in a coaxing kind of way that just seemed to melt some of the argument right out of Les, "I want to. Just let me do this, Les, okay?"

Les hesitated, and when he did not object, Buck began gently to wash the dirt and the blood off of his thick chest, pausing to dip the bandana into the trough again and wring it out. He rubbed it in little circular motions about one of Les's nipples, russet-colored and surprisingly plump for a man's chest.

Down below Les's prick took notice of the attention the nipple was getting and began to puff up indignantly. Les cleared his throat. "Buck ain't no real name," he said, to take his mind off what was happening.

"Stands for buckaroo," Buck said. "That's bastard Texas talk for *vaquero*. *Vaquero* means cowboy in Mexican."

"I knew that," Les said. "But it still ain't no name. No real name, is what I mean to say."

"It's really William Horse. My name I mean, but I been Buck since I was a tadpole." He rubbed the other nipple, his hand moving slower now, his thumb brushing it back and forth. "What about Les? What's that stand for, that ain't no real name, either?" Les mumbled something he couldn't hear. "Didn't catch that," Buck said.

"Sylvester," Les said sharply. Buck laughed out loud. "What is so goddam funny?" Les wanted to know.

"Well, it sure ain't no cowboy name, is it? Sylvester? Sounds like some prissy city dude, carries an umbrella and walks funny and all."

Les laughed too, but he quickly grew sober as Buck's hand left his chest, paused to run a fingertip about the basin of his navel, and moved slowly downward over the washboard of his abdomen. Les's foolish dick was definitely making a spectacle of itself now.

"What I did, the other night," Les kind of stammered. "When I come by your room. Don't that, well, don't it hurt, having that big old thing shoved up your ass?"

"Hurts some, right at first." Buck said. "Feel's better, though, the longer it goes. Lots better."

"Huh," Les grunted, which Buck figured could mean just about anything. Les looked past him, over Buck's shoulder into the far distance, like there was something over there that greatly interested him. He seemed not to be aware that Buck had let the bandana fall to the ground and was now caressing that enormous bulge down below.

After a moment, his breath sounding ragged, still looking into the distance, Les said, "What if someone was to try it once, what you been talking about, you know, up his butt, and, say, well, like he decided that he didn't like it and wanted to stop? What happens then?"

"I always promise first-timers I'll take it right out if it hurts them any," Buck said.

"Do you ever?" Les asked, "Take it out, I mean, if they say they don't like it?"

"No-o-o." Buck dragged the word out. "Never have yet. Happens by the time we have talked it over a little bit, they decided it wasn't so bad after all, and generally they'd as leave I put the rest in. It just takes a little getting used to, is all. Once they get used to it, they always like it well enough to finish what we got started, seems like."

Les laughed, but it caught in his throat as those determined fingers undid his buttons and pulled him free of his trousers. *That damn traitor,* he thought. It hadn't never been so hard in his life, nor so often. He could have pounded nails with it if he had a mind to.

"He been whinnying again?" he asked hoarsely.

"Yep," Buck said. "I heard him plain as day."

"What if I was to say he is lying?"

"If he is, he is doing one hell of a good job of it."

Buck was looking down at it, his fingers sliding up and down, and Les looked down too, to watch. The time before, in the buckboard, he hadn't looked, and he found the sight exciting to see. In Buck's brown hand, his dick looked as white as snow by contrast, and he thought again how different it felt to have somebody else's hand working it.

Then, as if it was on a signal, they both looked up at the same time and their eyes met, and everything seemed to stop all at once, like time was frozen. Les held his breath, and it seemed, even, like his heart had stopped to beat. For a long moment they stood like that, motionless, just looking at one another. Even Buck's hand had stopped its gentle stroking.

Then, out of the blue, Les surprised both of them—himself most of all—by suddenly grabbing hold of Buck, pulling him roughly close and kissing him, tentatively at first, then their mouths were grinding violently together, teeth scraping, bodies trying to find ways to get even closer.

It was like nothing he had ever experienced before, Les thought, their embrace felt so, he didn't know what, exactly, so natural, so right, and their mouths, and the way their bodies were grinding together like this. His bare dick chafed against the rough fabric of Buck's trousers, and even that felt fine, because he could feel the answering hardness there, and without even thinking what he was doing, he shoved a hand down between them and felt Buck through the cloth, and Buck made a low moaning sound deep in his throat, and kissed him harder.

They had to come up for air eventually, and when they did, Les put his cheek against Buck's cheek, his lips at Buck's ear. Les hadn't yet shaved, and his stubble scraped against Buck's cheek, and even that felt good to Buck, as worked up as he was, and he rubbed his own cheek against it in answer.

"There's some new hay up in the loft, yonder there," Les said, whispering as if someone might hear them. "Soft as feathers."

"I ain't never saw hay that soft," Buck whispered back. "Was you saying you was wanting to show it to me?"

Les was so long in answering that Buck had begun to think maybe he wasn't going to, there was just his breath, fast and rasping in Buck's ear. Then a shudder went through him, Buck could feel it the whole length of him, so violent that for a moment Buck thought he might have come, only there was no wetness in his hand.

Les gave a long sigh, so broken that it almost sounded like he was laughing. He took the lobe of Buck's ear between his teeth and bit down gently on it. "Guess maybe I was," he said, still whispering, so softly that if his mouth hadn't been right at Buck's ear, Buck might not have heard it at all. "If you was agreeable."

"Oh, I am agreeable, all right," Buck said. "I truly am." He laughed deep in his throat, and before Les could even think about changing his mind, Buck half walked, half danced him into the barn, Les's big prick still out of his pants, jutting out in front of them like a drum major leading the parade. Buck paused inside to close the door after them, but Les headed straight for the ladder, like a man in a hurry, and began to clamber up it.

Buck watched him as he climbed, his dick bobbing up and down, and he let his eyes feast briefly on the beautiful fullness of that manly ass as it disappeared into the loft.

He laughed again, his head fair to swimming with his excitement, and turned to bolt the door, in case anybody come back from town early. Or, hell, he thought, even if they came back late, on account of he wasn't planning on having this over with in any big hurry, after waiting so long for it. That cowboy in the loft might not know it yet, but he was in for a night of it—one hell of a night, if Buck had any say about it, and after the way Les had kissed him outside, he was pretty sure now that he did. Didn't seem to him that a man could kiss like that if his nuts wasn't burning up, however his mind might be thinking.

There was a can of axle grease, with its lid off, sitting on the floor where one of the boys had been greasing the buckboard, and he took that with him, and climbed quickly up after Les, in a hurry now himself.

Chapter 15

By the time Buck topped the ladder, Les was on his back in the hay wearing nothing but his union suit. With his eyes shut tight, he looked scared and grimly determined. He looked, Buck thought, cute as a bug's ass, and about fourteen years old.

"Whyn't you get them long johns off?" Buck said, shedding his own clothes as quick as he could.

"There's a trap door in the seat of them, and my hole's about where you would expect it to be," Les said without opening his eyes. "I reckon you can get where you're wanting to go with no trouble, seems like."

"This ain't just about plugging no hole," Buck said firmly. "What it is, is I got me a beautiful man in the hayloft with me, and it's took me some doing to get him here, besides a sock on the jaw, and now that I got him here I damn well want to see what I got me."

"I ain't never heard no man called beautiful before," Les grumbled, but he peeled the union suit off obediently and threw it aside in the hay and closed his eyes again and lay back naked, his big dick pointing at the roof. An owl in the rafters overhead saw it and fluttered his wings nervously.

Buck knelt and straddled him. "Dammit, open them eyes," he said, and when Les did, blinking in surprise, Buck said, "Tell me, what do you see?"

Les shrugged. "I see a naked Indian sitting straddle of me," he said, and when Buck just waited, staring him in the face, Les looked at him again harder. Buck's cock was standing straight out from his thick black bush, eight inches or so, it looked like, with a thick, tawny-colored shaft and a spade-shaped head on it, red-purple, like wine, or like it was bruised. Looking at it like this, thinking what they were getting ready to do, Les felt himself tighten up, but it felt all tingly too, and kind of hot, like. "With a big boner," he added.

Buck just continued to kneel there over him, though, smiling and staring at him and waiting without a word, so Les figured there was something more he was supposed to say, but damned if he knew what. Damn fool was all the time wanting him to say something, it seemed like, but how was he supposed to know what it was? He wasn't no mind reader.

He thought all of a sudden about the way Buck had made him notice those flowers out on the prairie, the bluebonnets, and think about how much he loved Texas—stuff he had never seen or thought of before.

He looked Buck up and down more carefully, at his flat little belly and his chest looking like it was carved out of some kind of rock, with those two little copper pennies on it, that he wondered what it would be like to run his tongue over them. He looked at Buck's face, at the dark curls that tumbled over his forehead, and his eyes, black and glinting in this light; his long nose with the slight hook in it, made Les think of an eagle, now that he noticed. Especially, he looked at his mouth, wide, with lips that were full and red and soft like a girl's, and he remembered how sweet they had been when he kissed them a minute ago.

And finally, something came to him that he would never before have even imagined thinking, let alone saying. He swallowed hard and said, "All right, goddamit, I see a beautiful man astraddle of me. Does that make you feel better, damn you?"

"Yep, it sure does," Buck said with that shit-eating grin of his. "'Cept you forgot some of it: a beautiful naked man with a boner who is fixing to fuck you raw, cowboy."

"Well, then, I guess we better get to it, 'stead of just talking about it," Les said hoarsely. "Am I supposed to turn over, or what?"

"Whyn't you just leave this to me?" Buck said. "I'm the one here knows what he's doing, ain't I?" He moved between Les's long legs, spreading them wide with his own, and lifting them to rest on his shoulders, took some of the axle grease on his fingers, and reached down to grease Les up.

Les grunted at the unfamiliar feel of a finger slipping inside him, and when, a minute later, Buck moved closer and tried to force his way in where the finger had been, he said loudly, "Shit! God damn, you said it didn't hurt."

"I said just at the start. It gets better as it goes."

"Well, how long does that take?" Les wanted to know.

"Are going to be a baby about this and start in boo-hooing 'fore I even get going, or are you going to take it like a man?" Buck demanded.

"Shit," Les said again, and gritted his teeth. "Well, I reckon if you know so damn much about what you are doing, you ought to be able to get that bitty thing in there without too much trouble."

"Fuck you," Buck said, and he did. But he stopped and rested about halfway in, to give Les time to get used to it.

It felt to Les like he was being split in two from the bottom up. Buck's cock must have doubled in size since he had looked at it a moment before. Maybe he had shoved his damn leg up there instead, he thought, thinking probably this had just been a mistake after all, only he knew if he tried to quit now, Buck would just call him a sissy, and he never would quit pestering, once they had gone this far.

Buck leaned down over him then, keeping his dick buried but motionless, and kissed him, his tongue exploring Les's mouth. At first Les made no response, his attention focused on that thing down there tearing him apart, but then he began to savor the taste of Buck's mouth and to welcome Buck's tongue with his own, and to kiss him back. That much he liked plenty well enough, anyway. He reached up and put his arms about Buck's shoulders, and his hand on the back of Buck's head, and crushed their mouths together, and concentrated on kissing him ferociously.

After a minute or two, Les was surprised to feel his butt muscles begin to relax the way Buck had said, and to stop resisting the invader. Buck felt it too. He began to fuck him, slow and gentle, and not going too deep, but he knew by instinct when the pain had turned to pleasure, and he began to fuck him harder then, and deeper.

"Shit," Les said, "That's—that's . . ." But he didn't have any words to describe what it was like, and he settled for a long, low groan, half a sigh, that sent a thrill of excitement all through Buck.

Buck bent down further, limber as a cat, and took Les into his mouth. Les moaned with pleasure. All those different sensations—he wanted everything all at once: to kiss him, hug him fiercely, to fuck him too. He raised his ass up to welcome the assault, and grabbed hold of Buck's narrow hips to pull him in tighter, till he had all of him in there. He was on fire now, like a grass fire raging across the prairie, spreading all the way through him, till it was scorching his balls, burning its way up . . .

Something changed suddenly inside him, Buck seemed to swell enormously, and then to explode, and he realized with a shock that Buck was firing off in him, where nobody had ever come before. Knowing it, feeling that erupt deep inside him, made him go off too, like molten lava, a load like none he had ever shot before, it seemed to go on forever. Buck choked and swallowed furiously—but the fucker never spilled a drop, Les was pleased to note.

They lay locked together for a while. Les ran his hands over the sleek young flesh next to his, and thought how amazing it was, the way their two bodies just seemed to fit perfect together, who would have imagined it? And Buck's dark curls laying on the golden hair of his chest—hadn't he dreamed that, or something?

It seemed funny, now, that he had resisted this so long, only to find out how special it was. Were other men like that, their minds fighting what their hearts must have wanted all along? There were other fellows that he might have done it with. Red, even, though that idea had never so much as crossed his mind until now. But no, it wasn't what they had done just now, it was Buck who was the gift.

Les was no philosopher. He had never struggled much with questions of right or wrong. He had always just gone ahead and done what it seemed to him was the right thing. He had thought for so long that what Buck was suggesting was wrong, but now that he thought about it, who had said that it was? He remembered reading something in the Old Testament, but that was about crooked priests or prostitutes or something like that, but what had that got to do with what had just happened here?

On the other hand, there was that story about David and Jonathan. It seemed to him as if maybe they were partners, like, too. Course, it didn't say anything about their private business, but if they had ever gotten around to trying it out, he felt pretty certain they would have found it about as pleasurable as he just had.

Or, maybe his mind had been right all along, he thought, remembering. Maybe what they had just done was wrong. But how could it be wrong, holding Buck in his arms like this, when it felt so right?

He turned his head and kissed Buck's brow, and when Buck looked a question up at him, he kissed his mouth, gently this time, tenderly, and ran a big, meaty hand down Buck's back. What a pretty thing Buck's body was. He had known that when he saw him naked at the creek, only like a fool, he had pretended to himself that he hadn't. Course, he himself wasn't no beauty.

He knew that, but damned if Buck didn't seem to like everything well enough.

"You think my butt's too big?" he asked out of nowhere.

"What makes you ask something like that?" Buck said, surprised.

"Well, you got this pretty little one, hell, I can hold it in my hands," Les said. He reached and cupped one of Buck's round little cheeks in his massive hand, to demonstrate. It seemed to fit just perfect, filling his hand like it was made for it. "Mine ain't like that, for sure, it's big and broad, seems like to me."

Buck reached beneath him to cup one of Les's cheeks in his own hand, but his hand didn't cover it the way Les's did with his. It felt good, though, firm and hard-muscled. It felt to him like just about the nicest butt in the world, the way he saw it.

"Fellow I knew down in Galveston, he used to say, you can't drive a railroad spike with no tack hammer," Buck said.

Which Les had to admit was pretty funny. He laughed and gave Buck an affectionate hug, and raised his head to look down at his dick. "'Cept it's bigger than a railroad spike, I reckon, if I do say so myself."

"Way bigger," Buck said. "And sweeter, too."

Les had never thought about a dick tasting sweet. Hell, he'd never thought about how a dick tasted at all. He looked from his own to Buck's, with that big purple head, and sort of wondered. He had never thought about a dick being pretty, either, but now that he looked good at it, he saw that Buck's was, pretty as all get out.

After a pause, though, he remembered what had crossed his mind a little bit ago, and he said. "I got to start driving them longhorns up to Wichita, to the railroad. Figured I'd be setting out the day after tomorrow, maybe. I'll take some of the boys with me, and leave some of them here to look after things." He hesitated for a moment, feeling kind of shy about asking, and unsure of himself. He cleared his throat and said, "Was you fixing to come along, or what?"

Buck raised up to kiss him again, lovingly, their lips brushing softly together. It had never occurred to Les either how soft a man's lips could feel. You would think they would be hard like the rest of him, wouldn't you? There sure was a lot to this stuff that he was learning.

"Darlin," Buck said, "ain't you figured out yet about you and me? You ain't going nowhere I ain't going too, not if you was to go to hell and back."

And, just like that, damned if Les's prick didn't jump right up with joy and start wagging for attention, like it hadn't just been sucked plumb dry. They both looked down at it.

"That damn thing sure has developed a mind of its own lately," Les said.

"Seems to me like he knows what's what," Buck said, "sooner than some folks I could mention."

Buck took hold of it, and turned about in the hay and began to suck on it noisily, but after a minute he lifted his head to say, "You best know from the start, I'm a man likes getting it pretty regular."

"I reckon you won't suffer none from any lack," Les said dryly.

For a few minutes there was no sound but their ragged breathing and the faint noises Buck was making. Les lay back and enjoyed the skillful ministrations, and the sweet scent of the new hay and their sweat and the semen and the faint, old odor of horses from below. The owl in the rafters murmured his approval at the way things had progressed.

After a bit, though, something occurred to Les that he had been worrying about, and he had been distracted from.

He said, "You think the boys'll guess? About us, is what I'm asking?"

Buck snickered and took his mouth off Les's cock to say, "You damn fool, them boys been rooting for me since the first day I come along. Hell, they been taking bets, if you want to know."

Les snorted indignantly. *Taking bets?* That didn't seem right somehow. What kind of tomfoolery was that, for grown men to be playing around at? He gave Buck's head an angry push downward.

"If you are gonna suck, suck," he said sharply. "You can jaw anytime." Buck obeyed enthusiastically, redoubling his efforts.

Darlin, Les thought about that. Nobody'd ever called him that before. He rolled the word around on his tongue, savoring it. It felt nice.

He slipped his hand across Buck's hard little ass, fondling it, and Buck made a funny, gurgling kind of sound in his throat, like a cat purring.

That was it, Les thought, he had kept calling him a puppy, but he wasn't a puppy at all, he was a cat, a *gato montez*—a Texas wildcat. Hell, he even walked like a cat, now that he thought about it. Les lifted his head and looked down, watching Buck's mouth slide up and down, and savored how ripe and kissable Buck's lips were, cock bruised and berry red by now.

He hadn't ever kissed nobody before, either. Maybe his mother when he was a baby, but surely not the way he had just kissed Buck, and them girls down at Yolanda's weren't into kissing their customers even if he had wanted to, which he hadn't. Fact was, he couldn't remember ever even *wanting* to kiss anybody before, until he had kissed Buck just a little bit ago, and that had just come over him all sudden like, he hadn't even known where the idea came from until he was doing it.

Remembering it, though, he had this funny wish that Buck could somehow kiss him and suck him at the same time. Hell, now that he thought of that, he wished he could do everything at once, all of it: fuck him and kiss him, and get sucked, and, shit, even just ride their horses fast over the plains side by side on a hot Texas day, with the smell of the range land and them bluebonnets everywhere, and the gray mountains on the far horizon, and the distant sky. He wanted to yell to the whole damn world how good it was, cowboys together, the two of them like this, him and this horny little half-breed of his.

For the moment, though, he decided that the sucking took precedence. He ran his thick fingers through Buck's curly hair, and gave Buck's head another shove, gentler this time, in case Buck might want to take it a little deeper. He did, it seemed like.

Darlin, Les thought again, and said it aloud softly, testing the feel of the unfamiliar word on his lips: "Darlin."

Buck heard him, and wriggled happily and, to Les's surprise, interrupted himself, to say, "I was sort of thinking, Les, us working together the way we do, and riding together, and all, and now we're doing this, maybe we could be . . ."

"Dammit, boy," Les interrupted him, "you are always in such an all-fired hurry all the time, if you would let me get a word in edgewise, I was about to make me a proposal, about us two."

"Well, go ahead and make it, then," Buck said. "Who's stopping you?"

"I was thinking," Les said, getting all serious, "seeing as how we are working together already, and riding together, and now that we finally got around to it, seeing as how we both seem to enjoy doing this shit together, well, what I was going to say, was maybe you and me ought to just up and be partners, like. I don't mean like no man and a woman settling down together kind of thing, I mean, well, like cowboys, only doing stuff together."

"Sounds good to me," Buck said. "Sounds mighty good, partner."

"Only thing is," Les said in a no-nonsense voice, "you got to understand, boy, I will be the boss between the two of us. That's just the way it will have to be."

"Seems like you already are, I reckon," Buck said.

"Well, what I was meaning to say is, like, for instance, say I was to say I wanted it sometime, you know, being took care of, I wouldn't want to hear no argument about it, or nothing."

"Won't get no argument from me, not about that," Buck said.

"Well, then I guess that's settled, the two of us, we will just be partners. I guess I'll be like your old man, kind of. If you are agreeable, that is."

"I surely am," Buck said enthusiastically. "Shit, you just made me the happiest man in the whole damn world, I could just about . . ."

"Oh, now, don't be getting all sappy on me," Les snapped. "It ain't like we was getting married and raising children. We'll be partners, is all I'm talking about, and fuck around together, we can do it every night, like, once or twice, is what I am thinking."

"Sounds just fine to me, just like that," Buck said. "And, I swear, anytime you was to want it, you just tell me so."

He grinned up at Les, but Les raised his head from the hay and looked down somberly at him. "I was kind of wanting it now," he said. "If you ain't got nothing else to do while you are down there."

Buck laughed, that throaty sound of his that made Les's balls tingle in a funny way, and he began to suck again, but after a minute he interrupted himself once more and lifted his head to look up at Les.

"I wasn't figuring on tying you down none," he said. "Case you was worrying about that."

"You neither, course," Les said.

"I mean, about them women. Won't bother me none if you have a mind to get yourself a woman now and again."

"Wasn't planning on being roped like no calf. If that is what I feel like I want, that is what I will have, it won't have nothing to do with you and me. That's just something you will have to understand. Same goes for you."

"A cowboy has got to be free," Buck said, "Way I see it . . ."

"Suck, boy," Les cut him off.

"Yes, sir," Buck said, and added, "Boss," and went back to his sucking, but after a minute, he paused yet again. "I guess you know, old Red's been riding me some."

"Well, shit, I ain't blind, boy," Les said. "I doubt there is anybody on the ranch don't know about that. Probably nobody in the state of Texas."

"You don't mind none?"

Les thought about it for a moment. "Well, I did some, at first, if I was to be honest," he said. "That's one thing I will swear to you, boy, us being partners now, I won't never lie to you about nothing."

"Me neither," Buck said. "That's how come I was telling you about me and Red."

"Which I knew already, but it is right that you said about it," Les said, nodding his head. "Man ought to know if somebody else is riding his bronc, seems to me."

"Well, shit, yes, of course he does. I didn't know it was making you sore, or nothing. You tell me to, I will put a stop to it."

"Didn't say you had to, and I didn't say it makes me sore, except at first, a little bit," Les said. "That is just being honest, like we said. But, see, Red and me, we been riding together for a long time, done just about everything else together, 'cept we never done nothing like this, him and me, but he is kind of like my right hand, so to speak. Ain't much else Red and me ain't shared over the years, including a woman or two. What I mean to say is, I reckon if you and me are going to be, well, you know, like this, only doing it regular—case I didn't say it already, I will be wanting took care of steady like, you best settle your mind on that, boy, if we're fixing to be partners—anyway, if we are going to, well, then, it looks to me like it would be better all around if you and him was kind of like partners, too, wouldn't it? Seems to me it would be friendlier for everyone."

Buck smiled and nodded and began to suck again, but damned if he didn't just raise his head again a couple minutes later.

"Well, I sure am glad to hear you say that, 'cause old Red and me, now . . ." He started to say, but Les could feel his sap beginning to rise, and it made him testy and impatient with all this palaver.

"You fucking crazy half-breed," he interrupted him sharply, "ain't you got some business down there needs seeing to, if you ain't too all fired hung up on old Red just at this minute to take care of it."

"Yes, sir," Buck said snappishly, and added, "no, sir."

"Suck, damn it," Les said.

Buck dutifully began to suck again, but he began to make loud slurping noises while he was at it, like a pig at a trough.

Les's testiness melted quickly, but his nuts were aching something fierce now, and he was of a mind to finish off. He took hold of Buck's head firmly in both his hands and, holding it steady, began to go at it hard. His juices were boiling up by this time, so that it didn't take but a minute before they boiled over.

Even when he had drained it completely, though, and Les had let go of his head, Buck kept it in his mouth, just savoring the lingering sweetness of come and spent dick. He laid his head on Les's belly, the thick copper bush—like a cloud of gold, it looked like to him—tickling his chin, his nose filled with Les's heady scent. Man, he had sure got himself one prize longhorn, he guessed there wasn't another one in the world as good as this.

After a minute or so, Les said, "I expect maybe I was kind of rough there," which was as close as he had ever come to an apology, that not being his way. "Even though I reckon it's some of it your own damn fault. You about drive a fellow crazy, the way you do that."

"Don't fret yourself none over nothing like that," Buck said. "However it suits you is just fine. I ain't no damned sissy."

"Didn't think you were," Les said.

"What I mean to say, is, a man wants it how he wants it, and if it don't make his partner happy too, him pleasuring himself, then it don't seem to me like he is any kind of real partner, as I see it. I reckon you and me is going to be real partners."

"Reckon we are," Les said.

Les sighed happily. An astonishing feeling of contentment like he had never known before seemed to spread through him—laying together like this in the hayloft, in the afterglow of sex, his little Buck's head in his lap. Damned, if that kid of his wasn't something.

Partners. He thought about that. He hadn't never had him a partner before, not a real partner, like they was. Didn't seem like it could be much handier than that for a cowboy, working the range the way they did, and seeing as how pleasurable it had turned out to be.

He reached down and ran his hand affectionately through the tangle of Buck's hair and twirled one dark curl between his fingers. When he looked he saw that Buck's eyes were closed, his expression one of dreamy contentment. He was making that sound in his throat again, like he was purring.

"One thing's for sure," Les said aloud, "My bedroll's gonna be a lot less lonesome this cattle drive."

Buck smiled and thought of something, and scrambled up on his knees between Les's muscular legs. "You was saying earlier about how you might like it pretty regular," he said. "And I was just thinking, if that well of yours wasn't dry yet, my . . ."

"I swear, if you ain't the talkingest damn fucker I ever heard tell of," Les said sharply. "Maybe if you would just roll over there on your back in this hay, I could get a thing or two off my mind 'fore the night is over, if you ain't got better things to do."

"Can't think of nothing better than this," Buck said. He grinned and rolled onto his back and spread his legs wide, and Les climbed over him and got between them, and lifted Buck's legs to his shoulders, the way Buck had done with him earlier.

"There is some axle grease over there, in that can," Buck said, and Les said, "Whyn't you let me do this for once? I think I know how it is done now, and didn't we say I was the one who is running things here?"

He got the axle grease, though, and greased himself up, and Buck, too. Buck grunted a couple of times when it began to inch inside him and grimaced, and he said, "Maybe if you was to . . . ," but when he looked up and caught sight of Les's expression, he changed his mind and clamped his lips shut and closed his eyes.

Les worked it in real slow, watching the frown on Buck's face to see how he was doing and worrying that maybe he really was hurting him. Well, shit, though, he'd said he wasn't no sissy, hadn't he, and his dick was his dick, it wasn't ever going to get any littler, and if they were going to do this, he would have to get used to taking it—but he took his time getting it in there, holding himself back with all his concentration and being as careful as ever he could. He hadn't ever in his life fucked anybody so careful.

He looked down between them, savoring the view, but that got him too excited, and he looked at Buck's face instead to distract himself. Buck's eyes were still closed, his lips parted. His tongue slipped out, and he ran it over his lips, and Les suddenly thought how damned pretty he really was, them long lashes resting on his cheeks and them pouty lips, just made to be kissed, and all of a sudden something seemed to pierce Les's chest, like someone had shot an arrow into his heart.

It almost seemed as if Buck must have felt it too, because he opened his eyes at the same moment like something had surprised him, and looked up at Les, and smiled, the sweetest smile Les had ever seen, and whatever was inside Les's chest seemed to burst into fireworks at the sight of it. Les bent down and kissed him, hard as he could, putting all his happiness and all the love he couldn't name into his kiss, and when Buck kissed him back and pushed his butt up to show that he was ready for the rest of it, Les was mighty glad to oblige.

Buck raised his arms up about Les's shoulders and hugged him tight. He was thinking, he wondered if anybody in the history of cattle ranching had ever looked forward to a cattle drive the way he was looking forward to this one. Three months, maybe four, out there on that wide prairie, all them nights to come, and not one but two horny cowboys to keep company with.

He began to think about some things he had heard of but hadn't ever had the opportunity to try out before, as they took more than one partner to do them, and it got him so excited that he took hold of himself and began to jerk himself off in rhythm to Les increasingly forceful poking.

Les watched him for a moment, and when he looked back at Buck's face, he had a funny kind of expression on it.

"What's that look come over your face?" Les asked.

"What look?"

"You got a look on you like a cat just stumbled on a bowl of cream," Les said.

"I was just thinking," Buck said, "About some things this fellow told me about once, down in Galveston."

"What fellow?" Les asked. "What kind of things?"

Buck looked up at him and said, "Are you going to talk, or are you going to fuck?"

"Damnation now, don't you be getting smart with me, buckaroo, 'less I take something else to your ass 'fore I am done," Les said, but he wasn't really mad—hell, he couldn't stay mad at that boy if he tried—and he forgot about being gentle and about being jealous, and set himself to fucking with a vengeance, deep and steady, the way he liked to do it, and it seemed now as if that suited Buck just fine as well.

While he fucked, he thought in a kind of a daze about everything that was in store for them in the time to come, and his heart felt as big and as full as his balls, and just as like to burst.

And the crazy fucker was as horny as hell, too, he thought happily, couldn't seem to get enough of it, which Les personally thought boded real well for their future.

Partners. Who'd have ever thought it?

About the Author

Lecturer, writing instructor, and early rabble rouser for gay rights and freedom of the press, Victor J. Banis is the critically acclaimed author ("a master storyteller . . ." Publishers Weekly) of more than 140 books, both fiction and nonfiction, and his verse and shorter pieces have appeared in numerous journals and reviews, including Blithe House Quarterly *(Winter 2006), and various anthologies, among them* Paws and Reflect *(Alyson, 2006) and* Charmed Lives *(Lethe, 2006). A native of Ohio and longtime Californian, he lives and writes now in West Virginia's beautiful Blue Ridge.*